I0627830

Spirit Sight

Last of the Gifted
BOOK ONE

Marie Powell

A WOOD DRAGON BOOK

Spirit Sight

Copyright © 2020 Marie Powell

Inside and cover art: Callum Jagger
Inside design: Adin Nelson, Amaya Editing Inc.

ALL RIGHTS RESERVED. No part of this publication may be reproduced, stored in or introduced into a retrieval system, or transmitted in any form or by any means (mechanical, electronic, photocopying, recording or otherwise), without the prior written permission of both the copyright owner or the publisher of this book. For permission requests, contact the author at: http://mariepowell.ca. Reviewers may quote brief passages in reviews. Neither the author nor the publisher assume any responsibility for errors, omissions, or contrary interpretations of the subject matter herein. Any perceived slight of an individual is purely unintentional.

Published by:
Wood Dragon Books
P.O. Box 429
Mossbank, Saskatchewan Canada SOH 3G0
1-306-591-7993
www.WoodDragonBooks.com

Library and Archives Canada Cataloguing in Publication
Powell, Marie 1958—
ISBN: 978-1-989078-28-0

Author Contact:
Marie Powell
http://mariepowell.ca

An earlier version of this book, under the title Hawk, was published by Five Rivers Publishing.

What readers are saying about Spirit Sight

Spirit Sight is an imaginative novel that makes clever use of medieval Welsh history and legend. Young adult readers will be drawn to the magic powers of Hyw and Cat, transporting them back to a tense and pivotal moment in the history of the United Kingdom, when the last Welsh princes faced down the mighty English army. Readable and well-researched.

— Danièle Cybulskie
Author of *Life in Medieval Europe* and *The Five-Minute Medievalist*

Marie Powell is a writer that is able to pull readers into her world and not let them go.

— Eileen Cook
Author of *With Malice* and *You Owe Me A Murder*

Marie Powell cleverly explores the possibility of a "gift of seeing" and has written an intriguing, enjoyable historical fantasy.

— Marion Mutala
Author of *My Dearest Dido*

Folklore, history, adventure, romance – Marie Powell's Spirit Sight has it all! The novel is beautifully written, full of lilting language and true-to-the-times characters that made me believe I was right there with them in 13th century Wales. The storylines switch back and forth between Hyw, who can meld his mind with the minds of animals – and a murdered prince – and his sister Cat, who can see the future in water. But are her visions sure to happen, or can they be changed? And can Hyw master his gift in time to save his country and the people he loves the most? Marie's masterful writing kept me engrossed right up to the final twist ending, which fulfilled the promise of everything that came before. I look forward to learning the rest of Cat and Hyw's story in the upcoming sequel, *Water Sight*.

— Sharon Plumb
Author of *Draco's Child*

This is a spell-binding, riveting YA historical fiction alive with character, conflict and action. Definitely a blow-your-mind debut novel. Loved it!

— **C.M. Janz**

Other worldly. History and magic, blended together in such a subtle way that I just wanted to stay in that world. Not only are the characters engaging, especially the two main characters—brother, Hyw, and sister, Cat—and the setting exotic...the castles of 13th century Wales...this book is also well plotted. As the tension builds towards war in the second half, I found myself eagerly reading chapter after chapter. A most engrossing way to appreciate a bit about the history of Wales. It's obvious that a lot of research went into this book and I look forward to the sequel. I also very much appreciated the glossary and historical note.

— **Gabriele Goldstone**
Author of *The Kulak's Daughter*

Well researched and well written. *Spirit Sight* is a unique retelling of Welsh history from the points of view of Hyw and Cat, siblings with special gifts. I cannot wait for its sequel – *Water Sight!*

— **Maureen Ulrich**
Author of *Power Plays*

I've had the pleasure of reading the first in this series and will soon read the second. They are fabulous. If you love magic, and history, and Welsh mythology, these books are for you. Spirit Sight is a fast-paced historical fantasy for young adults. This story blends Welsh mythology and magic with just enough historical detail to fully immerse you in the narrative world. A quick read that will leave you eager to read the sequel, *Water Sight.*

— **Leslie Wibberley**
Award winning author

Character Guide

Hyw and Cat's family

Hywel (HUH--wel) or Hyw (huh-oo) ~ Welsh warrior-in-training
Catrin (KAHT-rrin) or Cat ~ Hyw's younger sister
Bran (brrahn) ~ Hyw and Cat's father, Llywelyn's steward
Adara (uhd-EHRR-uh) ~ Hyw and Cat's mother
Gawain (GAH-wayn) ~ Hyw and Cat's uncle
Rhys ap Cadwgan (hrrees ap cad-OO-gan) ~ Lord of Meirionnydd
Cat's betrothed

The House of Aberffraw

Llywelyn (thluh-WEH-lihn) ap Gruffydd ~ Prince of Wales
Elinor de Montfort ~ Llywelyn's wife (deceased)
Gwenllian (gwen-THLEE-an) ~ Llywelyn's infant daughter
Dafydd (DAHV-ith) ap Gruffydd ~ Llywelyn's brother
Elizabeth ~ Dafydd's wife
Gwladys (GLAH-duhs) ~ Dafydd & Elizabeth's daughter
Llyw (THLUH-oo) ~ Dafydd & Elizabeth's eldest son
Owain (OH-wayn) ~ Dafydd & Elizabeth's youngest son
Margred (MEHRR-grred) ~ one of Dafydd's illegitimate daughters
Rhiannon (hrree-AN-on) ~ one of Dafydd's illegitimate daughters

Other Welsh characters

Aeneus (eh-NEE-aas) ~ Head of Llywelyn's teulu (personal guard)
Cynfrig ap Madog (KUN-vrig) ~ Rhys' steward
Dai ap Rhys (die ap hrrees) ~ warrior
Drem (drrehm) ~ butcher's son from Criccieth
Enid (EH-nid) ~ wet nurse
Emrys (EM-rris) ~ warrior, Hyw's childhood friend
Gwilym ap Einion (gwihl-ihm ap eye-NEE-on) ~ noteworthy bard
Ifan (ee-van) ~ warrior in Llywelyn's teulu
Maelgwyn (MYLE-gwin) ~ Welsh priest

The English

Edward I (Longshanks) ~ King of England
Edmund Mortimer ~ heir to Baron Roger Mortimer (deceased)
Gilbert le Clare ~ Marcher Lord (from the Welsh-English border)
James ~ Shrewsbury's son, Hyw's friend, half-Welsh
Lord Shrewsbury ~ Marcher lord, Hyw's foster father
Robert ~ training to be a knight, son of Shrewsbury's cousin
Roger Lestrange ~ commander in King Edward's army
Stephen de Francton ~ a Shrewsbury knight
William de Valence ~ Marcher lord
Alan Acton, Gerald ~ soldiers who befriend Hyw

Don't forget to look in the back of the book for:

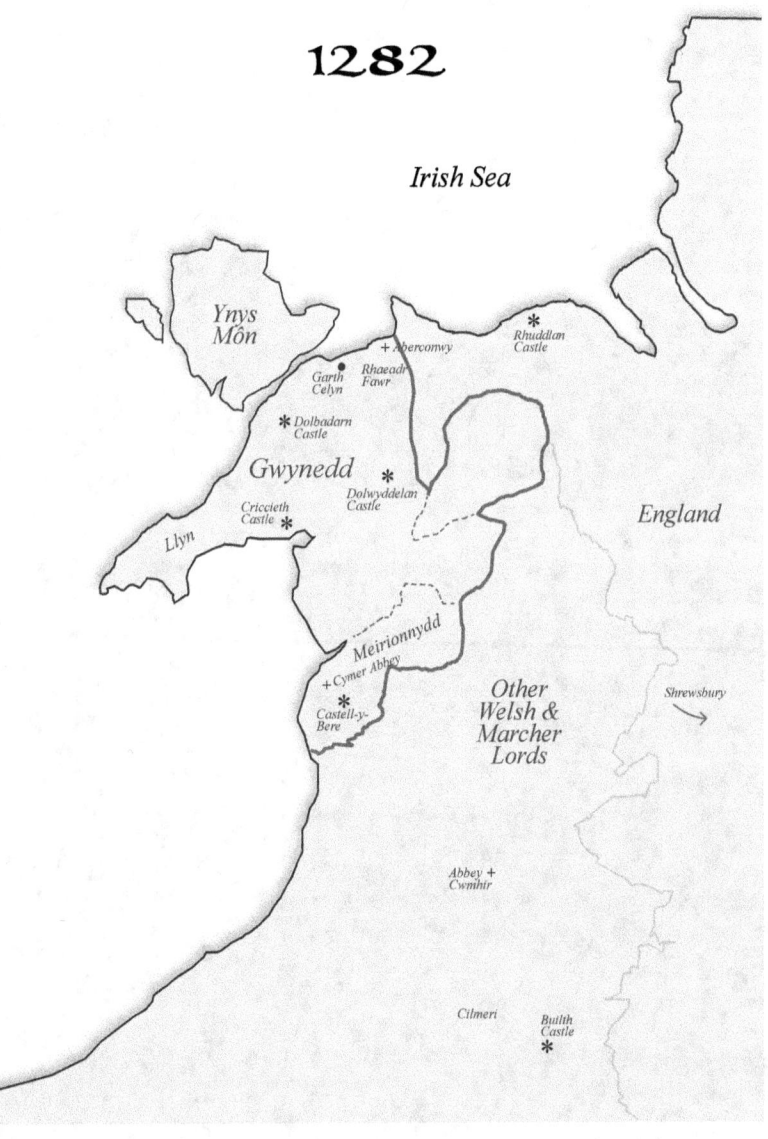

1282

Irish Sea

Ynys
Môn

+ Abercomwy

Rhaeadr
Fawr

✱ Rhuddlan
Castle

Garth
Celyn

✱ Dolbadarn
Castle

Gwynedd

✱

Dolwyddelan
Castle

Cricicieth
Castle
✱

England

Llyn

Meirionnydd

+ Cymer Abbey

✱
Castell-y-
Bere

Other
Welsh &
Marcher
Lords

Shrewsbury
→

Abbey +
Cwmhir

Cilmeri

Builth
Castle
✱

1

December 1282, Gwynedd, Cymru (North Wales)

He raised his arms, feeling bone and feather flatten against the wind, and knew himself tethered to air currents that smelled of salt and fish, somewhere off the horizon.

He ran below the bird, yet his mind and the hawk's mind moved as one. He could feel the dry December grasses beneath his bare feet, but he saw as the hawk saw: a flash of grey fur in the stubble, the swaying pattern of a tree branch.

He tried to turn the hawk's mind—his mind—to his will, and for a moment he succeeded. In the distance he could see the stone watchtower of his home at Garth Celyn, seat of the royal court of Wales. But the hawk's need was powerful, turning him back to scan the ground they circled. If he squinted—just so—at the yellow and russet clumps, he could make out the leaves of each tree. A shadow flitted from branch to branch.

Prey!

His talons ached for the soft flesh and his beak thrust forward—

No, not his. It was the hawk's beak that longed to rip the flesh from bone and feather. Hyw grasped the bird's thoughts again and turned its head toward Prince Llywelyn's tower. There! A streak of movement across the grass. Was it some grotesque beast from the

1

past? He urged the hawk to circle until he could see it more clearly. A single horse and rider galloped toward Garth Celyn.

A messenger! Fast horses in wartime never bring good news. Had the English broken the peace again? Hyw gasped, and his connection to the bird faltered.

The hawk gave a piercing shriek. Hyw felt himself falling, as if he'd dropped from its talons rather than its mind. His feet—the same feet that had seemed to barely skim the ground a moment ago—thudded against the earth. He stumbled and the momentum of his running threw him, over and down until he braced his hands against the mountainside. He almost flipped again and bit back a cry as his fingers buckled, but his shifting weight came to a stop. *Tears have no place in a warrior's world,* his father had told him when Hyw had sprained his ankle five years ago. He flexed his fingers. Each one moved, painfully. Nothing was broken.

When he shared the mind of an animal or bird, he often lost the sense of his own physical body. He was becoming familiar with the consequences of coming back to himself. This time, though, he'd taken it a step further. He'd done it! He had made the hawk turn, so he could see what he wanted through its eyes, if only for a moment. It was easier with horses, because they loved him and he them—but they couldn't see any farther than the men riding them. Hawks and other birds would be more useful in a battle. Now he had proven it. He scarcely felt the dry spears of grass as he pushed himself up.

Hyw's first thought was to tell his father. But would his da listen? His da was Bran ap Maredudd, a trusted warrior of the prince's bodyguard. When Da bid him learn the ways and customs of their English enemy by going to foster at the court of Lord Shrewsbury, Hyw had gone. He spent four long years in the borderlands. But he had returned over a week ago. Every Welsh boy in training at Garth Celyn received a red sash on his fourteenth birthday, to mark his warrior status. Hyw had turned sixteen before he left Shrewsbury's court. All last week he'd waited, but his father had not brought him a sash. Hadn't even mentioned it.

On Hyw's first evening home, his mother Adara had seemed glad that his ability had manifested while he was away. It was his inheritance from her family, similar to her brother's, she'd said.

She'd even called it a "gift" that could help them. Bran had nodded but shushed her, glancing around at the priests and other wagging tongues in the Welsh royal court. He had not called on Hyw to serve the prince at Garth Celyn. But now Hyw had something to offer. Surely, now that he could control the minds of the creatures he bonded with, he could change his father's mind.

And what word did this messenger bring? If this meant war, Hyw would be needed. Wouldn't he? At the same time, Hyw felt a nagging doubt. What of James? They were best friends, but James was Shrewsbury's son and one of the *Saeson*—English. The enemy.

Fie on it! If his father rode with the prince, Hyw must be by his side. He would work harder to master his gift and to prove its value. He could prove himself—he would—if he could make his father listen. He would win his red sash. His cheeks burned as he sprinted for Garth Celyn.

As Hyw passed through the gates, he heard an anxious neighing. He sprinted across the courtyard toward the barns in time to see a young groom, holding the reins of a lathered horse. The sunlight caught a gleam of metal and Hyw saw a heavy English saddle, rather than the darker leather gear of the Welsh. The messenger's horse! The man who'd been riding it must already be inside the longhouse.

The groom crooned softly to the horse, but it blustered, jerking its head down. "*Hogyn da,*" he repeated, but the horse reacted as if he was cursing it instead of saying "Good boy." Hyw caught sight of its wild eyes as its head reared up again, and its hooves skittered on the packed courtyard. Could it be reacting to the language itself? Hyw felt the wrath beneath the horse's bay coat like a fist in his own gut. Warhorses were bred to be fighters too. How often had he dealt with their tempers in Shrewsbury's barns? He took a deep breath and held out his hand.

"Would you like me to try?" he asked in Welsh, and the groom passed over the reins.

"Why not? He's one of the *Saeson* too, after all."

Hyw took the reins and ignored the slur. It was mild compared to some he'd overheard since his return. After so many years away, he was like a stranger to his own people. He'd had to prove himself to the English in Shrewsbury's court, but it stung to have to prove himself again here at home.

He turned his attention to the horse, reaching out with his mind to make contact with the animal. He relaxed, probing the horse's mind to find the link that would bond them. He gasped as he felt his head lengthen. His back stretched. His nostrils filled with the smell of sweat and dust. Sunlight filtered across his blinkered eyes. He was all but overcome with a wild urge to kick out and pull away. He bared his teeth and snarled.

At the sound, he opened his eyes. It always felt real, but he knew it had occurred inside his mind and not in his body. He was able to join with the animal's mind, to see and think as it did. Yet from the look on the groom's face, he had seen nothing more than another boy calming a horse. Hyw stared into the dark intelligence reflected in the horse's eyes. Its skin shivered, but it stared back at Hyw with pride and defiance. As if he were an enemy, Hyw realized. Because he was Welsh? Hyw reached out once more, crooning in English as he had to the horses in Shrewsbury's barns. Gradually it calmed.

"I'll take care of him," Hyw said quietly in Welsh, and the horse tossed its head again. The groom held his hands up in a gesture that clearly said he was leaving Hyw to his fate and backed away to attend other duties.

As Hyw turned, he spied his father's lean frame by the doors of the longhouse at the other side of the courtyard. Bran was standing with Prince Llywelyn, easy to recognize in his black mourning clothes. The prince had no doubt been training with his men when the messenger arrived. Bran must have carried the news to the prince. Even now, they would be on their way to hear the messenger's words.

The two men appeared to be watching him. For a moment Hyw felt a faint hope that his father had seen him use his gift. Then he realized the groom standing right beside him had not known what Hyw was doing, so how could his father from that distance? Perhaps he could do it again, and use this horse to convince his father that his gift would be useful to the prince. But before Hyw could wave, they turned and made their way inside the longhouse.

2

"Deep breath," Cat's mam whispered, standing with her back to the heavy embroidered draperies that kept the cookhouse separate from the rest of the longhouse. She held a thin bread platter with an assortment of meats and a mug of the prince's best ale. Cat stood facing her mam, balancing her platter of cheeses and honeyed sweetbreads. Then her mam backed through the heavy curtain, holding it open for Cat to go ahead of her into the large open room.

Their guest sat cross-legged on the floor. He was one of the *Saeson*—English—but Cat wasn't prepared for how awkward he looked, knees akimbo, waiting for his refreshments. She managed to turn her smile into a welcome. After all, Cat and her mam had been hosts of Garth Celyn since Princess Elinor's passing last summer, and good hosts were expected to serve their guests. True, a messenger would most likely have been sent to the kitchen, but Mam had said this one was a special case. Messengers came and went often at Garth Celyn these days, and most were friendly and courteous. Hadn't the English Archbishop even stayed with them a fortnight ago? The English priests had looked much the same as the Welsh, and messengers were used to travel and adapted quickly. This tall, silent man in his riding coat and boots looked more like a knight than a messenger.

Cat placed the platter on the matt of rushes in front of the messenger and sat to his left. Her mam set her platter to the right, as she handed him the mug of strong Welsh ale. Then Mam knelt and took up the thicker piece of bread with the hollowed out middle that she'd had Cook save for their English guests—a "trencher" just as Cook used to make for Princess Elinor and her ladies—and Mam chose the best pieces of meat and cheese and set them into it. Mam was proud of the way she could adapt their Welsh fare to suit English tastes, but when she handed it to him, the man only grunted.

Cat wrinkled her nose and almost *tsked* before Mam caught her eye. Mam had asked Cat to make the traditional threesome for his meal, but he hadn't even greeted her yet. She knew Mam would expect her to make an effort, but before she could think of a question to ask, the messenger downed the ale and gestured with his head towards the door.

"Where is the prince?"

"He will attend you shortly," Mam responded, smiling. "My husband has gone to let him know of your coming."

At that moment the longhouse door opened for Prince Llywelyn, with Cat's da close behind him. The messenger stood, heedless of the platters, and Cat and Mam followed suit. Cat took a few steps toward Da, but something made her hesitate. The prince cast a deep shadow as the door slowly shut behind them. His black mourning clothes made him stand out against the colourful tapestries that adorned the walls.

Cat stared up at the prince's face, noticing for the first time the lines on his forehead and around his mouth and eyes. He had always seemed ageless, but Mam said he had been the country's leader for thirty years.

The prince smiled briefly at her as he passed, and Da laid a hand on her head in blessing. Cat touched the black band around her sleeve, a sign that she and her family shared in mourning for the Princess Elinor, who had died giving birth to the prince's first child, Baby Gwen. Cat still missed the princess and her ladies, who had brought so much colour and laughter to the longhouse. Cat ducked her head and said a silent prayer for the princess' soul, as Da began Llywelyn's formal introduction, tracing the prince's lineage back to Troy itself.

Her prayer and Da's voice were cut short when the bowing messenger began to speak, in English. "My Lord Llewellyn—"

"Prince Llywelyn," Da corrected, pronouncing the prince's name in the Welsh way.

"Erhm—My apologies, but time presses. I bring greetings from Baron Edmund Mortimer, lord of the March, the newly returned heir of Wigmore Castle."

"Yes, I knew his father and respected him," said the prince, his deep baritone echoing in the hall. "I trust the new Baron is well?"

The messenger faltered for a moment, his mouth gaping like a fish pulled out of the lake. Cat realized he must have forgotten his memorized message. What manner of messenger was he? Frowning slightly, the prince gestured for the man to continue.

As he began again, Mam leaned down and whispered in Cat's ear. "Go and see to Gwenllian for me, if you please."

Cat started to remind her mam that she'd already checked on Baby Gwen when the messenger first arrived. What could change in an hour? Besides, she wanted to stay and hear what the Englishman had to say.

"Please, Catrin," Mam repeated firmly. Cat knew better than to argue when her mam used her full name. She moved toward the kitchen, but as she passed the draperies separating it from the main room, she lost herself in their heavy folds and stood very still. She often hid there to listen to the kitchen gossip, but today she was more interested in the strange Englishman.

"Attack!" she heard the Englishman say. She knew that word well enough. Those *Saeson*! They should have learned their lesson by now. Hadn't Da and the prince turned them back, time and again? But now they were coming once more. Why couldn't they just go back to their *Saeson* hovels and leave Cymru alone? Maybe Hyw would know. He'd spent years and years with them.

Then she heard the word "alliance." Did that mean friendship? She remembered the old Baron Roger. They'd had a feast when he visited last year, and she'd tasted her first pigeon pie that night. Cat frowned. She remembered another messenger a few weeks ago, bringing news of the old baron's death. That made the prince very quiet. Had they been friends? Maybe his son Edmund, the new baron, would visit and they could have another feast. She put a hand over her stomach and willed it not to growl at the thought.

"...this letter," the Englishman was saying. Cat peeked from between the curtains in time to see him step forward to hand a parchment to the prince. Llywelyn took the parchment, examined the seal, and opened it. He scanned it, then handed it to Bran. The messenger fidgeted as they read.

"Tell Baron Edmund that Wales accepts his offer of friendship," the prince finally said, in a commanding tone. "We greet him warmly as the heir to Wigmore Castle. He will be welcome here at Garth Celyn."

"My lord—" the messenger began.

"Your Royal Highness," Da corrected again, his voice threatening. "As befits the Prince of Aberffraw, Lord of Snowden, and still the Prince of Wales." Cat noticed her Da's hand move to his sword, but Llywelyn shook his head slightly.

"Yes, er, your highness, my master beseeches you to attend him at Builth," the man said, bowing formally.

Llywelyn stood with his arms folded. Da turned to him, and they exchanged a few words too low for Cat to hear. She was listening so hard, she didn't notice her mam returning to the kitchen with the platters and ale jug in her hand. Mam opened the curtains and Cat almost fell through them into the other room. Mam shifted the platters, took Cat by one arm, and pulled her through the kitchens to the outside door. The frown on Mam's face warned Cat not to argue.

"Gwenllian," Mam whispered loudly, and pushed Cat towards the hut next door, where Enid nursed the baby.

As Cat stepped into the hut, she found Enid twisting wool threads into yarn on her spindle as she crooned a wordless lullaby. "Lullay, lully..." The wet nurse had lost her own baby a few days before Gwenllian was born, and she'd moved down from her farm near *Rhaeadr Fawr* to nurse Baby Gwen instead.

Cat sidled up to the baby's cradle and stared down at her pinched little face. Baby Gwen's eyes were tight shut, and she held one fist up to her closed mouth. Cat felt a sharp pang of sympathy for Gwenllian, who had no mam to show her the way, and for Enid, who had no daughter of her own.

On her deathbed, Princess Elinor had made her mam promise

she would keep Baby Gwenllian safe. Hadn't Cat even heard it, when she'd carried more water and blankets to Mam and the other ladies? They had shushed her from the room, but she had waited in the hall. She could hear the princess groan and plead and finally scream until Cat ran outside of the longhouse and wept in the gardens. The next time she saw Elinor, she was laid out for burial, her body shrunken and her face pale and still.

Baby Gwen was all that was left of her princess now. Cat's thoughts took another turn. If Enid's baby could die, what about Baby Gwen? *No!* There had been too much death lately, and it would not touch this baby. Didn't she have Cat and her mam to protect her? And Enid, too. Between them, surely they could protect one tiny baby. Cat moved the baby's coverlet gently around her and sat nearby to listen to Enid's sad contralto.

3

Hyw was brushing the bay's hide to a mahogany shine when the kitchen boy found him.

"Lord Bran says to fetch ye," the boy panted in Welsh. Hyw wondered if his father had news of his placement at last. He told the boy he would come as soon as he stabled the big horse, and the boy ran back to the kitchens without another word.

At Shrewsbury, Hyw would have been expected to call another groom to look after the horse and immediately attend his lord's summons. But at Garth Celyn their lives were so dependent on the livestock—especially the horses—that he would be expected to finish with the horse before he reported to the longhouse. Besides, this horse would not respond to the Welsh groom. Hyw let the big stallion loose in an empty pen near the geldings to avoid friction between this aggressive visitor and the Garth Celyn stallions.

Then he quickened his pace to the longhouse, where he found Bran sorting his gear.

"There you are, Hyw," his father greeted him. "We must ride hard, and we need a squire who can manage the mounts. Are you up for another journey?"

"Yes," he said, and then shifted uncomfortably. He had still been a page when he left Shrewsbury. Saints knew he would have become a squire soon enough had he stayed, but he'd rather be a warrior and serve the prince and his father. This trip might be the way to show them what he was capable of, and so finally win his sash!

Bran turned to him. "Your prompt response makes me proud, Hyw," he said. "But you have my leave to reconsider. I know you've just returned, and you might want time with your mother and sister before—"

"No—that is, I will say farewell to them if I may, Tad." His father flinched at the formal term, but Hyw pressed on. He was the best choice for this job, whatever the circumstances, but he wasn't sure how to say it. "I know there is risk in any journey, with the English on the march, but I would go with you. Besides, none other has my gift—with horses."

His father scanned the room, even as the corners of his mouth turned up briefly in a smile. "Yes," he replied, "if your mam speaks truly, yours is a gift we will find most useful on this journey." Before Hyw could ask more questions, Bran returned to his sorting and dismissed him with a parting comment. "Best sort your gear and say your goodbyes tonight. We leave at first light."

Hyw's first thought was to find his mother. Adara was spinning near the window to catch the sunshine. When she saw him, she stood and moved to him for a hug. As she released him, her smile was genuine.

"How have you settled in, Hyw?" she asked as she drew him to the window seat, holding his hands in hers.

"Well enough, Mother," he said, loathe to tell her that he felt like a stranger again. During the years of his fosterage, thinking of her round, smiling face had brightened his heart. Shrewsbury's older lady had taken little interest in him, save the one time she referred to him as "yon Welsh cur." She spat those few words like a bad taste in her mouth, and the others of her court had taken her cue. He wondered what his mam knew of what had befallen him in Shrewsbury.

He blushed and tried to turn his head away. Adara dropped his hands quickly. "I forget how near a man you are already. Forgive me, Hyw."

"Do not fear it, Mam," he said, wishing he could reach for her hands again. She reached up then and brushed the hair from his eyes.

"That's what I was hoping for," she said. He looked at her in surprise, and she laughed. "For you to call me Mam again, instead of mo-ther." She emphasized the English pronunciation and he smiled, realizing he had been using the English words. Maybe he'd been acting like a stranger.

"Ah, what brings that flush to your cheeks, then?" she continued. "An English maid, left behind?"

"Nay, Mam," he answered quickly. "No English girl would have me." He spoke in Welsh, using "geneth" for girl with a smile, but at her look of concern he wished he had kept silent. The English girls had found little to their liking in his wiry frame. His copper hair earned its share of jeering from them, but it came, like his own gift, from his mother.

"Well," she brightened, "there will be time for a' that, now that you are home again. And glad I am of it." She laughed again, patting his folded hands.

He made a pained face. "Now is not the time," he told her. "I must take my leave shortly, to go with my father and the prince."

"So soon? But I had thought—" Adara broke off, realization dawning in her eyes. "Well, that is good news, is it not? Your da asked for you at last?"

Hyw nodded, on the verge of telling his mother that he was neither a squire nor a warrior yet, but she continued with a look of delight.

"I prayed he would call you to the prince's service, and now I will not need to prompt him," she said. "I am not pleased to see you ride to war, Hyw, but I believe this mission may help prevent one. If your da and the prince can bring the new Baron of Wigmore to their side, it may give the English king a reason to hold his advance at Rhuddlan. And I am well pleased to see you serve the prince."

"It is only one mission, Mam. I am not yet *teulu*," he said, referring to the prince's special bodyguard.

"And why should you not join your da there too?" she asked. He dared not admit he hoped to prove himself worthy, but she gave him a look as if she had read his mind. "Ach, we have tomorrow for goodbyes. Today we will make you ready. I have a fresh tunic for you."

"Not red, Mam," he admonished her, referring to the red tunics worn by Prince Llywelyn's *teulu*.

"Not yet," she answered, meaningfully. "And how does your surcoat?"

"Well enough, Mam," he mumbled as she looked his clothes over for tears to mend. As a page, he had learned to mend his own clothing in emergencies. But Adara's attentions also showed how much she cared for him, and for a moment he longed to throw his arms around her again. She often said she could call her gift when she needed it, and he wondered if he should ask her advice on using his to help him win his warrior's sash.

Before he could find the words, Enid entered, carrying Baby Gwen. Adara held out her arms for the child and began to hum softly. His sister Cat came in behind Enid and sidled closer to him. He reached out and pulled a strand of hair that had come loose before she could push him away. He had been surprised at how much she'd grown in his three-year absence. She would soon be fifteen. He wondered if arrangements had been made for her wedding, or if the war would delay that as well.

"Cat, your brother has news," Adara said. "And he needs his new tunic. Would you take him to fetch it?"

4

Cat drew her brother toward their mam's basket of sewing projects, while Enid and Adara took the baby to be admired by the other women. The tunic was neatly folded on top, waiting for the servants to come and put it with his things. As Cat shook it out for him, he told her he would be going to serve the prince as squire.

"You will be a warrior now, surely," she said, half listening. "Your gift can only help you get there." Hyw was lucky to have gained such control over his gift already. What would it be like to connect with animals like Hyw, or charm bees like their mam? Her own gift had not appeared. Some of Mam's family had no gift at all, but surely she would not be one of them.

Cat put that thought aside as she handed the tunic to him. "Don't fret. It will be red soon enough."

"It's fine," he said, taking it from her and unconsciously wringing the fabric with his hands.

"Then why aren't you smiling?"

He grimaced then, as if he was trying to smile. She made a face at him, and finally coaxed him into a grin. Then he shook his head.

"Your words reminded me of something," he said.

As his voice trailed off, Cat realized what he must be thinking. "James!" she said.

Hyw nodded, looking miserable. It was not the first time since his return. He often seemed stuck between the *Saeson* world and his own. She touched his shoulder.

"I cannot imagine it, Hyw. What it must be like to know you might meet a friend in battle."

"It's more than that," Hyw said, staring at the tunic in his hands. "James helped me forge my gift."

"He knows?"

"He guessed, one day when I worked with a nervous filly in Shrewsbury's barn. And instead of turning away or raising the alarm, he urged me to try with other animals. He helped me build something like a wall in my mind, to protect me from connecting with animals by accident. He kept my secret. It was—like a bond between us."

Cat wasn't sure what to say. Their mam had long warned them never to tell anyone outside the family about their special abilities. Did Hyw think of this *Saeson* boy as a brother, then? She almost felt jealous of him. Hyw went on to explain that James was the son of one of their father's cousins, so he was half-Welsh. Then she brightened and put her hands over Hyw's.

"I heard the messenger when he told the prince. You do not ride to war, Hyw. You ride to make an al- ally-" She paused to think of the right word in English. "Alliance."

"What else did you hear?"

Cat told him everything, even her thoughts about the strangeness of the man's dress and bearing, and his poor skills at delivering the message. "I could have done it better," she declared.

"Where is he?" Hyw craned his neck to look around the room.

"He is gone already," she told him. "Fret not, brother. The man was so anxious to leave he saddled his own horse for the journey." They both grinned at that.

"It seems strange that he would not break bread with us before he left."

"*Saeson*," Cat said with a dismissive shrug. She reached for his hand again. "Here, I made this for you," she said, taking a colourful finger bracelet from the basket and knotting it onto his wrist. "I made it for your birthday, thinking you would be here with us. Look, I braided in a few strands of my hair. The princess said everyone does it in France. For remembrance." She looked up to see him watching her, a look of concern in his eyes.

"Do you miss her very much?" he asked.

She raised her hand to her black armband again. Adara had called Cat into service when the princess first came to court. Princess Elinor and her ladies spoke only French and English and Cat's job was to sing children's songs and poems to help them learn Welsh. The princess had welcomed her. Later, Cat learned the complex meters of the bards so she could sing Welsh poetry to them. At the princess's insistence, Cat travelled with their itinerant court to visit the prince's holdings and castles. During one of these trips, Princess Elinor introduced Cat to Rhys, the boy she was promised to marry. If she had married Rhys, Cat would have become the Lady of Meirionnydd, but when the princess became pregnant, she asked Cat to put the wedding off and stay with her. Yet in the end, there was no help. Cat could not find the words to say how much she missed her princess, so she said nothing.

"I wish I had something for you in return," Hyw said. His face looked so serious.

"What of a deed instead?" she suggested. "Come and see *Rhaeadr Fawr* once more, before you go." Would he recall their old childhood races to the waterfalls? Before he could reply, she tagged him and ran off toward the path.

"No, you don't!" he cried from behind her as he followed, laughing.

The night's grey clouds had parted, allowing the wakening sun to slant off Tŷ Hir, the longhouse at the heart of Garth Celyn. This was her favourite time of the day. A wave of love for the peaceful and industrious *llys* washed over her. She shielded her eyes as she looked up, hoping to savour the moment, but she caught sight of the armed warriors pacing on the tower and shivered.

Sturdy wood and stone buildings fanned out from Tŷ Hir, creating a small town that made up the royal *llys*. Already people filtered into the courtyard to bid farewell to Llywelyn's *teulu*, the trusted warriors who made up the royal bodyguard. Cat stood with her mam, counting the warriors. At first, she was surprised not to see more of them: only about twenty men, counting her da, wearing his gold torque around his neck and red sash across his coat of mail. Her brother held the reins of the prince's horses. Of course, it took fewer warriors to make friends than to fight off enemies. She felt a small swell of pride that her brother and father were included in this select company, twenty out of one-hundred sixty warriors.

Then she was struck by an overshadowing greyness, almost a feeling of dread. No! She almost said it aloud. But her da was already embracing her mam before he bent down to her. She snuggled into the warmth of his heavy fur cloak and put her arms around his waist.

"Tada," she whispered, using the phrase she had not used since she was a small child. He hugged her closer for a moment before releasing her and ruffling her hair.

"Worry not, little Cat," he told her. "We will be back before you know we're gone."

Hyw moved to hold Aeron, their da's brown warhorse, as Bran mounted, and then held the prince's huge black stallion steady for him. As she watched, Cat wished the messenger had remained to guide them. She suddenly thought of Father Maelgwyn. What had he said at Mass? Something about being rewarded by the "fruit of his mouth" while a transgressor would only "eat violence." She shivered.

"Are you cold, sister?" Hyw asked, draping his soft cloak around her shoulders.

"No, Hyw," she said, trying to give it back to him. "You will need this."

"I have another." He held it on her shoulders a moment before pinning it in front with the gold clasp from her woolen surcoat. "This cloak was a gift to me. It is much too fine for where we are going."

She felt the soft fabric, dyed a rich blue and lined with blue-grey squirrel fur. It was a mark of wealth. "Was it from James?"

Hyw nodded and began to turn away from her. Her earlier feeling of greyness returned and threatened to overwhelm her. To escape her thoughts, she flung her arms around him in a final hug.

"Fare ye well, Hyw. May God protect you and Da," she whispered, "and may you keep the prince from harm."

"We will," he told her, kissing her cheek. His mouth twisted into a lopsided grin. "You look after our infant princess." The grin lapsed into seriousness again. "And our mam."

"I will." She hugged him fiercely another moment before he turned to mount his horse.

5

Through the morning they rode hard when the land allowed, dismounting to lead their horses through denser brush. As he rode his father's gelding, Cadarn, Hyw clicked his tongue and the horse's ears flicked forward in response. He had taken special care to groom Cadarn the previous evening, and the horse remembered and trusted him. In his free hand, Hyw held the reins of Llywelyn's fresh mount, ready in case of ambush. Vox was a stallion, powerful and used to action. Hyw connected with him often to keep him calm and quiet. He found himself glad that, since this was to be a short trip with no hunting, Llywelyn had left the dogs behind—which meant fewer animals for him to marshal.

At first, it was a matter of keeping the horses abreast and not letting the stallion take the lead. The ground in several places was already covered with snow, making the narrow trail increasingly dangerous for the horses. As the path twisted, Hyw had to make Vox fall in behind Cadarn.

Vox pushed against the lead, snorting. Hyw didn't need his gift to know the stallion was not pleased to follow the gelding, but both horses were well trained. Hyw created an image in his mind of the bushes and thickets around them, projecting his sense of urgency to Vox in a strong command: *Enemies. Be watchful.* Vox's head veered from side to side once, as if he was scanning the terrain. After that, he followed, ears forward.

The men spoke little, and the prince even less. No one sang, as they would have on most journeys. Often the prince had surprised his enemies with the swiftness of his response to battle. His warrior *teulu*—the men he often called his true family—had it down to a discipline.

Hyw scanned for birds in the trees, especially the hawks with which he felt special connection. His gift would help the men avoid danger if it came. But with Bran riding behind Llywelyn, and Hyw at the other end of the line of warriors, how could he give the alarm without explaining his gift? How receptive would his father be, with the prince and his warriors so near?

They stopped to water the horses, which most of the men accomplished without dismounting. He'd forgotten what the *teulu* were like, but he soon learned what it meant to ride hard through the mountains. At one of these stops, he made his way to his father.

"Da, I am able to see farther than most," Hyw began, holding Vox's reins as the horses drank their fill. At his father's raised eyebrow, Hyw pointed upward at a hawk circling nearby. "I can see what he sees. But how can I let you know if I spot the *Saeson*?"

Bran looked around at the wooded stream, patting Aeron's broad neck. "Once, when you were young, you and I disturbed a nest of red-tailed hawks near Aber Falls. Do you recall the sound they made?"

Hyw nodded. The chicks had made a shrill near-whistling sound with a slight warble in its centre. He felt sure he could reproduce it. "If you hear that sound today, Da, it will mean trouble," he promised.

Bran nodded as he turned Aeron's head back to the path.

The day waned into the next morning as they pressed on. Years of early training under Aeneas served Hyw well. He set his mind not to feel the cold or the hunger that gnawed at him. They needed speed and stealth. There would be no stopping to hunt or make a fire. His mam had slipped him extra bread with dried meat strips from her pocket. He ate these from the pack he'd tied to Cadarn's saddle as he saw the other men do, and he would need to make them last as long as he could.

Several times he had to jump down to wade beside the horses as they crossed treacherous fords with fast currents. Hyw had to shake himself more than once, as he began to slide from the saddle in sheer weariness. Then in panic he connected with the hawks again, making certain no enemy was near.

They were forced to a halt at the River Wye, black and swollen to the level of its banks. Impassable.

The remnants of a bridge clung to the near bank.

"*Saeson*," one of the warriors grunted, and spat on the ground.

Llywelyn motioned for Bran and a younger warrior named Goronwy to walk aside with him. They stood contemplating the river. Hyw could see the younger man gesturing down the bank and across the river. Hyw dropped from the saddle and led the horses to the water to drink.

"What can you see?" Bran asked.

"There are two armies." Hyw stood staring at the sky, seeing through the eyes of a hawk as it spied on groups of men milling about a field. Some cleaned weapons, while others put armour on each other and their horses.

"Can you see the sigils?"

Hyw drove the bird closer and described what he saw on the banners of the enemy. Bran quizzed him carefully and then nodded.

"Giffard the Saxon," Bran said. "And Roger LeStrange. We must tell the prince."

Hyw watched anxiously as his da spoke with Llywelyn, just out of earshot. He had learned about the allies and enemies of his prince's house almost from the cradle. Giffard was Llywelyn's cousin by marriage. How must the prince feel to have his cousin turn against him yet again? Llywelyn questioned Bran and then abruptly turned toward the others. Bran nodded and smiled at Hyw as the prince rallied his men.

Llywelyn's response was decisive. "The English king is upon us. We must send word to our allies."

A wave of relief flooded Hyw. The prince had believed them, although Bran would never have named Hyw or his gift as the source of the information. Llywelyn was known as a modern Welshman, with tolerance but no fondness for the old ways. The prince acted quickly, sending a man back to Garth Celyn for his army, and others to muster his allies in Gwynedd and Powys Fadog.

"We will meet at Garth Celyn in no less than three days. All haste is necessary."

As the men rode out, Llywelyn turned with a gesture to Bran and the few men remaining. Hyw's heart was pounding as he brought Vox forward. He must go with them. He could use his gift to watch the enemy, to help protect his prince—and his da. But how could he convince them?

Then he heard his da's low voice. "We must bring my son."

Prince Llywelyn stopped for a moment and looked back at Hyw. The expression in his eyes was unreadable. Finally, he nodded.

The next morning, they arrived at Abbey Cwmhir. The imposing building sprawled across the field in front of them. At Llywelyn's gesture, Goronwy remained near the gatehouse with the horses in readiness for their departure. Hyw followed Llywelyn and Bran through the gate to the church and down the long stone nave, the main aisle of the church. The vaulted ceiling rose high above them, and Hyw counted fourteen bays.

"Impressive," Bran said softly, crossing himself and bending one knee as they came in sight of the altar.

"Yes," Llywelyn responded, kneeling also. He bowed his head for a moment and rose to continue down the aisle. "After this skirmish, by my troth, I will finish it." As Hyw knelt, he realized this abbey reminded him of the abbey at Aber, near Garth Celyn. The familiar look and style of this nave meant these were the White Monks, Cistercians, who believed in the simplicity of prayer and work.

The abbot saw them and came forward with two other monks in their characteristic white robes. Llywelyn turned the abbot aside, and they spoke in a low voice for a few moments. As Hyw politely turned to look again at the church, one of the monks clasped Bran by the arm, warrior style. The two embraced briefly, and then the monk turned to Hyw.

"He has certainly grown," the monk said, using his hand to mark a space by his waist, and then by the top of Hyw's head.

"Uncle Gawain!" Hyw threw his arms around his uncle in a bear hug that was heartily returned.

"We are grateful to have this chance to see you again," Bran added.

"And lucky, for I am traveling to Aberconwy this week," Gawain said. "Now I shall have an excuse to stop in on my lady sister."

"That would please her, I am sure," Bran said.

"Enough of this family reunion," Llywelyn said, clapping Bran on the shoulder. "The abbot has given me a blessing for our actions and a brother to ensure our success."

"You have missed the morning service, I am afraid," said the old abbot with a kind look. "I must remain, but I will give Brother Gawain a special release to attend you, to aid your mission if he can."

Llywelyn offered Vox to Gawain, since the horse was already saddled and their need to get back on the road was pressing. Hyw helped him check the cinches on Vox's gear before they mounted.

"Shrewsbury treated you well?" Gawain asked quietly, using the horse to mask them from the other men.

"He did, uncle, but—" Hyw broke off, unsure how to tell his uncle. "It seems I am like you."

"Oh? In what manner?"

"Mam says you and I have a similar—gift."

Understanding dawned in Gawain's eyes. "Then I may be able to advise you, Hyw." He asked a few quick questions, and Hyw answered as well as he could. Gawain paused to look at him. "I have such a gift, but only with horses. And I have never felt what you describe, as if you are becoming one with the creature."

Hyw was unsure what to say. His dismay must have shone on his face.

"I recall our grandfather speaking so of his early years," Gawain went on quickly, placing his spare robe into the soft leather bag attached to the horse's saddle. "Perhaps I will journey to Garth Celyn for Twelfth Night, so we can spend some time together. I do not promise to have all of the answers to your questions, but what I know I will share." He tousled Hyw's hair. "Together we may sort out your strengths. Meanwhile, we must get the prince into Builth Castle to meet his allies."

Hyw expelled a breath in relief, although he had not realized he was holding it. His uncle would make good his promise as soon as their mission was complete. Other questions crowded into his mind, and he blurted out the first one almost without thinking. "Is that why you packed a second robe, uncle?"

"You have sharp eyes, I see." Gawain looked into the distance, his expression almost sad. "I forget you children were born in war and weaned on watchfulness." Then he smiled a little as he continued checking Vox's saddle and gear. "And Llywelyn himself may be your model for it, forced to be watchful for so many years. This second robe may prove its worth. With a castle shut as tight as Builth, a simple monk may travel with less notice than a rival prince."

Hyw nodded, beginning to understand his uncle's role in helping Llywelyn. The prince would dress as a monk and the two would pay a call on the castle. Gawain turned his attention to Vox. It was strange to watch his uncle use their shared gift to make contact with the skittish stallion. Hyw wondered if he looked as intense when he used his gift, and if that's how James always knew. He wondered if others could tell, or if he could school his expression to hide it.

When Vox quieted, Gawain mounted. Bran motioned for Gawain to join him farther ahead in the line of men, and there was no more time for talk.

Later that day they neared Builth and stopped to make camp. Llywelyn and Gawain moved aside to speak together. Bran and the other men began to tend their horses, and Hyw took Vox and Cadarn to the stream. He dunked his own head in the cool water as the horses drank. As the waning sun glinted off the surface, he stared down at his reflection. With one hand he fingered the threads of the bracelet his sister had woven around his wrist.

Then he stood and moved onto the bank with the horses to remove their saddles. He took his brushes from Cadarn's saddlebag to groom them. He finished Vox first, and then turned to Cadarn. His father's gelding nickered softly as Hyw came closer and nuzzled at his side to take the small apple he kept hidden there. Hyw smiled, stepping easily to Cadarn's side as he had so many times before. He had been grooming Cadarn since he was a boy, before he went away to England. Sometimes it seemed the horse remembered him better than his old friends or his family.

As he finished brushing Cadarn's shaggy winter coat to a shine, he heard the clashing of armour in the distance. Could the men be practicing, with the English army so near? Cadarn nickered uneasily, swinging his head around and twitching his ears. Hyw put away the brushes and looked up, choosing a rook from a flock hovering overhead to be his eyes. The bird could hear the faint sounds of clanging armour as well, and he willed it to look closer. Its vision caused his stomach to fist: men fighting and bleeding in a clearing.

He released the bird, left the horses grazing on the bank, and sprinted toward the clearing.

6

At first, all she saw was water.

Cat was in the chapel with her mam and some of the other women, listening to Father Maelgwyn's baritone as he sang the prayers. She had worn the cloak Hyw gave her, and she stroked the rich material with one hand. The ever-present rain drummed steadily on the stone chapel walls.

"Let us pray," Father Maelgwyn sang. Cat focused on the raindrops dripping into the chapel through the arch of the window, as she drew in a breath—

—and suddenly she could see the wide, dark expanse of a river. Was she dreaming?

She tried to open her eyes, but the picture became clearer. Black water rumbled, swollen and churning against the banks. This wasn't her familiar Aber. What river was it? Where was it?

She turned as if to ask someone, and saw her brother standing on the bank, staring into the water.

"Hyw!" She called his name, but he didn't look up. Couldn't he hear her? He snapped his head up but looked past her. And then he ran.

Things began to move around her. It was as if the scene broke apart and came together again. She was standing in a meadow. The stench of blood and death filled her nostrils. She heard a high-pitched whistle—no, a scream! Someone screaming. She raised her hands to cover her ears—

—and she found herself back in the church, kneeling. She

could feel the wooden balustrade in front of her, and hear the chant rising and falling around her.

"*Dominus vobiscum,*" the priest sang in Latin.

The Lord be with you, Cat thought automatically, the familiar words anchoring her in the ritual.

"*Et cum spiritu tuo…*" she sang back. *And with thy spirit.*

Cat looked up and found her mam's eyes, which slipped from smiling to alarm. Without dropping a word of the prayer, Adara touched Cat's forehead and then drew her into her side for support.

"*Sanctus, Sanctus, Sanctus,*" Adara's clear soprano rang out. Holy, holy, holy. This was always the part of the *Te Deum* that Cat liked best, and she joined in, harmonizing automatically.

"*…Pleni sunt caeli et terra gloria tua.*"

Heaven and Earth are full of thy glory. Had she just seen some of it? Or was it a dream? She felt a chill like the spray from the waterfall on a wintery day. Father Maelgwyn warned of darker forces. Was that what caused her vision? Was her gift evil? But how then could it come to her in church? She turned to her mam, but Adara shook her head slightly and touched one finger to her lips.

When the service was finally over, Adara drew Cat aside to walk with her toward the waterfall. They had often walked together after church when Cat was younger, but they had been too busy of late. When they had gone far enough to be out of earshot, she told her mam what had happened in the church and what she'd seen.

"What—what is it?" Cat asked. "Do you think I really saw Hyw?"

Mam thought for a moment and then nodded. "It seems clear to me that you saw him. And possibly more."

Cat shivered, thinking of the churning water and the smell of blood. "What can it mean?"

"I know not, Cat. The meadow in your vision marks a change. If this vision is of something yet to come, if it is the future, then you must have seen it for a reason."

"What reason? What can we do?"

"Often a vision is a warning. If your gift is the Second Sight, we must not ignore it."

"Second sight?"

"It's an old gift, Cat," said Mam slowly. "One I haven't seen for a long time. My grandfather used the term 'seeing beyond the veil.' There are different ways that comes to us. We each bring our own nature to it. Like the connection your brother has to animals. My own brother—your uncle Gawain—has such a gift as well."

"And you, Mam." Cat thought about the way her mam could take honey from beehives without ever being bitten, and the way no gnats or insects ever bothered their banquets and campfires. "You're a bee charmer."

"Bee charmer." A smile played around Mam's mouth. "Yes, I suppose I am. I like that, Cat. And our grandfather had a strong gift. His started with matching his mind to the creature, as Hyw does. Later he learned to fully transform into the creature. My great-aunt—rest her soul—could see the future. Our grandfather called that the Second Sight."

Cat hesitated, unsure she wanted such a gift. "But I have no gift. Or at least, I thought I didn't. Why did this happen now?"

"Maybe because we need it now," Mam said. "I've watched for your gift too, but there has been no sign. It comes to men and women in our family, but it does not come to all. I thought you might be like my youngest sister, your Aunt Cadi. One or two of each generation have been passed over, and sometimes the gift will skip generations and pass to the children or grandchildren. My mam used to say it was to balance the scales. But perhaps that can change, if the need is great. As it is now."

"Then we must do something."

"We will send someone to give the warning to your da, that he may pay special heed to your brother." Mam put her arm around Cat and turned them both back toward Garth Celyn.

7

Hyw arrived panting, more with alarm than exertion. The reek of blood and sweat surrounded him. He crouched, looking around him for soldiers, but nothing stirred. Spotting one familiar figure lying on the ground, he ran to it. He turned the body without thinking. It was not his da's face. Relief so strong it made him giddy washed over him, before he recognized the man was one of the prince's *teulu* from Garth Celyn. The warrior's eyes were open and unseeing, and his skull above shorn off. Hyw crossed himself and reached forward to close the man's eyes with a blessing. Then he turned and retched into the grass.

"Help," someone cried behind him. Hyw turned to spy another warrior lying a short distance away. "Help the prince."

The man pointed over the hillock and Hyw ran, leaving the fallen warrior to bleed into the hillside. His neck prickled with panic. He raced heedlessly over the hill and almost into the arms of an armoured man. The man grabbed Hyw instinctively and swung him around with the momentum of his charge.

"Here now," an English voice said. "What's this?" Hyw found himself dangling in the air. He stared at a group of armed soldiers, who seemed to be merely standing on the hillside together.

Then he paled: Llywelyn was there, kneeling on the ground. A spear pierced his body from front to back. Yet the prince supported one end of the stake aloft, or perhaps it held him upright. Hyw realized the prince must have been surprised by the English soldiers.

Where was his da? And his uncle Gawain?

"He's just a lad, Mortimer," said another voice to his right, this one strained and thick. "Leave him be. Has there not been enough killing this day?"

Hyw dropped roughly to the ground as the soldier laughed. "This from the man who struck down the Prince of Wales? Have you a woman's will, de Francton? Bah. Take him then. Enough of this. It ends here, prince or no."

Before the men could stop him, Hyw leapt up and ran to the prince. His knees hit the ground in front of the dying man.

"Get me a priest," rasped Llywelyn, in English. Then his black eyes focused on Hyw, and he seemed to recognize him. In Welsh, Llywelyn said, "Protect my daughter. She is all my future now."

Hyw met the prince's gaze. Llywelyn's dark eyes never wavered. As Hyw stared into them, blood roared like a dark river in his ears and his mind seemed to expand. His consciousness opened to the prince. He saw himself kneeling in the field. He must be seeing through the prince's eyes, as if he and the prince were one.

The prince cried out, "God have mercy on our souls!" And the dark eyes broke contact even as the prince's head was cleft from his body.

Hyw saw as if through a veil as the English knight held the prince's head high in the air, roaring with triumph. Blood gushed from the prince's headless body, still kneeling in the field, impaled by the spear. And blood dripped from the knight's sword onto the grass.

Something like mist spread over Hyw's mind. Clouds appeared from nowhere to dim the sun. The world turned ashen, and then as red as blood. Stars fell toward him and birds plummeted from the sky like rain as the ground thundered and rose up in its place.

As if from far away, he heard someone screaming and did not know it was himself until he felt a blow on the side of his head. Then he heard and saw—nothing.

He floated in a sea of cool water and soft cloth. He thought of Elinor, her scent and the softness of her skin. But when he opened his eyes, he saw her not. Instead, he saw a blue-eyed man in a monk's cowl.

"Hyw, glad I am to see you waken," said the monk.

"Who is Hyw?" he asked. His voice croaked, and the monk sponged his lips with a wet cloth, dripping some of the water into his mouth. He swallowed.

He recognized the monk's voice. Or did the boy recognize the voice? He shook his head and almost swooned from pain. How could it be that he, Llywelyn, could see at all? Was he not dead at the hands of the traitorous Mortimer?

Was he in hell then? He almost laughed. Had he not already been there? Any place was hell, without his wife. Again, the anguish of her loss threatened to drown him, but the monk laid a cool cloth upon his brow. "Rest, Hyw."

"Nay," he rasped. "I am not Hyw."

"He is bemused," the monk turned to an armoured soldier at his side. "But he is strong. He will rally."

Llywelyn recognized the mounted soldier who had struck him down. Somewhere inside his mind he heard the echo of a name: de Francton.

"Murderer." He tried to rise, but his head felt thick. "I am not Hyw."

The monk looked at him deeply then, into his eyes. Llywelyn read a mix of shock and horror in his face.

"Can this be?" the monk half-whispered. Then his expression became thoughtful. He moved closer and spoke the next words into Llywelyn's ear. "Fear not, my liege. All will be well."

Llywelyn's eyes began to close. He heard a voice singing and thought of Elinor. He whispered her name as he sank beneath consciousness again. It was like floating underwater.

As he sank, he saw a lad swim past him, pulling hard for the surface. Why, it is Bran's son, he thought, and slept again.

8

Cat knew before the kitchen boy came to get her.

She was kneeling in front of Baby Gwen's cradleboard, shaking a clay rattle Llywelyn had made for his daughter. It was cleverly fashioned in the shape of a smiling pig, and whatever tiny stones he had placed inside clinked cheerfully. Baby Gwen reached out her chubby fists to the rattle—which Cat held just out of reach—and giggled. Cat sang a short rhyme about patience as she gave the pig to the excited baby. Enid smiled at them.

Cat took a drink to clear her throat and leaned forward to set the cup down, adjusting her new cloak to a more comfortable position. Her eyes caught the glint of the swishing liquid as her fingers brushed the fabric—

—and she found herself in a meadow, kneeling in front of Prince Llywelyn instead. The prince's face was contorted in pain. Then she saw her brother's face. The two faces merged so she could not tell one from the other as they fell into the raging waves of a dark river. Then she saw a head raised high in the air by a mailed gauntlet. She could not see the face. Was it her brother?

She heard an echoing laughter, a man's deep spiteful laugh, and it sent a shiver down her back—

—and she was kneeling in front of Baby Gwen again.

"Hyw!" she cried out. "Where are you, brother?"

But the vision was gone.

Startled, Enid set down her mending and stood. "What is wrong, child?"

Before Cat could answer, the boy appeared at the door.

"Your mam sent me," he said. "Ye must come—right now!"

A familiar young man looked decidedly uncomfortable in the hall, a small figure turning his cap over and over in his hands as he answered her mam's barrage of questions. Aeneus was there as well, his arms crossed over his chest and his face a grim mask. Mam paced in front of them. Cat had never seen her so anxious.

"We must go at once," Mam began as soon as she saw Cat.

"Hyw is hurt," Cat said.

"As you have guessed," Mam said, casting her a warning glance. Cat, flustered, turned to Berwyn. The son of another warrior, he had left recently to join the Cistercian order, but the abbot must have sent him back to tell the family the news. Cat's knees buckled as she recalled the mailed fist and the raging river of her vision.

"What of Hyw?" Cat broke in. "Is he alive?"

"Hyw lies in a sickbed in the abbey."

"Sickbed?" What good was the Sight, if it came too late to save those she cared about? She could not make sense of what she had seen. "What happened to him?

"The abbot did not say, and I could not tarry."

"And Bran?" Mam asked. "What of my husband?"

"I am sorry, my lady," the stable boy stammered, shaking his head. "There was no word."

"No word," Mam repeated, a worried frown creasing her brow. Cat flew to her.

"Lady, the *Saeson* will come to claim Garth Celyn," said Aeneus. "We will fight them." He turned to Berwyn. "Did your abbot tell you how many troops Edward brings with him?"

"Th-th-thousands," stammered Berwyn.

"How's that?" Aeneus stepped back and swung his arms expressively. "Tell me truly, boy. How many?"

"Th-the monk said, begging your pardon, sir," Berwyn stammered. "He said to tell ye they mean to—to—"

"Monk?" Mam broke in. "Was it my brother?"

"It was, Lady," Berwyn stammered. "He was with the prince in the field, he said. They let him go because he was in his robes, and because he demanded to look after Hyw."

"My brother lives," Cat whispered.

"God be praised." Mam kept her arm around Cat, who leaned into her familiar warmth.

"He said Mortimer comes in force, and to tell my lord Aeneus that your only hope is to flee Garth Celyn."

"We must secure Llewelyn's daughter. Tell Enid to get Baby Gwen ready for travel." Mam released Cat and turned to Berwyn and Aeneus. "Aeneus, you know my brother. He would never interfere if he was not certain. See to the men."

"I will see you to safety first, Lady," the warrior answered. "Whither thou goest."

Mam frowned and then nodded. "I know you will." She put one hand to her brow. "We will take Gwenllian to Criccieth Castle. Word came yesterday that Dafydd has sent Elizabeth there, with their children. The babe should be with her family."

Dafydd was the prince's brother and heir, and Cat realized he would now be the Prince of Wales.

"Aye." Aeneus nodded. "Criccieth is more fortified than our *llys*, and the garrison is loyal. With its twin towers between us and the English, the babe will be safe."

"Dafydd will protect her as he does his own children. Send to Anglesey for more defenders to make a stand here, lest the *Saeson* get through to burn our winter stores as they tried to do five years ago."

Aeneus nodded. "I will see to it."

"Once Gwen is safe, I must go to Builth." Mam turned to Cat, her unspoken concern for Da and Hyw bright in her eyes. She seemed about to ask something, but Aeneus took a step toward them.

"Nay, you must stay with the babe," he said. He raised his hands before she could protest. "I will see you both to Criccieth, and after I will go to Builth and fetch your son. And I will find his da or bring his body home to you. On that, I give you my word."

Hyw rose to consciousness only to sink again into a place he could not remember on waking. He sensed himself rising and falling, like the tides surrounding Garth Celyn. Yet he was not near his home at all; he was in a monk's cell, stark and cold. Whenever he woke, his uncle Gawain was there, sponging his brow or holding his hand.

"My da? I did not see him. Was he—?"

"Shh. There's no news, Hyw. I will tell you as soon as I hear. Try to sleep."

"Where am I?"

"You are in my room, Hyw. In the abbey."

Hyw glimpsed a soldier standing behind Gawain. "Who—?"

"Hello, boy," the soldier said, smiling at him. "Glad I am to see you waken."

"This is Stephen de Francton, Hyw. He brought you to us."

The man's name was lost inside him for a moment, as he struggled to remember. Yes, this was the man who had spoken for him on the hill near Builth. Instantly, rage flooded Hyw, bursting from inside and outside of him at the same time. He remembered someone hitting him on the head. And something else—a spear, blood.

Gawain saw his agitation and shooed de Francton from the room. Hyw closed his eyes and slept.

He could not tell whether hours or days flashed by this way. Finally, he surfaced in a cavern pool. He was able to float gently on its surface and was surprised when the water did not splash with his movements. It was blue, and thick, and as warm as a goose-feather quilt. He looked about to see reflections of light on the stone walls. Was he somewhere deep under the mountains of his home?

At the edge of the pool, he saw his uncle Gawain standing with his head bowed. His lips were moving, but Hyw couldn't hear what he was saying.

You, lad, he heard a deep voice rumble to his left. At the same time, he felt his own breath vibrate with the words. *You are Hyw.*

He turned to find the prince sitting on a rock at the pool's edge, staring at him. Hyw frowned. It couldn't be the prince. For a moment he couldn't remember why he knew that. Then his mind flooded with the sights and sounds of the hillside again. He saw the knight, sword raised, with his other hand grasping the prince's head.

Hyw flailed in the water. Sputtering. Drowning. As he disappeared underneath the blue surface of his consciousness, he heard Gawain's voice, and clung to the sound.

Hyw heard singing. The voice was low, as if from far away. It must be his uncle. Gawain sang of the mountain and its sleeping spirits. His words were not the Latin of Cistercian monks, nor the language of English lords, but the soft words of old Cymrae*g*:

"*Cysgu mae ysbrydion o dan y mynydd...*"

"*Spirits sleep beneath the mountain...*" Gawain sang of the world that had been, and the world to come. He sang of the pool at the edge of the world, and he sang of Hyw and of the gift they shared.

When Hyw broke the surface of the thick blue water again, he saw Gawain standing at the edge. His uncle raised his head, and

Hyw watched as Gawain's eyelids fluttered and opened. For a long moment they stared at each other.

"Where are we?" Hyw wondered.

"A safe place," Gawain told him, as if he could hear his thoughts. Or perhaps Hyw spoke aloud; he could not tell. Goose down seemed to fill his mouth. He concentrated and tried again.

"How came we hither?"

"The old songs," Gawain said, smiling. Hyw couldn't understand what he meant and thought he must be dreaming. Then he remembered the other dream, of English soldiers standing over the prince. He began to shudder. Gawain reached out to him with one hand.

"The prince yet lives, Hyw. He lives in you, if you will it."

"How can it be, Uncle?"

Gawain shook his head. "'Tis true."

Hyw reached out, and felt himself pulled from the pool, although he did not touch Gawain's hand. Then he realized he was not wet. What appeared to be a pool was not one at all. Hyw stood on the rocks at the cave edge as Gawain continued.

"It would seem that in the moment of his death, your minds joined. Whether you are kindred spirits, or whether it was mere accident, the true-born Prince of Wales is here with us. With you. When his spirit left his body, it entered yours."

What magic is this? The prince's low rumble came again, and Hyw turned quickly. He opened his eyes—eyes he thought were already open—and found himself in a bed in the bare monk's cell.

His uncle stood motionless, with his cowl hiding his face. Gawain had his head bowed and he was reaching forward, one index finger touching the middle of Hyw's forehead. Inside his mind, Hyw heard his uncle's voice, calling to him as if from far away: "Close your eyes, Hyw."

Hyw did and saw Llywelyn seated on a rock in front of him. Gawain appeared to be standing with them again, at the edge of the same pool-that-was-not.

"If I close my eyes, I can see you here."

Gawain nodded. "This is where the prince lives. Inside your mind."

38

Will you sell me to the Tylwyth Teg next? Llywelyn spat the old words for what the English would call "fairies" with contempt rather than fear. His voice echoed as if it were drawn from deep within the earth. *Is this some demented OtherWorld?*

"Nay, my lord," Gawain replied, his voice low and even. "It is but the gift with which our family has served yours all these years. As we serve you still."

The prince stood. *I told your great-grandfather I had no wish for your gift. I freed you—all of you—from those old bonds of fealty. I want freedom for all of our people. An end to these superstitions that cripple us.*

Gawain waited in silence. The prince moved restlessly and spoke again.

Was I wrong then? Am I being punished? Must all of Wales suffer, because of my mistakes? Because I chose to follow God, and not the old ways? Is that why—why my Lady Princess had to die?

"Nay my lord, I cannot think it. I also choose to follow God in this life, and to put my gift to His service. Our gifts are strong, but they are natural. Part of nature."

Then why did you not prevent her death? Llywelyn's voice thundered on the cave rocks, but Gawain did not shift his position.

"You know our family, my lord. You know our hearts are true. We believe human beings can be evil, but the gift has no power over the one who wields it. We bear no ill towards your Lady or any other. She was a pure and good woman, and as a woman our Maker called her home."

Gawain fell silent as Llywelyn's shoulders shook. The prince wiped his hand across his face. Hyw drew in a deep breath. He was not sure it was his place to speak, but he must.

"My mam says—" He faltered.

Go on, lad. The Lady Adara was Elinor's truest friend in life. What says she of my lady wife's demise?

"Mam would have acted to prevent it, if she had known. She told me childbirth is the most natural of events, and just as natural for a woman to give her life to save her child's."

For a moment Llywelyn did not speak. He turned from them, and they heard him groan. When he turned back again, his face was drawn, and his dark eyes glittered. *You, lad, you have the power to keep me here. Is that true?*

Gawain nodded. "If he agrees, you may share this time with Hyw. At least, until Nos Galan Gaeaf this autumn, when we must lay all restless spirits, for their sake and our own."

Then I will have ten months. The prince shook his head. *Mortimer did not act alone. It bears the mark of my old enemy, Gruffydd ap Gwenwynwyn—*

"My lord," Gawain said. "I must caution you. If you stay for vengeance you will corrupt your immortal soul, and this boy along with it."

Llywelyn stared at Hyw for a moment and slammed his fist into his hand. *To know, and not wreak vengeance! How can you ask me that? How can I not act?*

"You must not, my lord."

And who will stop me? This boy?

Gawain stepped closer. "In peril of your soul, and Hyw's, you must act only in justice while you remain among us."

The prince's face was red, and he snarled like his namesake, the lion. *Cannot vengeance for a wrong be a kind of justice?* His will was as powerful in death as his body had been in life. It was the first time Hyw had seen the prince's fiercer nature, but he had the sense to fear it. Would saving the prince's soul damn them both?

"You are no longer part of this world, to decide this world's justice," Gawain was saying. "How can you be sure what is God's will, and what is your own?"

Llywelyn struggled to bring himself under control. *Release me from this torment. I demand it.*

"I—I cannot, my lord," Gawain replied, faltering.

"Can I do it?" Hyw asked. "Can I release him?"

Gawain shook his head. "I cannot tell. In truth, much of this lore has died with those who knew it, in these past years of war. I have not seen it done since I was a child, myself, and then only on Nos Galan Gaeaf. All I can do is guide you to abide together until then, as best I know how, if you will accept my guidance."

"What will happen to us, if we do not?" Hyw asked.

Gawain shrugged. "Madness, perhaps. Or worse. It is a thing of legends. All I know is to follow the way as I was told it. There may be those who know better, but I know them not."

Then, from the centre of his fear, Hyw felt his gift begin to stir inside him like the pure bell tone of the harp. He began to see what had happened in the final moments of his prince's life in a new light.

From the beginning, Hyw had followed his gift. He let his instinct guide him. It stood to reason that what had happened on the hillside had been his gift again. But it was also his choice, and he had chosen to act. Wales needed her prince now more than ever. And Hyw had chosen to save the prince in the only way he knew. His family had always served Llywelyn's. And without thinking, he had chosen fealty. He, Hyw ap Bran ap Maredudd ap Rhys ap Eineon, chose to stand with his prince. And he would pit his gift, his fealty, his will, all that he was, against his prince's rage. He concentrated again and managed to make his thoughts known to the prince.

"You must let me act for you, my liege. As I saved your spirit that day, so will I act to save your soul."

Llywelyn contemplated Hyw for a moment before he spoke. *Some would call the Prince of Wales the soul of the country. Verily, may you save all Wales, master Hyw.*

Hyw nodded, crossing himself. He had taken the Church for granted. He understood the Latin, but he had never really stopped to think deeply about what the priests said. He hesitated now, unsure if he could remember the words properly, and heard Llywelyn's voice again, first in Latin, and then in Welsh.

For what does it benefit a man, if he should gain the whole world but lose his soul?

Hyw turned to Gawain. He noticed his uncle frowning.

"Uncle, with your help the prince and I will make peace between us until Nos Galan Gaeaf. But what will happen then?"

"We will lay the prince's soul to rest, God willing," Gawain said, keeping his eyes averted.

"Will it be difficult?"

Gawain glanced at him. "If God is with us, we will prevail."

Then God be with us. Llywelyn bowed his head a moment, and when he raised it to look at Hyw, his eyes were determined. *Until then, let us work for peace.*

41

10

When they heard the clamour at the gates, Cat was kneeling in front of her chest, choosing what to take. She dropped her things and fled to her mam's chamber.

"Quickly," Mam said, and they ran to the main hall where they found Enid. She had finished feeding Baby Gwen and wrapped her soundly for sleep. Aeneus rushed into the hall, followed by four warriors.

"Lady, we are sore pressed at the gates," Aeneus said. "We must make you safe."

Mam hesitated a moment, and then gestured for them to follow her toward the kitchens. Cat was no stranger to war, or to secret escapes from Garth Celyn. She took Enid's arm, careful not to jostle Baby Gwen, and their small group made their way to the centre of the longhouse.

Opening the trap doors to the cellar, Aeneus helped Cat drop down into it. She lifted the wooden ladder into place for the others. Mam held Gwen as Enid stepped down it, and then handed the baby down to Cat before she descended. Three of their warriors came after, making little sound. Before Aeneus dropped through the trap door, he clasped the final warrior's forearm firmly. Aeneus descended and nodded grimly up at him. The warrior's face showed no emotion as he dropped the trap door into place. They heard a scraping overhead, and then light footfalls as he ran from the room. Cat realized he would rejoin the other men at the gate, holding the *Saeson* off as long as he could to cover their escape, even if it cost his life.

Baby Gwen stirred with a small cry, but Enid placed her little finger in the baby's mouth to suckle, soothing her. Aeneus replaced the ladder on the ground as an extra precaution. Mam and Cat each lit a torch from a bundle stored against the cellar wall. Mam pressed one hand on the wall. The release would not be found easily. It had confounded would-be attackers in years past, and Cat was not even sure she could locate it.

"We must hurry, my lady," Aeneus said softly.

Mam handed her torch to Aeneus and placed both hands against the wall. She kept her head bowed as she carefully felt along the wall with her fingertips and palms. Finally, a section of rock scraped aside. Cat jumped back as their flickering torches revealed a small, dark opening.

Mam nodded as Cat handed her the torch and led their way into the darkness. Enid passed the baby through and followed close behind. Cat paused for a moment to return the baby to Enid, as Mam pressed another hidden catch near the opening. The rock swung closed behind them, scraping a little louder than the table had along the floor earlier.

Aeneus lit another torch from the one he held and distributed it to a man behind him. Cat again led the way as their small group started along the dim passage, moving noiselessly. There was a familiarity to their movement—almost a ritual, a disappearing act they had mastered through long years of strife with English siege-masters. Their leather walking shoes barely disturbed the pebbles on the worn stone floor.

The long dark tunnel seemed to stretch ahead of them forever. Cat's mind raced. How many times as a child had she fled in the night, to hide with her mam at dawn? This time, there was no prince to rescue them, and her brother was injured. Would he live? And what of Da—where was he?

In one section, the walls had crumbled to rubble, creating a small opening barely large enough for the taller men to go through. Cat was the only one who would not have to go on hands and knees. With Cat holding the baby, Enid took her own triangular nursing shawl and placed it around Cat's back and shoulders, and then tucked both ends around Baby Gwen in the traditional style. Cat bent only enough to clear the rock ceiling, with Gwen cradled snugly to her chest in the shawl, and felt her way forward with her toes to keep her balance. Finally, the tunnel opened wider again. Enid took Gwen, who sighed and turned a little in her swaddling. Cat had barely felt the baby's weight, in spite of the awkward position.

When they came to the end of the tunnel, Mam touched Cat's shoulder and the group halted behind them. Cat's heart thumped in her chest. This passage ended at the top of the hill outside the castle walls. Always before Hyw had checked to be sure the English soldiers had not discovered it, using his gift to protect them. Mam must wish her to take Hyw's place this time.

But my gift is not the same, Cat wanted to say. Instead, she reached up and groped blindly until her hands grasped a length of leather twine hanging near the top of the low wall. She flattened her palms and pushed up against twigs and brambles. A smattering of old sealing wax flaked into her face as the curtain of thatch covering the entrance gave way. She marvelled again at her mam's ingenuity in hiding the tunnel entrance from prying eyes. Cat pushed the thatch aside, to be replaced later. She stepped through, stopping beneath an overhang of shale.

Late afternoon had turned to night while they made their escape. A sudden fork of lightning split the sky. Cat crouched, drawing her cloak around her. All she could hear was her own hushed breathing and the light patter of raindrops. She looked down at the reflection of the half-moon in a shallow puddle of water at her feet—

—and found herself in a thicket of trees. In front of her, she saw a small mound, and realized it was a man sleeping on the ground. She looked around her, and saw a group of sleeping English soldiers, with their horses tethered near. One man sat awake, his back against a tree, keeping watch.

They must be scouts, she thought, or perhaps a small group sent to capture the women.

She spotted Aeneus crouched in the underbrush, leading their small party through the forest and along the Aber River, straight toward the group of men. The soldier on watch spotted them as well. He stood, waking one of the others with his boot and motioning toward their small party. The group of sleeping soldiers was suddenly awake. The first soldier drew a knife from his belt with a grim smile. Cat tried to cry out a warning—

—and she was back at the mouth of the tunnel.

It was another vision, she realized, but not about Hyw this time. Armed *Saeson* soldiers set to prevent their escape. Surely they had to take another road. She frowned. Something else from her vision played at the edges of her mind: the soldiers had horses. Horses could hasten their journey and help them get Baby Gwen to the safety of Criccieth.

Was this vision sent to her for a reason? Was it to give her knowledge of their fate, or could she influence the outcome? As the others hovered near the tunnel entrance, she gestured to her mam. Quickly she whispered what she had seen. Mam's eyes opened wide in alarm.

"We must not take the path," she began.

"But we have no time," Cat said, and quickly explained about the horses. "These visions, Mam, are they a certain fate? Or can they be changed?"

Her mam's brows knit together, as if she was trying to recall what her grandfather had said and what she had heard in her own childhood. "We must find out." Then she nodded to Cat and took Aeneus's arm to draw him into their circle.

"When Cat first stood here, she spotted a band of men ahead on the path," Mam whispered to him. "They have horses tethered, and only one guard watching. What think you?"

He looked at Cat strangely, and then his eyes became thoughtful, roaming past her toward the dark mountain path ahead of them. "How many men —and how close?" He kept his voice lower than a whisper. "Can you point to where you saw them?"

Cat tried to recall her vision as clearly as possible. "There were eight, I think. As to how close—I cannot be certain now," she admitted.

"How is it that you came to know this?"

"I—" Cat faltered, unable to explain.

"The moon revealed it to her," Mam told him, and they exchanged glances. Aeneus nodded grimly and Mam continued, "Let

Cat lead us, and she will know the place."

"Fear not, Lady," he said. "I will see to the rest."

Cat nodded and willed herself not to think about the implications of what she was about to do.

"This way, Mam," she whispered, and the others followed her, bending low to hide their passage as best they could. When they neared the spot she had seen, she turned back and caught Aeneus's eye.

He took out his knife, placed it between his teeth, and without a word gestured to two of the men to follow him. He waved the other, a younger warrior Cat knew as Ifan, back toward the women.

Cat, Mam, and Enid sank to the ground to catch their breath. Baby Gwen stirred again, and Enid spread her cloak over the baby to feed her. Cat didn't need her gift to know they would reach Criccieth the next day, on the backs of English horses.

11

The ringing of the bells woke Hyw the next morning. Bells marked the daily routine of prayers in the Abbey: *vigils* in the early hours and *lauds* at daybreak. After each, he was soothed back to dreaming by the faint voices of the monks chanting prayers in the nearby chapel. Gawain came to Hyw's room shortly after *terce*, the third prayer of the morning.

"We buried the fallen on the hill," Gawain told him, "but rest easy, Hyw, for your da was not among them."

"Is there no word from him?"

"Nay, but take hope," Gawain put his hand on Hyw's arm. "A villager brought in a wagon of supplies to trade. He told us he saw wounded warriors in the forest on the other side of the River Wye."

Hyw's next thoughts were for the horses, Vox and Cadarn, but Gawain shook his head. Hyw felt some relief that his da's body hadn't been found on the hillside, but he worried for Bran's safety, and for the fate of his sister and mother at Garth Celyn. "What news of home?" he asked.

Gawain had heard nothing, but tried to reassure him by reporting news from the handful of villagers who had taken refuge inside the monastery. Before long, Gawain bade him rise. "We must begin," he said, placing two fingers on the centre of Hyw's forehead. "Close your eyes and call yourself to the cave where we saw the prince."

Hyw's initial attempts failed. The cave he imagined was a pale image, lacking the depth it had during his meeting with Llewelyn.

Gawain showed him how to slow his breathing and focus his mind. After one more try, he was able to feel the cave around him and see the prince again.

They fell into routine quickly, helped by the disciplined life of the monastery. Gawain recommended that Hyw not leave the room until he and Llywelyn found a way to co-exist. The first day was difficult. At first, Hyw would move about the room as he moved about in the cave in his mind. He bruised his knees on the bed, and once even banged his body into the wall.

By the second afternoon, Hyw had nearly mastered the trance-like state and could call the cave into his mind's eye as soon as he closed his eyes. Gawain worked with Hyw until the bells rang *sext* at noon, then returned until *nones* at mid-afternoon, and again until *vespers* at sunset. In between his sessions with Gawain, Hyw rested in his room, echoing what he could hear of the brothers' prayers.

Gawain seemed to have more energy when he returned from the chapel. "It's the prayers," he told Hyw. "Each hour has its own colour and feeling. Singing the hours with my brothers, even in this time of trouble, restores my strength."

Gawain had also been released from manual labour to help Hyw recover. The Cistercians, a new order, were devoted to working the land, and Hyw soon realized Gawain missed the physical and outdoor part of his daily routine. Yet his uncle did not complain, and Hyw took that as his example.

He also had Llywelyn to consider. After their sessions, the prince was often angry. Hyw thought he had seemed aloof or preoccupied when he was alive, and now he seemed to resent his dependence on Hyw. There was a sadness in him, as well. Llywelyn had bound himself to Elinor when she was young, even before they had met in person. The prince had lived a life of strict discipline, especially after the English king had captured Elinor and held her in house arrest for three years before finally allowing them to marry. Llywelyn was almost fifty years old by then, and she was twenty. Elinor was the first person he had allowed himself to trust. Now that she was dead, Hyw could sense a deep loneliness in him.

Hyw said nothing, mindful of his family's obligation, and tried to be patient. He was surprised the prince did not expect him to bow or humble himself.

A warrior is expected to fight and die for Cymru and should be treated with deference by all, said Llywelyn, *and with gratitude by his liege. You are a warrior's son, and I am asking more of you than ever I have of your father.*

Hyw worked to separate his thoughts and actions in the trance-world he shared with Llywelyn from the real world of his physical body. The more he concentrated, the more his mind's landscape seemed to come into focus. When they moved in the cave, his body remained still. Gawain reported that Hyw's lips no longer moved in the physical world when he spoke to Llywelyn in his mind.

At this sign of progress, Llywelyn began training Hyw. They trained every day, the Prince's weapon appearing in his hand as it might in a dream: a sword one day, a bow and quiver of arrows the next. Hyw stood alongside him, matching his movements and trying to learn what Llywelyn knew of fighting. When they took a break for a drink, they needed to wipe the sweat from their eyes and faces. Yet in the physical world, Hyw's face was barely flushed.

"How can this be?" Hyw asked Gawain.

"It must be as the legends describe: the OtherWorld seems as real as our physical life, but exists inside our minds." Gawain shook his head. "I believe few could call up that plane in the way you are doing, Hyw. It leads me to wonder, if we were not so pressed by the English, how far this skill could take you."

Hyw marvelled that he could be one of those few. Unlike Gawain, he wondered how much of this he would recall when he was able to train in the yard again.

Llywelyn would often ask Hyw questions about his life. Hyw told him about fostering in Shrewsbury, about the horses he tended, and about the way he first learned of his gift. He even told the prince about his friendship with James, Shrewsbury's son and heir.

Hyw longed to ask the prince about himself, especially whether the whispers of Shrewsbury's court were true: had he really hugged his cousin with one hand and driven a knife into his body with the other? And how could he imprison his own eldest brother? Hyw dared not ask. Llywelyn offered only advice on how to place his feet, or how hard to pull the bow string.

12

Criccieth Castle rose white and majestic against the morning sky. One of the men pointed out its twin towers on top of the rocky headland.

"No worries, Lady Cat," Aeneus told her. "The wee lass will be safe inside those stone walls."

The path to the gate wound around the mountainside. They dismounted. Ifan and another warrior had been leading the remaining horses to prevent them from returning to the English. The two now took the leads of all their mounts, to leave Aeneus and the other two soldiers free to defend them. Cat offered to take Ifan's horses, but he shook his head.

"The way is treacherous for the horses, lady," Ifan said. "Best that I lead them."

Two Welsh guards appeared, dressed in armour. Aeneus sang out the opening of a Welsh bardic poem. He and the guards spoke for a moment and then one clasped forearms with Aeneus in a warrior's greeting. Then the guards stepped back and waved them on.

Enid tucked Baby Gwen into her cradleboard and let one of the warriors sling it onto his back for the walk along the rocky path to the gatehouse. Cat made the climb nimbly enough, helping her mam and Enid as they needed.

When they gained entry into the courtyard, they were taken to Princess Elizabeth, wife of Dafydd, who had rightfully claimed the title Prince of Wales after Llywelyn's death. The new princess received them in her private solar, wrapped in a light blue shawl that showed off her fair hair and light skin. She embraced each of the women, including Enid and Baby Gwen.

"You have done well to come," she said. "Dafydd left for Dolwyddelan yesterday. You might have passed him on the road?"

"Nay, we passed no one," Mam shook her head. "Has there been any news of my husband Bran, your highness?"

Elizabeth frowned and turned slightly away, rocking the baby. "How strange it is to think of myself as Princess of Wales now. Please, among ourselves, please continue to call me by my name."

Mam took a step toward her. "If I may be so bold, Elizabeth, to put my heart at rest. Will you tell me what you have heard?"

Elizabeth spoke quietly. "Our messenger said—Adara, I am truly sorry. He said all perished with Llywelyn."

Mam went white, and turned her eyes to Cat. Cat moved to support her, feeling the tears coursing down her own cheeks.

"I am most sorry, Adara," Elizabeth said. "You are weak from your journey." She called to her servant. "Make room for Cat with the girls. Lady Adara and the baby will stay here in my rooms. The men will be welcome in the guardhouse." Turning back to Cat and her Mam, she added, "I will have food and drink brought to you. Come, Enid, let us see to Baby Gwen."

Elizabeth herded Enid and the baby from the room along with her own servants. For a moment, Cat and her mam found themselves alone. Mam sat in front of the fireplace and gestured to Cat to come closer.

"He is not dead. I would know. Or you would, surely. Cat, tell me again what you saw."

Cat recounted her vision again, but she had seen nothing of Bran or his fate. For the first time, Cat noticed how frail and thin her mam had become in the past few weeks; or perhaps it was that she herself had grown. Finally, perched on a low stool at her feet, Cat stroked her mam's hand and they comforted each other.

Two of Elizabeth's three children were with them at Criccieth. Gwladys was a cheerful toddler and Cat enjoyed playing games with her. Owain was a serious boy of about ten or eleven, but Cat soon discovered he knew a wealth of information about this part of Wales. He told Cat his older brother Llyw had joined the garrison at Dolbadarn.

A group of six girls in varying ages and sizes shared the nursery with them. Mam quietly explained that these were Dafydd's children by other mothers, and Elizabeth showed great charity in taking them in to protect them during the past few months. Cat noted that Elizabeth was not unkind to the girls, but she did not pay them the same attention as Owain and Gwladys. Owain called them all sisters.

The day after their arrival, Cat rose early while the other girls slept. She crept downstairs and found Owain having breakfast with a few of the other boys.

"How fare you?" he asked, as he grabbed more bread and cheese.

"Well enough," she answered, "but I look forward to working out the stiffness this morning."

He raised his eyebrows as if he wasn't sure what she meant, so she continued, "I will join you for the early exercises today."

"But you are a girl," he said.

"Yes, of course," she said. He laughed then, as did the other boys. Aeneus had always included the girls in the exercises and defence training at Garth Celyn. "Surely your sisters will join us?"

At that, the boys began to laugh in earnest. Before Cat could take them to task, Aeneus walked through the doors. He had already been in the yard, tending his horse and preparing for the morning's training sessions. He smiled at Cat and then turned to the others.

"Share the jest?" Aeneus said to them.

"They seem to be laughing at me," Cat told him.

"She thinks she will be training with us today," Owain said.

"Aye, so she will," Aeneus said. "You boys should always be ready to protect your families, and any woman who comes within your company. But we must also help our women prepare for anything they may face in the days ahead. May it help them against the devil-spawned English," he added with a grim look that sobered the boys.

Cat filed out to the yard behind Aeneus and the other boys, but Owain disappeared. As Aeneus began a series of daily exercises to improve their agility and toughen the muscles of feet and legs, she saw Owain return with his two older sisters. He grinned at her as his sisters joined in the drill, and she smiled back at him.

That night they joked with each other, flexing their sore muscles as they climbed into their shared bed.

"Sleep here," said Margred, indicating a spot between herself and her sisters. She was the eldest, and close to Cat's age. "That way when Rhiannon pulls the covers, you'll still be warm."

The other girls settled quickly, but Cat had a restless night, despite the down-filled quilt. When she closed her eyes, she dreamed of people running and screaming through the halls. Were these prophetic dreams? She wanted to ask her mam, but Adara was impatient for anything but news of Hyw and Bran. Of them, Cat had seen nothing more.

What good was this gift if she could not control it?

Aeneus left the next day to search for Bran and Hyw as he had promised. Criccieth's man would not let Cat and the other girls join in weapons training, as Aeneus had, so they spent their afternoons inside with Elizabeth, Mam, and the other women.

A few days later, while Cat played with Gwladys and Princess Elizabeth tended Baby Gwen, another messenger came. He told of troops that took every Welshman prisoner on the road. With a glance toward the children, he whispered something in Princess Elizabeth's ear that made her face go white. A prickle of fear crept up the back of Cat's neck, for her da and brother, and for Aeneus in his search for them.

Burdened by bad dreams, Cat threw herself into the festive preparations to take her mind off her fears. Princess Elizabeth was determined to give the children all the Christmas cheer that could be had, with their father and elder brother away. Cat decided to make something to cheer her mam. Elizabeth allowed her to look through her stock of woolens and fabrics, and Cat settled on making a scarf of bright Italian red. She embroidered a small tree in one end, with initials for each of them fanning out from the trunk like branches: Adara, Bran, Cat, and Hyw. It took several tries to finish, since her stitches were as loose and poorly formed as ever. She sighed and rolled it up, hoping Mam would find it useful as well as comforting.

At the Feast of St. Stephen's, they sat at the high table with Elizabeth and her children. Cat reached forward to take some roast duckling from the platter and glanced at her cup of light wine. Elizabeth always drank English wine rather than Welsh ale and served it on feast days. The liquid seemed to be swirling—

—*and she found herself at another table, in a room much more Spartan than Princess Elizabeth's domain. She looked up at the sound of a familiar voice, and on the stairs, she saw Prince Llywelyn.*

"For Cymru, let them bring us peace!" he sang. And then his face and voice seemed to melt into the face and voice of her brother Hyw as he sang the line again. Then Hyw seemed to look right at her and smile. She did not see his lips move, but she heard him as if he whispered in her ear.

"I live, Cat, and the prince lives within me." She turned toward him—

—and dropped her knife onto the table with a clatter.

Her mam turned to her, and Cat smiled and took her hands. She could hardly wait to finish so she could take her mam to a quiet corner and tell her the vision. Now she had a proper gift to give her this Christmas!

13

Gawain worked every day to help Hyw and Llywelyn develop the ability to communicate in a way no one could detect, a way that would not change Hyw's appearance or actions in physical reality. Gawain also cautioned Hyw against bonding with the minds of birds or animals while he held Llywelyn's spirit.

"You may be able to put yourself between the prince and the beasts in time, but for now focus on maintaining the space between you. Let your skills grow as they must."

During one training session, Hyw opened his eyes to find Gawain asleep on the small bed despite the bright sunlight streaming in the window. Hyw hadn't realized how exhausting the work must be for his uncle. He resolved to let Gawain sleep, and worked on his own with Llywelyn for the rest of the day.

When Gawain woke again, it was late afternoon. Gawain looked guilty, but Hyw explained what he had been doing. He couldn't help but smile when his uncle clapped him on the shoulder.

Gradually, Hyw moved more easily in the physical world while keeping his mind open to the prince. Hyw could always sense Llywelyn and hear his voice, but unless he closed his eyes, he was unable to see the prince.

He also discovered they were not restricted to the cave beneath the mountains. In the trance, he "took" them to an open field like the one outside Garth Celyn, and once into a wooded meadow. Llywelyn could also suggest new landscapes for their training, as long as the areas were familiar to Hyw. The prince had only to think of a place, and Hyw could see it in his mind and create it almost as if he was transporting them there.

Once, when Hyw closed his eyes, he found himself on a flat field of green and red squares. It was familiar, but not a natural field. He saw what looked like stone statues surrounding the prince, some upright and others on the ground, broken in pieces.

Hyw blinked: it was the chess set Llywelyn brought back from the Holy Crusades. Llywelyn had kept it in the study where he met with his councillors and nobles. Hyw had often served his father in that study when he was younger, and again since he'd come home. The pieces were carved in stone, each forming a different human figure that might live in a castle. His father had explained the figures and their placement and had begun playing the game with him in the evenings.

Now he and Llywelyn were the size of pieces on the board. Hyw turned to the prince. "This is how you see the world? As a game of strategy?"

Llywelyn stood with his arms folded across his chest and nodded. Showing this board was a gesture of trust, and one not given easily. Hyw stared at the figures carefully. Llywelyn stood in the king's position. Hyw remembered his father talk of a secret move called castling that could only be done if the king-piece had not moved.

Then another piece caught his eye. It had fallen away from the prince and broken into two pieces. Hyw connected with Llywelyn's memories as if the prince had opened a door for him: the grizzled face was Simon de Montfort, Elinor's father and Llywelyn's best friend. Hyw could even hear the knight's laugh booming off the walls at Garth Celyn. Yet de Montfort had died a decade earlier at Edward's hand, before Edward became king of England.

Like you, I fostered with the English, Hyw, and came to appreciate their ways. De Montfort was more a brother to me than any of my own.

Hyw looked up and saw an empty space behind and to Llywelyn's left. It almost seemed to glow. The Queen's position. Elinor had been Llywelyn's wife for three short years, but she had changed the game entirely for him. He could not present her fallen or broken, as he had her father. The space was empty but luminous.

Llywelyn was dressed in black. The stone figures near him shone ebony against the colourful landscape of the chessboard. That meant the prince was not the first to move, but rather the defender of the board. It was easy to guess that the board was Wales.

Few pieces remained around Llywelyn. The castles stood in their spots at either end of the board: Garth Celyn, and a large, imposing stone castle.

That is Y-Bere, Llywelyn said.

One piece in the robes of the councillor or bishop had moved into a protective position a little ahead of Llywelyn. The piece seemed to change shape in front of Hyw's eyes. Once it looked like Gawain, his uncle; then it changed to a likeness of Bran; and once he glimpsed his mother's face as well. He realized the piece represented his family and felt a flush of pride that Llywelyn saw them in this way.

Slowly, Hyw swiveled to face the enemy. As expected, the white king stared back at him: this could be none other than Edward, King of England. Beside him a white knight was poised in his advance, sword raised, grinning. Hyw shuddered and turned to Llywelyn, who answered before he could ask.

Edmund Mortimer.

Hyw was shocked to see other familiar faces in the white army: the face of Dafydd, Llywelyn's brother, crouching as a pawn in front. Several Welsh courtiers crouched with him, identifiable by their coloured emblems and coats of arms.

Their in-fighting serves the English king. Llywelyn's voice held more sorrow than anger.

"It seems they do not know a pawn cannot be crowned king," Hyw quipped, and heard what might have been a snort of laughter behind him. Hyw realized there were no black pawns on the board; in fact, no other black pieces at all.

Now you see the game for what it is. What part will you play, Hyw?

He turned back to Llywelyn. "I will not be a pawn. Even for you, my lord."

The prince studied him and nodded slightly. He unfolded his hands and gestured at the board. *Choose your piece.*

Hyw looked around him again. Then he crouched beside the fallen de Montfort and took the hilt of the knight's sword. With a *zing* he pulled it from the stone and held it high. Instantly he found himself dressed in black like his prince, and under his legs was Aeron, his father's warhorse. Hyw raised his sword, as Aeron rose with hoofs drawn, and found himself and the horse frozen in attack formation. Behind him, he heard the welcome sound of Llywelyn's gruff laugh.

"Have at us," Hyw yelled.

By Christmas Day, Gawain pronounced Hyw fit to make an appearance for the Feast of Saint Stephen the following evening. The abbot had taken in many people displaced by the fighting, and this feast honoured the saint known for his service to the poor. Llywelyn was pleased by the chance to see his people and discover how they fared. Gawain thought it would be a good test for their alliance, since many people would attend, and they could pass unnoticed in the crowd. Still, he hesitated.

"My lord, you will hear of our continued defeat at the hands of the English," he warned. "You must be careful to give nothing away."

The monastery was full of people as Hyw descended the stairs to the common eating area. He felt Llywelyn's anguish at the austerity of the room. Cat had written to him the previous year of the festivities at Garth Celyn. The newly pregnant Princess Elinor had decorated the halls and corners of the longhouse with traditional holly and ivy, along with bits of ribbon and bells, until the whole world seemed alive with the promise of the Christ child. Hyw was glad to concentrate on the stairs so he could not close his eyes to see the prince's face.

Supper was quiet and spare: roots, breads, and mutton stew with few spices, as befits the frugal Cistercian table. As Hyw ate, he looked more closely at the people around him. They were speckled with mud and their clothes were in tatters. Some had old blankets wrapped about their heads and bodies, and many were barefoot.

Their hands, faces, and even feet had been washed clean for the meal, but they sat with slumping shoulders and lowered heads. Hyw felt the prince's grief turn to anger. *Let me up, boy.*

Hyw stood and walked back to the stairs. He moved up a few steps to be visible to the crowd of peasants below. When he opened his mouth, Llywelyn's voice came from it.

> *Open your ears to my words, and*
> *Lift your head from your arms.*
> *Let the old poet lend me his voice.*

He began an old song of the brave three hundred who stood together against an army they could not hope to defeat, to protect their people. At the end of each verse, the poet named a fallen warrior, so they would not be forgotten over time. Hyw had heard the song enough to have memorized the words, but Llywelyn changed the words to praise each of the warriors who had fallen with him at Builth. He created a new verse for Bran and the others whose bodies had not been found, bringing hope to his listeners.

Hyw fingered the cord Cat had tied around his wrist and thought of his sister, and Christmases when they were children.

> *Let the mountains hide their voices,*
> *Let forest and fountain keep them safe.*
> *For Cymru, let us bring them peace.*

"The boy," someone whispered in the crowd. "Look to the boy."

Hyw did not know if they heard their prince's voice in harmony with his own, as he did, or perhaps saw the prince's shape mix with his in the way he had seen figures shifting on the chessboard. But one by one other voices joined with his. Soon the cold stones of the Cistercian monastery rang with their voices.

Shortly after Christmas, the abbot again broke into his stores for the Feast of the Holy Innocents. That night a band of weathered soldiers banged on the abbey door, demanding tribute to feed Edward's army.

Hyw was in the hall with the others when the soldiers clanged in and sat, expecting service from the hardworking Cistercians. In the spirit of the season, the abbot had welcomed them at the door. His concern showed on his face as he entered the hall with them, and Hyw wondered if the English soldiers returned a full measure of seasonal goodwill. Hyw wondered if he should try to fight, so as not to shame his lord. Then he felt or heard Llywelyn's voice, as if whispering in his ear. *Live to fight another day, lad. Yet tarry, that I may listen to their prattle.*

Gawain gestured toward their rooms, but Hyw shook his head and remained seated with the others. Gawain and another monk brought in the trenchers and served the soldiers.

"Ugh," complained one soldier, who looked to be the captain of the rest, as he sopped up the stew with bread. "Sodden tasteless mess. I thought you Welsh crusading went. Brought you nothing back to spice this gruel?"

The abbot shrugged. "We are but simple brothers here."

"Simple indeed," another soldier guffawed. "Simpletons."

"Leave them be," another said. At the man's voice, Hyw could sense Llywelyn bristle. Hyw glanced over to recognize his champion on the hill. From his dress, the man appeared to be a minor English lord. Hyw remembered his name as Stephen de Francton. Hyw closed his eyes to find the prince in full war armour. Hyw placed himself in front of Llywelyn to hold him back.

"Why do you hate this man so?"

He it was who ran me through with his spear. Lucky chance for him, but not so lucky now.

"Yet it was not he who finished you," Hyw pointed out. He remembered the look of remorse on de Francton's face as Llywelyn knelt on the hillside. "He saved me on that day—and you with me."

Llywelyn shook with rage, but made no further move. Hyw opened his eyes again. De Francton was speaking with the abbot, as the captain sloshed back the abbot's ale.

"Ah," the captain said, banging his cup down on the wooden table. He wiped his mouth on the back of his hand. De Francton cringed a little, but said nothing. "Well, good man, have you Welshmen here?"

The question caught the abbot by surprise. "We are all brothers here," he began.

"Aye, but have you Welsh brothers, Father?" The other soldiers guffawed with him at this poor jest. "For you know, do you not, that every Welshman's head will fetch a shilling at Rhuddlan?"

Hyw felt Llywelyn stiffen. *So, the fool lets slip the whereabouts of his king. Let's see what else we may glean from his manly ignorance.*

Hyw understood and slipped to the kitchens to bring more ale for the soldiers. The night wore on, and the men were fully in their cups before they uttered the words the prince had been waiting to hear.

"We took the silver seal from that devil's own pocket, before we sent the body to his cousin's wife," a soldier offered. "It seems he will receive a Christian burial after all. What's left of him."

They mean me! Llywelyn's voice grated against Hyw's ear.

"Aye, and his seal now awaits its companion at Rhuddlan," the captain added. "We hear the babe has one too, and as soon as Garth Celyn falls, we will have it."

Garth Celyn stands! Hyw was impatient to hear more of his family home, but he dared not speak. Instead he poured more ale and listened to what poured forth.

"Of what use is this silver to the king?" the abbot asked.

"Of no use, I would say." The captain laughed loudly and burped. "Save never to give these Welsh devils an excuse to rise against their betters again. He will march against them within the fortnight."

The talk went on a little longer, before the captain's face fell snoring against his arm. His men left him half sitting at the table and bunked down on the floor by the fire. The abbot showed de Francton to a guest room.

We must learn more of their plans, Llywelyn said in Hyw's inner ear. *Make haste to Rhuddlan. Afterward, if we can get word to Dafydd, we may yet stop this war.*

Hyw continued cleaning tables until he heard the other soldiers snoring too, then made his way to Gawain. "I must go to Rhuddlan."

"I heard them," his uncle whispered back. "We can leave at dawn."

"Nay, Uncle." Hyw laid a hand on his arm. "Not with a shilling on every Welshman's head. I must go. They will not notice me."

"Hyw, I cannot—"

Llywelyn again whispered to Hyw, and the boy reached out to touch his uncle's arm, concentrating. *"Then consider it an order from your liege,"* said a low, deep voice from somewhere inside him. It felt odd to have Llywelyn speak through him in that way, although he had allowed it. Hyw added in his own voice, "It will be fine, you will see. I can pass for much younger than my years. Even Edward cannot countenance killing children. And we—the prince and I—have a plan."

"What will you do?"

"Nay, 'tis best you not know, Uncle. Take my thanks, and I will take your love to my mother when I see her next."

"Tell her she has but to send word, and I will take her and the babes to the Sisters of Light for sanctuary."

With that Hyw continued clearing food to the kitchen. In the process, he gathered bread and cheese in a brown cloth wrapper that would travel in his tunic.

Before Hyw left the abbey, Gawain handed him a cloak. It was frayed but warm, with thick, serviceable lining. "I am due another soon." Hyw wondered how long that would take, given the scarce supplies of the monastery. He thanked Gawain and drew the cloak around his shoulders. They hugged and moved separately toward the doors: Hyw to the kitchen, and Gawain to his plain monk's cell.

Dawn found Hyw slipping through the hedges to the old Roman roads that led to Rhuddlan Castle, as his mind wandered beyond it to Garth Celyn.

14

On the first day of the new year, as they sat working together in Princess Elizabeth's solar, Cat heard her mam begin humming a familiar tune under her breath. Cat looked up from her attempts at embroidery. It was *Y Calan*, the traditional song of New Year's celebrations. Cat and her family—and the entire court of Prince Llywelyn—had celebrated the Christmas feasts with Princess Elinor and her ladies for the last four years. But the traditional Welsh holidays were always Cat's favourites. Mam shot her a rare grin and touched the scarf around her neck, before she changed the tune and began to hum a more traditional hymn. Cat ducked her head, pleased and embarrassed that her mam had chosen to wear her present.

At dusk, Cat heard the song echoing again at the castle gate, in a chorus of men's voices loud enough to reach them inside the castle.

"We beg your permission, we beg your permission, we beg your permission to sing…"

The sonorous three-part harmony gave Cat a thrill of recognition and a sense of safety, as if their rituals and traditions would continue no matter what threats the Welsh faced. She couldn't help running for the castle door, along with Owain, his older sisters, and the servants. Mam stood to follow, but Cat noticed Elizabeth sniff and take up her embroidery again.

"Will you not come to see the *Mari Lwyd*?" Mam asked, using the Welsh term for the Grey Mare.

"Nay, not I," said Elizabeth. "But it's important to the servants."

"And the children, apparently," said Mam. "I will go and make sure they stay out of trouble."

Mam smiled and touched Cat's shoulder as they went through the doors. Perhaps Elizabeth's English background made her reluctant to take part in the more bawdy Welsh traditions, Cat thought. But at least the princess wouldn't stop the mare, or the luck she would bring the castle once she was allowed inside. The other children ran for the gates as the singers began the third verse, and Cat couldn't contain herself any longer.

She got to the gate in time to hear the last of the ribald insults that accompanied this ritual.

"What's that? Didst thou say thou art a pathetic, pigeon-livered, pribbling pignut?" called a lusty voice from behind the gate. "A mewling, milk-livered, maggot-born miscreant?" A chorus of neighing followed his words. "What's that, my lady? Ah, the mare says she would not have credited thee to speak such truths!"

She saw the castle bard draw himself up and turn red in the face, barely able to control his rage. The man's ample girth and jiggling belly made Cat worry if his rage would do him more harm than it could ever do the mare and her merry men. Up to that point, she had heard him recite the family's genealogy and a few children's rhymes in the nursery. She leaned forward intently to hear how he would fare in the verbal sparring with the mare's merry men.

"Woudst thou try to match wits with me, thou bear-biting, beef-witted churl," the bard began, but a booming voice from the mare's entourage cut him off.

"Nay, not beef, but mare, thou clod-brained cockerel. If brains were beef, thou wouldst not have enough to feed the porcine strumpet who shares thy bed."

The bard balled his fists and hoisted himself toward the gate.

"Grab him!" called the captain of Criccieth's guards. Two warriors took the bard by both arms, dragging him back toward the castle courtyard. "Give him another flagon of ale for his trouble," the captain called. Musicians launched into another tune, and singers on both sides joined their voices in the traditional welcome songs.

The final notes turned from a hoot to a laugh as Criccieth's warriors opened the gate wider for the Grey Mare and her entourage. One of the players led the mare by a long halter, and the pipers piled through the gates behind them.

Although Cat knew what to expect, she gasped at the sight. The "mare" was over seven feet tall. Its bone-white skeleton head and long neck led to a white cloth body. Like a macabre legend, it walked on a man's legs. Harness bells jangled as the head shook its mane of bright-colored, fluttering cloth ribbons. Its long snout clacked at the children as it came through the gate. Owain screamed along with his sisters. Cat ran around the mare with the children and singers, their laughter ringing the stones.

The musicians played and danced once around the courtyard and into the castle hall where servants rolled out barrels of ale. Criccieth's warriors mingled with the four Garth Celyn warriors as well as Dafydd and Elizabeth's guard. Other women and children—the warrior's families, Cat guessed—streamed in behind the players as if called by the procession. One of the warriors tried to offer Cat a flagon of ale, but Mam frowned and bade her drink the less potent ale-and-water mix instead.

The Grey Mare cavorted around the ladies until one consented to dance a few steps. Cat laughed as the bells strung through its colourful mane jangled in time with the music to bless them all with luck and good cheer.

"Who is it?" whispered the girls, trying to guess the mare's true identity beneath the bone mask. "Who can it be?"

"Why, it's Drem, isn't it?" Margred breathed to Cat, pointing to the soft leather shoes on the mare's feet. "He's the butcher's son from town. Already he runs his father's business, they say." Although that meant little to Cat, her new friend's excited eyes told her Margred thought very well of Drem.

A niggling doubt made Cat uneasy. Margred was likely betrothed to another lord's son to form an alliance for her father, Dafydd. Cat thought briefly of Rhys, the young man she was pledged to marry. She had met Rhys several times while she traveled with Princess Elinor and the Welsh court, and thought herself lucky in the match. But being betrothed didn't need to stop them from enjoying themselves on New Year's eve, did it? They weren't doing anything improper.

"She's been eating mistletoe," called the woman leading the mare, and the warriors whistled. Cat saw sprigs of mistletoe sticking out of the skeleton mouth. The "mare" held out its bony muzzle for a kiss, and the older girls screamed and ran away. The mare lowered its head and shook its mane in mock despair. It tried to lay its skeleton head on Cat's shoulder until Margred coaxed it away to dance. When it turned to dance with another girl, Margred grabbed a flagon of ale from a passing servant.

Finally the mare removed its bony head for a moment to reveal the man beneath. Margred held up the flagon. That must be Drem. He grinned at Margred as he took the flagon and tipped it back for a long drink.

The battle of wits that had begun outside the gate continued with riddles and stories as the celebration got underway.

"Can you say the days of the week?" sang one of the players to the children. As Owain began to recite them, the player shook his finger at them and sang again. "Can you say the days of the week—but without naming them?"

The children stared at him and at each other, perplexed. Then the player turned to the adults and asked again, "Can anyone say the days of the week without naming them?"

The cook grinned. "That's a very good riddle, very good indeed. But I have guessed your riddle, if you please." The musicians stopped and the player turned toward her expectantly. The cook continued, "Why, it's the day before yesterday, yesterday, today, tomorrow, and the day after that, isn't it?"

The player bowed to her, and the crowd clapped.

"Your turn, Cookie," called out a woman's voice from the crowd.

"Oh, aye, verra well for you, isn't it? Let me think. Ah! I have in my kitchen a pot the whole sea cannot fill. Can you guess what it is?"

"Your stew pot when you make our supper, I hope," laughed a warrior.

"Nay, 'tis not, as you well know. Guess again. I have a pot the whole sea cannot fill. What is it?" She turned to the musicians and players, since it was their turn first. If they could not guess, the crowd would have a chance.

After a few unsuccessful tries, a musician sang out. "That's a very good riddle, very good indeed. But I have guessed your riddle, if you please. It's a sieve, is it not?"

The cook clapped her hands. As the musicians struck up a bawdy song, the castle doors flew open. A guard entered, followed by another group of people.

"Father Maelgwyn," cried Mam. Their priest from Garth Celyn and a bedraggled group of women, children, and older men entered. The music fell silent and everyone stood still for a moment. Then one of the castle warriors stepped forward and greeted them formally, welcoming them to the castle.

"Time to fetch a proper supper for them, isn't it," the cook said quietly, motioning to her kitchen boys and heading for the castle kitchens.

"Call the Princess Elizabeth," Mam said to a nearby servant, who dashed up the long stairs.

Cat felt as if she was waking from a strange dream. "Welcome!" she cried, as she ran to the priest and gave him a hug, and turned to hug as many of the others as she could reach.

15

Rain and the noises of the forest slowed Hyw's progress. He dared not use his gift to find out more this time, after Gawain's warning. Twice he followed sounds he thought were Welsh voices, hoping to find some sign of his da. None of the sounds led to camps or soldiers. The hair crept up on his neck as he peered at the dark thickets, but he persevered along the path at the prince's urging.

This way. Follow this stream and it will lead you to Rhuddlan.

When Hyw closed his eyes, he could see Llywelyn dressed in his fur traveling cloak, and without thinking drew Gawain's quilted one tighter around himself.

We must make haste.

Once his stores ran out, Hyw picked frozen roots and berries he knew to be edible, wrapping them in the cloth held next to his body to warm them. The stream was frozen, but he melted snow in a skin pouch the same way. A steady drizzle of cold wet snow melted around him as it fell, filling his shoes with slush. Before long, he was wrapped in mud and grime from the road. More than once he consoled himself by remembering he would soon be closer to Garth Celyn. He might at last reunite with his mother and sister.

At dawn on the fourth day of his journey, Hyw saw the spires of Rhuddlan. Sounds of clanking metal traveled across the still valley. Swords rang against armour, reminding him the English occupied the castle. He circled around to the gatehouse. As he tried to dash through the back entryway, someone grabbed him by the scruff of the neck and pulled him backwards.

"What do you think, Thomas? Worth a shilling?"

Hyw heard a short bark of laughter behind him.

"Nay, brother," said another voice. "Probably some village brat. You know the king won't pay for women and children."

"Just need to dip the heads in their own gore," came a third. "I hear they ain't looking too closely. These Welsh women with their short-cropped hair look like men anyways. Good for a tup and a shilling, eh? Boys the same."

"Oh, please, sir." Hyw mimicked the accent of the boys he'd fostered with as best he could and held up the roots from his cloth sack. "Cook sent me for som'at to spice the stew. These Welsh devils never use anything, and the king is plenty sick of bland."

"Ah let him go. He'll be in the kitchens when we need him."

The hand that held him let go abruptly. Hyw lost his balance but managed to scramble upright. One of the soldiers landed a kick on his behind that shoved him through the entranceway, and he ran without looking back.

He'd been worried what Llywelyn might think of his outburst, but he was reassured by the prince's laughter in his inner ear. *Quick thinking, boy. Now follow through and we might get out of this with our skins.*

Hyw followed Llywelyn's directions and slipped into the kitchen. He wiped the road dust from his face and hands with the traveling cloak. In case he needed it again, he folded it and stashed it in a corner by the door.

Two cook's helpers were already starting to prepare the evening meal while a third was setting up a tray of loaves and smoked herring for the breakfast tables. The English cooks would use peasant boys from the castle and villages, especially on feast days. Likely they hadn't looked too closely, and he could pass for a willing kitchen worker.

As he thought, the harried cook called out to him. "You, boy. Take this plate of eels to the high table."

Hyw picked up the dishes pointed out by the cook and followed the other helper into the great hall. Hyw glanced toward the centre of the high table and spotted a figure in purple silks that must be the English king. Edward lounged in his seat, fingers steepled in front of him, staring out over the tables of soldiers. Hyw closed his eyes and noted Llywelyn glaring in the king's direction. Hyw thought it was a good thing Llywelyn didn't have a real sword in his hand and opened his eyes again.

At the tables, people laughed and talked as they cut portions from the main dishes and set them on the thick bread trenchers that served as bowls, to be given to the poor after the meal. Hyw breathed a small prayer of relief that this meal was being served English-style with much ceremony, and several courses carried by many servants. He would never have escaped notice at Garth Celyn, with the simpler fare and more intimate groupings around a traditional Welsh meal.

Then he spotted a thatch of brown hair and a face that gladdened his heart: James, seated at a long table with a group of knights and squires. What luck! If he could get a sign to his friend, he might have an ally to help him discover the fate of Garth Celyn, and perhaps his father. Yet he must tread carefully so as not to give himself away and startle James into revealing his identity.

Hyw stepped up onto the dais and stopped near the end of the high table. He set the plate of eels between two lords wearing silk surcoats. He started when he heard one murmur thanks: Lord Shrewsbury.

Hyw ducked his head into his tunic, hoping his former lord would not recognize him in this setting. Lords and ladies rarely looked at servants, especially in another lord's home. As he hoped, Shrewsbury reached toward the plate without seeing him. The old knight had developed a lifelong habit of courtesy that had caused him to thank his host's servant, but he did not recognize that servant as his former ward.

Just then, James looked up toward the high table and his father. For a moment he merely chewed and watched. Then his mouth fell open and he stared right at Hyw. Hyw moved his hand to his lips in a shushing gesture. He had barely turned to leave the dais when someone thrust a pitcher at him. "Boy, fetch my lord more wine. Be nimble."

The voice made Hyw's blood run cold. It was Robert, the boy who had beaten him on his last day at Shrewsbury's manor—and beaten James as well. As squire, Robert now stood behind Shrewsbury's chair.

Hyw bowed and backed away. Robert moved to help Shrewsbury get a choice morsel for his trencher. Hyw moved swiftly down the tables toward James again. Many times at Shrewsbury they had helped each other escape to play after mealtimes, unnoticed by the bigger boys with table duties. One would touch the other on the shoulder as a signal, and they would leave separately to meet outside or in the kitchens. Hyw touched his friend on the shoulder as he passed, hoping James would remember the game.

Glancing back, he saw Robert's eyes following him. Had he been recognized after all? Then Hyw remembered the wine. Perhaps he could run the wine back to the table and arrange to meet James afterwards.

He filled the decanter and started back toward the dining room. As he reached the door, James appeared. Hyw drew him aside into a darkened recess.

"You didn't write or send word," James whispered fiercely. "I thought—I didn't know what to think."

Hyw whispered back, "Much has happened. I don't know how to begin. And I must return to Robert with this wine before he comes to find me."

James nodded. "We are housed in the wing across the courtyard, nearest the gates. The residences here were recently completed. My father fears the treacherous Welsh—oh, I'm sorry Hyw." James broke off, realizing what he had said. Hyw raised his eyebrows. "Sometimes I forget that my own mother was Welsh."

"You're not to blame for that," Hyw said. James had never known his mother, since she died in childbirth. Hyw had a keener sense of the depth of that loss through Llywelyn, though in a different way. He tried to think of a way to communicate that to his friend, but all he could think to do was lightly punch James' shoulder. "It is what both sides think of the other. Perhaps both are right."

"Can you slip away after the meal?" James looked hopeful. "There are many sheltered spots along the walls where we might talk in peace."

Hyw had come in through the back gate to the kitchens and was not familiar with the layout of Rhuddlan castle. Would Llywelyn know? He only knew one way to communicate with Llywelyn. Dare he take the chance, with James so near? Would James understand? Hyw had to chance it. He took a breath and closed his eyes. He found Llywelyn staring at him, arms crossed across his chest.

Aye, said the prince. *I know this castle well. 'Tis one of Edward's favourite holdings, and he has stolen it from me before. I was forced to submit to Edward here five years ago, to get Elinor back from him. No doubt he has changed it since. Never mind. We will find your friend this evening. Indeed, I would discover more of what Edward has done to the stronghold.*

Hyw opened his eyes again. Llywelyn planned to spy on the king, and his plan might compromise James. James, in turn, was staring at him. "What is it?" James asked. "Why did you stop in your tracks? You look like you've seen a ghost."

"I will explain anon. Tonight. I will find you, never fear." Before he could say more, Robert burst in upon them.

"I would not have known you, had I not seen James follow you here," Robert hissed. "Have you used your devil's craft to hide your shape?"

"He is no heretic," James said, standing up to the bigger boy.

"Let the priests decide."

Robert meant to turn him over to the English priests. Hyw had heard of their trials for heresy. Throw a man in the river: if he floats, he must be a heretic and is put to death; if he sinks, he is no heretic, but just as dead. He thought quickly. If he dropped the wine decanter would it create enough distraction that he could run? Then James stepped in front of him, glaring at Robert.

"And you will serve no master. My father will not have you as squire if you do this. And you will ne'er become a knight."

Robert stepped back from James in something like fear. Hyw felt a glimmer of hope. Then the bigger boy smiled. "But there is one thing they will believe faster than heresy." He shoved James aside and grabbed Hyw by the ear, dragging him back into the hall.

"A spy!" Robert shouted, throwing Hyw in front of the long tables of soldiers. "A Welsh spy in our midst."

16

Cat turned to see Princess Elizabeth sweep into the room, her golden hair down around her shoulders as if for bed. She looked like an angel as she offered Father Maelgwyn and their people sanctuary. The cook brought in plates heaping with cold meats and cheese, and the guards broke out another keg of ale.

As the people were eating, Elizabeth beckoned to Father Maelgwyn before starting up the stairs to her solar.

"Come with us, please, Lady Adara," she said in a low voice. She motioned to one of the serving boys to bring the priest's plate and follow them. Mam held out her hand for Cat to come as well.

The servant set the priest's plate at the table with the women around him. The boy brought wine from a decanter on the sideboard. As the door closed behind him, Princess Elizabeth nodded at the priest to tell his tale.

"We were brought from the castle by Llywelyn's man, one of those I had thought was to accompany you, Lady Adara," he began. "He managed to get us through the gates behind the fighting. He bade us to meet you here at Criccieth, and so we made haste."

"Have you any word of the English troops?" Elizabeth asked.

"The force that attacked was small, and from what I saw, our men held their own. But I fear it was merely a scouting force, with the army to follow."

"Had you any word of my husband, Father?" Mam asked. Her voice and bearing seemed calm and composed but Cat saw her

74

fingers clutched in her skirts. "Or did you meet Aeneus on the way?"

"Nay, we heard nothing of Lord Bran, although I heard your son Hyw was being tended in the Abby Cwmhir. A lad was later dispatched to Anglesey for more men, or so I heard. But we saw no one on the trail here, my lady. Neither Welsh nor English."

Mam nodded gravely and looked down. Cat frowned. He was telling them nothing new, since they had heard Berwyn's story before they left.

"The whole of the north will be at war if the English take Garth Celyn." Father Maelgwyn shook his head.

Elizabeth took a sip of her wine, and they sat in silence a moment. The priest pushed his food around his plate. Cat thought of the warrior who had replaced the trap door for them, and presumably joined the fighting.

"What happened to the warrior who helped you?" she asked.

Father Maelgwyn bowed his head and made the sign of the cross. "He went back to rejoin the fighting and said he would return if all was safe." He looked up at Cat, and she could see the sorrow in his eyes. "He did not return. We waited on the trail as he bade us, but no one followed. The following morning, we came here."

Cat said nothing. She felt her mam touch her fingers and took her hand, but she couldn't calm her fears for her brother and Da. Would Aeneus find them? Would she ever see them again?

After the Garth Celyn survivors arrived, Elizabeth sent her guards through the countryside to warn the people and offer to help any who would fight the English. Cat had taken to walking the battlements in the early hours to dispel her dreams, and she saw the first group of men making their way to the castle gate with grim expressions. That day and the next, many more followed. Some brought small herds of cows with them.

She discovered that these farmers, like the people around Garth Celyn, had fought the English many times. The guards spent their days teaching the farmers to fletch arrows, finish javelins, or curve long shafts of yew to be ready for longbows. Often, the men would train in fighting during the cool of the morning and spend afternoons sharpening weapons and scouring armour. Women from the neighbouring towns came to gather medicinal herbs such as willow bark for pain or moss to pack wounds, weave and sort linens for bandages, or help feed the growing numbers as the people prepared for war.

In the evenings, men and women gathered together for stories and songs near the fire in the outer ward. Cat, Mam, Enid and Gwen, along with Elizabeth and her family, shared rooms in the inner ward. Many of Dafydd's special bodyguards had remained with Elizabeth, including her loyal guards who had come with her from England to Wales when she married Dafydd. These guards slept near the women's quarters, as did the Garth Celyn guards who had come with Mam and Cat. If Cat got up to use the garderobe in the night, she often saw Sir Ifan patrolling the halls outside their rooms.

As January winds turned to heavy rains and sometimes snow, Cat was glad she and the girls had their fireplace, thick wall tapestries, and coverlets. The guards stayed in less fortified timber buildings of the outer ward. Horses and other animals shared one end of the timber buildings where some of the farmers and townsfolk slept. It was not surprising when sniffles and coughs made their way around the courtyard.

Eventually, Father Maelgwyn spotted the girls as they began their training. He had already joined Criccieth's more amiable priest in the chapel and was accompanying him on his rounds to fortify the guards and the people at their work. As they passed by the girls, who were warming up with stretches and exercise, Father Maelgwyn called to Cat.

"What is it you are doing here, Lady Cat?"

"We are training, Father," she replied.

"War is not the work for women," he told them. "Go about your business, ladies."

Cat tried to protest but he was adamant.

"I know you did thus at Garth Celyn, Lady Cat, but it was no more right there than it is here. And now you have no other guide but me, you must let yourself be guided." Cat wanted to say her mam guided her well enough, but the priest believed the male head of the household should be in charge. Without intervention from her father or brother, she could not change his mind.

"Come on," Margred said to her, and the sisters ran toward the castle. Cat shook her head, needing time to think things through. At one time, she might have found Hyw and enlisted his aid. Instinctively, she walked toward the horse pens where she had always been sure to find him. She leaned on the stone fence, watching the shaggy coated horses.

She had never disobeyed the priest, but she had a sudden flash of vision: Margred, her long black tresses streaming, being chased by an armoured horseman with sword raised. Cat could not let that happen! She was not really sure if it was the Sight, or her imagination run wild, but she had to do something. Surely training would make them fit and wary, better able to cope with what they may have to face.

She set out to find Owain then, and a plan hatched in her mind as she walked. By the time she found him lounging with the other boys, she had the details worked out. She drew him aside and explained what she meant to do. At first, he tried to argue, but he could see how determined she was.

"If you don't help me, I will find a way to do it myself," she said.

Owain studied her a moment, and then nodded. "Come with me."

They strolled casually toward the armoury, and he told her a riddle he had heard at the fireside the night before. She laughed, and he said quietly, "That's better. You cannot carry out a devious plan while you look so serious, Lady Cat. Trust me on that. I am the master of mischief in this castle."

She laughed again, glad he was helping her. At the armoury, he swept up a horse blanket from a bench and handed it to her. Then he began to inspect the children's wooden swords and blunted javelins, placing several on the blanket in her outstretched arms.

"What is it that you seek, Master Owain?" asked a voice. Cat turned to see Sir Ifan, the young warrior who had accompanied them from Garth Celyn, with his arms folded across his chest.

"Some of the boys mean to skirmish later, to please my Lady Cat and her friends," Owain replied smoothly, bowing slightly to him. "She is helping me choose the terms."

Ifan frowned for a moment, then nodded and moved toward the javelins. Owain turned to the light daggers then, choosing a few and hastily grabbing belts and sheaths for them.

"Come," he said, and wrapped it all in the blanket as he took it from her. He grabbed a thick shank of rope and tied the package. They made their way out of the armoury and he turned a sharp right, taking her toward the wall. He threw the blanket over the wall and turned to her.

"I will wait on the other side until you arrive. This field is sheltered from the town by the castle wall and should suit your purposes. Now you must gather the girls."

"Thank you, Owain," she began, but he cut her off with a wink.

"If you can beg a round of cheese from Cookie, that will be my reward."

She found Margred and Rhiannon, as well as a few of the other Garth Celyn girls. Owain stayed to help with their practice session and found an old squirrel hole in a tree trunk to stash their gear.

Although Cat could not manage one of the cook's prize cheese rounds later, she did get a quarter piece by saying she was taking the new girls on a walk around the castle to orient them to their new surroundings, which was at least partially true. From the look on Owain's face when she presented him with it, he was as pleased with their bargain as she was with their morning's work. He gallantly shared it with the girls and took the time to walk with them to the path on the other side of the castle where they could survey the town in daylight.

17

Hyw landed hard as Robert threw him down in front of the English knights in Rhuddlan's hall. With the agility he had regained under Aeneus' training, he recovered to one knee in time to see James step forward.

"He's not!" cried James. "Father!"

At Robert's first cry of "spy," many of the knights drew swords, and a gallant few clustered around the king. Edward stood on the dais, arms folded much as Llywelyn's had been moments ago, and glared down at him. Shrewsbury also stood with his fingertips on the tabletop, frowning intently at his son, his squire, and finally Hyw.

"Where is the spy?" Edward demanded. His voice boomed in the great hall. Several soldiers flinched, while those guarding the king moved their swords menacingly.

Fear not, lad, he heard Llywelyn whisper in his ear. *Hope is not lost, where life remains. Show them respect but no fear.*

Robert gestured toward Hyw, who had remained on one knee and turned slightly in a proper greeting to Shrewsbury, his former lord.

"That boy?" Edward's voice was incredulous. When no one moved, the king spoke again. "Are you Welsh, boy?" Hyw could only nod. Edward watched Hyw with narrowed eyes.

Hyw was unable to find his voice. Was he a spy? He had come to Rhuddlan to discover what he could about the English plans in order to help his people. Indeed, in serving one lord he had betrayed another. He was miserably aware of James, kneeling beside him, compromised.

"He serves my father, my lord," James said stoutly.

"And who is your father, boy?"

"Lord Shrewsbury, sir."

The king turned to Hyw again, more kindly this time. "Are you in service?"

In answer, Hyw held the decanter up. He looked toward Shrewsbury, unable to find his tongue.

"My lord king, if I may," Shrewsbury said. "I believe he was bringing me wine."

The king looked astonished. "He is your squire?"

Shrewsbury gestured toward Robert. "I believe my squire asked him to."

"Squire," the king boomed, turning back to Robert. "Am I to understand that you asked a Welsh spy to serve us?"

Robert, who had been mirroring Edward's stance, unfolded his arms and took a step back. His face flushed. "Nay, my lord—" he spluttered.

Shrewsbury took that moment to pick up his mug, gesturing for Hyw to come forward with the wine. "I apologize for my squire, my lord," he said graciously. "His zeal against the Welsh leads him to be ever watchful. These boys have both been in my service four years."

"And you vouch for this one?"

"He has been loyal to me."

"Then may he be so to his liege as well."

"I—I will, my lord." Hyw found his voice. His liege was Llywelyn, after all, and he served as well as he could. He sent up a silent prayer, thankful he could speak the truth, although it might not be the truth Edward heard.

Edward resumed his seat. Hyw stood, keeping his eyes on Shrewsbury, and walked around the dais away from the king. He relied on his training to keep himself erect and pour the wine into the old lord's mug with a steady hand. The soldiers soon lost interest in him and went back to eating. An old soldier cuffed Robert on the ear and sent him sprawling.

"Do not bother your betters with your boyish rivalries, lad," the soldier growled.

On the dais, Hyw bowed low to Shrewsbury.

"So, I find you in my service again, Hyw," the old lord said. "Come to me first thing tomorrow. I would have words with you."

"Aye, my lord." He stumbled from the dais. James stood as well, and moved back toward his own place at the tables. Before they could speak again, another kitchen boy grabbed Hyw's arm roughly.

"Come, Welsh," he spat, "we have work for you anon."

Hyw saw the boy nod over his shoulder toward Robert, as he dragged Hyw from the room toward the kitchens. Robert had recovered himself and was staring at them, his face almost snarling. The older boy would not soon forget the incident.

The kitchen boys kept Hyw busy cleaning grates and all the dirtiest places of the kitchen. All the while they cast insults and well-aimed kicks at him. He was able to dodge most, but his pride was wounded. Robert came to gloat once.

"Make sure he has too much to do to spy on anyone," he growled, handing a copper coin to one of the kitchen boys.

"Welsh devil," laughed the boy, excited to be noticed, lashing out at Hyw again with his bare foot. Hyw dodged easily and the boy fell on his behind as his foot connected with nothing but air. It was little help, though, because Robert kicked him instead and sent Hyw sprawling in turn.

Hyw gathered the last of the plates from the tables as the soldiers bedded down on the floor of the great hall. James had not come to see him before the old lord and his family retired to their wing. Hyw was both glad and sorry. Glad because James would have tried to defend him, and they would have both ended up being beaten—and sorry because they might have stood a chance together.

He closed his eyes, but Llywelyn was nowhere to be found either. Hyw wondered how the prince could hide himself. And whether he might be able to hide someday, if the need arose.

After the cook chased the other boys back to work, they more or less forgot about him. Hyw did the work they set him and said nothing. When the servants had taken themselves to bed, he curled into a warm corner of the kitchen. The cloak he had left there had disappeared, but he had little energy left to mourn its loss. He still had to face Lord Shrewsbury in the morning.

Hyw jerked awake again before dawn and made his way to the courtyard. Rhuddlan was an English castle now, and nowhere was that more evident. There was no ritual shaving while the English held court, or boys ready to help the men shave the hair from body and head. Hyw spotted a vat of cold wash water from the pots the night before and washed some of the grime from his face and hands.

He wasn't sure which direction to go to find Shrewsbury's rooms or how to make his way around the huge stone castle. It was larger and very different from the welcoming wooden structures of Garth Celyn. The stone was cold to the touch and felt menacing. He closed his eyes in the dark. Llywelyn reappeared, and Hyw was glad to find company. He sent his thoughts to Llywelyn as a question.

"Last night I sought you. How came you to disappear?"

I did not think you wished a witness to your ordeal, lad. Llywelyn appeared to turn away. *Many times, as page in an English house, I suffered so. I was younger than you are now when my uncle accepted me as part of his court, and I am glad of it.*

Hyw was a little touched by Llywelyn's consideration. He wanted to know how it was done, though. "It was a neat trick, to disappear."

The prince stared at him and then laughed. *You mean could you do the same if you tried? You know more of this process than I, boy.*

"We both act on instinct then, my liege."

Llywelyn showed him the way to Shrewsbury's rooms, but in the near-dark Hyw almost stumbled into Shrewsbury's new page. The boy slept outside the door. Hyw didn't recognize him. He felt a pang to remember this was his own position a few short months ago.

With a sigh he gave his name to the boy and asked him to tell Lord Shrewsbury he was waiting.

The boy disappeared through the doorway. When he returned, he gestured for Hyw to follow, sneaking glances at him as they went. Hyw couldn't help wondering if the child was trying to see the pointed ears or tail of a "Welsh devil." Yet he said little, more concerned with how to answer the old lord's questions.

Shrewsbury was dressed and ready for him, and Hyw knelt before his former master as custom demanded. For a few moments Shrewsbury looked through some rolls of parchment without acknowledging him. The older man wore a familiar wool tunic over his other clothing. Hyw remembered the soft texture of it, but also the tightness of the weft in its weaving. He wondered if the new page had enough strength to stretch it wide over the man's broad chest, as Hyw had when he'd dressed the lord for training exercises in the yard. It seemed much longer than four months ago.

His knee began to ache with kneeling. When Shrewsbury finally looked up, he did not smile. "So, Hyw, it seems you have found your way into my service again. Or do I flatter myself?"

"My lord, I could do no better." Hyw meant what he said, but felt his face redden.

Shrewsbury finally gestured for Hyw to stand. "Robert is no fool, Hyw, as you and I both know. I wonder why you did not come to me plainly last night."

Hyw raised his eyes as far as the garnet clasp at Shrewsbury's neck, but could neither speak nor look into his eyes.

"I promised your father I would foster you, Hyw, and I will keep that promise. Yet if it is a spy's game you play here, you must know it cannot come to good. Many young men are tempted by gold or glory, but this king does not take treachery lightly. And Robert's are not the only eyes that watch you now."

"Lucky none but my lord can see my soul," Hyw said softly. He was thinking of Llywelyn, trapped inside him, and was tempted to tell the old lord everything. Shrewsbury folded his arms across his chest.

"Many a lord would cuff you for speaking out so, Hyw. Lucky for you I know your ways from my own fosterage in Wales, where I met my first lady, James' mother. Yet know this: God can truly see your soul, and that is as it should be. Be faithful and do your duty well."

"Yes sir."

"If it is your intention to return to my service, know that I will not tolerate any action that stinks of spying. What is in your mind is between you and God, but your actions on this earth reflect on me. I cannot and I will not protect you, if you prove disloyal. Do you understand me, Hyw?"

"Yes, m'lord."

"Then we will not speak of it again." Shrewsbury stared at him a moment longer, before unfolding his arms. "What news have you of your father?"

Hyw felt his chest cave and kept his head down. He could not find his voice. Shrewsbury spoke more softly.

"We had news of Llywelyn's death before Christmastime. I thought your father could not have been far away. Is he also—?"

Hyw felt a lump in his throat, and swallowed it down, but his voice was much quieter than he intended. "I know not, my lord. No trace of him has been found."

"I am sorry to hear it, yet I fear worse. Wars in the borderlands come and go, but this time Edward will stay until it is finished. When that happens, the world may seem a topsy-turvy place for you, and for all with Welsh blood. For my son's sake, and the sake of his dear mother, you may have a place with our guards."

Shrewsbury reached out then and clasped Hyw's shoulder. James' mother, the first Lady Shrewsbury, had been a distant cousin to Hyw's father. They shared bonds of kinship as well as fosterage. She had died birthing James, but as eldest son he would someday be the lord of Shrewsbury. Hyw could think of no better fate than serving in James' guard—but that could lead to fighting against his own people in border skirmishes. Hyw's head whirled with divided loyalties.

Always I have liked this man, Marcher lord or no. He heard Llywelyn's voice in his ear again. *He has honour and kindness in him. I envy him that. You must stay with him, Hyw. He may be useful to us.*

At Llywelyn's last words, Hyw shrugged away, and out of

Shrewsbury's grip as well. Then he knelt again at the old lord's feet.

"My lord," he said, "I could have no finer master than you, and I will serve you in my heart long after I am a man. I know not what I might do, if this war ends as you say. I am Welsh and wish to please my father also. In good conscience, I cannot fight against my own people. But I pledge you this: if I become a knight hereafter, I will never take arms against your son James in battle. I love him like a brother, and will protect him as well as I am able, against all calamity."

The old man considered what Hyw had said. "Your honesty commends you, Hyw, and your bond with my son is well known to me. I appreciate your wish not to fight your own people, but your knowledge of Garth Celyn may compromise you." He paused, stroking his beard. "As soon as I am able, I would get James to Shrewsbury, away from this war. Perhaps you should come with us. Young Robert may win his spurs in the next battle. That will occupy him well, and he would be better served to forget your enmity in service to Edward. I would make you my squire, Hyw. You might then come to Shrewsbury again when this is done and serve me without betraying your own."

"So I will, if you will have me, my lord, and thank you." Hyw was surprised at the old knight's offer, and grateful not to be parted from James again.

"See you do your duty well." The old lord's arm was strong, and he cuffed Hyw on the shoulder. Hyw stood fast, anticipating the cuff he might receive upon knighthood would be much stronger.

That's right, Llywelyn spoke in his ear. *Do your duty, as you pledged you would.* Hyw wondered where his deeper duty lay: to his master Shrewsbury, who offered him a place and the chance to serve James after him, or to the dead prince he carried inside him?

Your purpose here is to find out what you can and get word to your people, Llywelyn reminded him.

Shrewsbury beckoned him to the door. "Come Hyw, let us find James, and try our skills in the yard, before we break our fast with the others."

"What happened to you after you left us, Hyw?" James asked that night. "When you did not send word, I was sore afraid for you. When we saw the prince's head–"

"You saw?"

"Oh, 'twas horrible. And all I could think was that your father may have been nearby. And you—?"

Hyw nodded but could not speak. He longed to confide in his friend about events on the hill, but he could not find words to explain. James patted his shoulder. "You do not need to say, Hyw. I can see in your face how it was with you. Know this: you can confide in me as you choose. I will not betray you. I would die first."

"Nay, never say it James. Have no fears for me, but protect yourself. For I am pledged to give my life for yours—and I am not ready to lie down yet!" Hyw grinned away his embarrassment.

"Come, you fat slug, let me teach you how to dodge the quintain again."

At that Hyw leapt up and followed James, glad for an excuse to run.

18

Cat quickly settled into the routine of training with the other girls each day after chores, explaining it away as a walk or a chance to show the newcomers around. Few noticed the girls in the bustle of activity and people milling about the castle yard. As soon as they got outside the gate, they would meet in their field, choosing a spot on the other side of the wall from the smithy to cover the noise.

Margred naturally led them in warm-up exercises, since she was the most agile and enjoyed the chance to show off a little as the others struggled to keep up. Cat, who had the benefit of Aeneus' tutoring at Garth Celyn, then led them in a series of exercises with the wooden weapons designed to help build their arm and upper body strength. Although Aeneus had never let the girls participate in hand-to-hand combat training, he had encouraged them to throw javelin and lightweight knives at targets. The girls tied planks of wood together to fashion a target, and took turns throwing the javelins and knives Cat and Owain had purloined from Criccieth's armoury.

Owain's younger sisters often joined them, as did several older girls from the Garth Celyn group and a few of the farm women and servants from Criccieth. Cat made a point of swearing them to secrecy, lest the priests discover their activity. With all the extra souls in the castle, she hoped Father Maelgwyn would be busy enough ministering to them to forget the girls—at least for a time. They often returned in smaller groups to begin their afternoon chores. For

Margred, her sisters, and Cat, that meant joining Elizabeth at her embroidery.

One morning the fierce rains and winds of January howled around the castle. Cat sat in the hall at breakfast, chewing staunchly and waiting for Margred. Beside her, Owain groaned.

"You're lucky to be born a woman, Cat," he said. "At least you can stay inside this fine day." He laid his head along his arm on the tabletop.

Cat bristled, recalling Aeneus' words to the warriors of Garth Celyn on wintry days. She repeated them to Owain now. "Do you think the sun will always be shining when our enemies attack?"

"You sound like our captain of the guards," he told her.

She worked hard to recall that he was several years her junior, and calmed herself. "We do not choose the trials that form us." She was quoting her da this time. Owain peered up at her, and she could not resist poking his arm playfully. "Are you going to let mere women show you up?"

"You're not going out in this, surely," he said, more statement than question, raising his head. "You cannot. You will be blown away."

"We shall see."

"You will be alone. My sisters certainly will not join you. I cannot allow it."

Prince's son or no, there were times when his arrogance irked her. Cat said nothing more, pushing back from the table and marching up the stairs to the room she shared with the girls. Owain trooped at her heels.

She burst into their room and shook Margred and Rhiannon awake. Owain leapt onto the bed beside them all, his eyes snapping with laughter.

"Awake, awake," he sang, composing an englyn on the spot:
"Awake, awake, my sisters here abed.
Now end your dreams of bliss.
Do not make the young Cat hiss.
For her, your moaning dismiss."

"You have little grace and less harmony," laughed Rhiannon, hitting him with the feather pillows. He laughed and pulled her from the bed into a heap on the floor, where he tickled her mercilessly until the servants came in and chased him from the room. By then, the girls were awake and there was no going back under the warm quilts.

For all Owain's teasing, only Margred went with Cat into the gale. After an hour lashed by wind and rain, the two girls had missed more targets than they hit and had fallen so many times their clothes looked and felt like a wall of slush and mud. But their energy kindled against the elements as they stowed their gear in its hidey-hole and raced each other back to the castle.

Margred burst through the doors a hair before Cat. Drenched and laughing, Cat almost didn't notice a man warming his hands by the fire in the inner hall. She thought perhaps he had just arrived. He turned toward them and bowed. The girls bowed in turn but refrained from speaking to him until they could be introduced. Cat thought he looked very familiar to her, and then recognized him as a bard who had travelled with Llywelyn's court the previous year.

"Good day to you, Gwilym ap Einion," she said, curtsying to him. "Pardon our appearance, but we were caught in the weather."

"I am sorry to hear it, young Lady Catrin, but glad to see you here," he responded. He made a strangled sound she thought might have been laughter, but he deftly turned it into a cough.

"May I introduce you to Margred, daughter of Prince Dafydd," Cat said. She stopped abruptly, realizing she did not know Margred's mother's name, and hoped he would not notice as she fully introduced him in turn. As they exchanged greetings, he gazed at Margred longer than seemed polite. Margred made their excuses, grabbed Cat by the arm, and turned toward the stone staircase.

The two girls slogged up to their room to change from their wet things, and Cat all but forgot him as they combed their hair by the fire in their room. She showed Margred how to plait her long black hair the way Princess Elinor and her ladies had preferred. Cat still missed them, but after Elinor died they had asked to return home to resume their own lives. Cat moved back to admire her handiwork.

"You are so beautiful this way, Margred," Cat said.

"Mam says beauty is a curse for a poor woman," Margred said. Before Cat could ask her anything more, she grabbed the bone comb and began to brush Cat's unruly copper locks for her. Rhiannon and the younger girls demanded to learn the new braiding style. By the time they were finished all of them sported the new look, and Margred had mastered it also.

Afterward, Cat and Margred went to Elizabeth's solar, where Cat planned to resign herself to better her skills at embroidery. But the servant making Elizabeth's bed said the ladies had both gone down to entertain "a gentleman"—although the quirk in her mouth told them the girl was not altogether certain he was a gentleman. Wandering bards had a reputation in the Welsh countryside, but a bard of Gwilym's stature and skill had always commanded respect at Llywelyn's court. Cat frowned a little, wondering what had happened to make the girl think badly of the bard.

Margred grabbed her hand and they raced down the stairs again. Princess Elizabeth had joined Gwilym to sit near the fireplace, and they stood to greet the girls. Elizabeth frowned at them as Cat and Margred came to a clattering halt. Mam, holding Baby Gwen, stood too, hiding a smile as she held her free hand out to Cat. The girls came closer.

"It is a pleasure to greet the daughters of the house," he said, bowing to them.

"My husband's daughter," Elizabeth said quietly, her face frozen in a polite smile.

Gwilym turned to her with an encouraging smile. "As we protect all of our children now, may they return to aid us in our nether years."

He smiled at Cat and she liked the twinkle she saw in his eye. He certainly did not seem much like the disreputable wandering bards she had seen come through Garth Celyn, or on her travels with Princess Elinor in past years. As he turned to Margred, his expression changed again. Before he could say anything, Princess Elizabeth spoke.

"Gwilym brings us good news this day, Cat."

"Aye," he said, turning from Margred with what seemed like reluctance, before he smiled at the other women. "I had been across the borderlands these last few months, working out the details of a land settlement for Prince Llywelyn. When word came to us of his untimely murder, I travelled through Builth to learn as much of the truth as I could. I discovered two pieces of information that may interest you.

"First, Prince Dafydd survived the loss of Hawarden and is still at liberty. I have it on good authority that he is safe at Dolwyddelan Castle and intends to prevent King Edward's troops from massing farther north.

"Second, I passed through Abbey Cwmhir, and spoke to a man who claims to be your brother, Lady Adara. He tells me that no trace of your husband was found after the fray. We may surmise that Bran leads the Welsh army against the remaining English."

"And my son? Was there news of him?"

"Aye, Lady. Your son Hyw has taken the northward road to Rhuddlan and come under the protection of his former foster father, Lord Shrewsbury."

"He is with the English?"

"It cannot be." Cat spoke without thinking and ignored her mam's signals. "He would not return to them."

Gwilym turned to her. "I have it on reliable authority," he said. "Yet have no fear. He is not a traitor to his country. Nay, rather, he plans to return with news that may help his people."

She frowned, scarcely listening to her mam's questions. Could the poet be right? Would Hyw betray his friend to save his country?

"—and you are welcome to share our hospitality, such as it is, for as long as you may need it," Princess Elizabeth was saying.

"Winter's bite can scarce be felt with two such early roses to brighten the room," Gwilym said, turning back to Margred and Cat. Gwilym's bow included them both in the compliment, but his eyes never left Margred's face. Cat felt her own cheeks go warm on her friend's behalf, and she wondered if Margred's mam had been right about her beauty.

19

War came upon them swiftly. One afternoon, when Hyw and James were sparring with the other squires, Shrewsbury was called away to Edward's chambers, along with several of the other Marcher lords. When the old lord returned, the boys saw him gesture to his soldiers and they scrambled to prepare to march the following morning.

At dawn a priest gave a hasty blessing, and they formed up in companies. The knights around them were keyed up. These were mainly personal guards, set to meet the bulk of their companies in camps outside the castle gates. Hyw noted many of the more seasoned were quiet or even surly, lacking the enthusiasm of the younger men.

Hyw's heart thumped to the rhythm of hooves pounding the cold ground as he rode out of the gates at James' side. He couldn't help but wonder whether the Welsh were nearby. Where was his da? Would he be with the warriors? Would he have to fight one of his own countrymen—or his own Da? If he did not, would harm come to James, or to Shrewsbury?

Llywelyn spoke in Hyw's ear. *Remember your duty.* Hyw nodded, keeping his thoughts to himself.

He needn't have worried. Shrewsbury sent them as far from the fray as he could. Hyw and James waited with two of Shrewsbury's soldiers

on a hillside near the English camp. Around him, he could hear the clanking of arms and men's shouts. Llywelyn whispered again. *If only we had a bird's eye view of this field.*

At those words, Hyw looked up and saw the sky full of black rooks. Then, circling with outspread wings, a huge and beautiful hawk. *Boy, if you use your gift, can we become this bird?*

Careful that James and the other soldiers did not notice him, Hyw closed his eyes to make contact with Llywelyn. "My liege, while I cannot take its corporeal form, I can see through its eyes. Its world can be as real for me as mine own. Or as yours."

Then we must do so.

"But this is what Gawain warned us against. It poses danger for us both."

Llywelyn considered his words. *Always the paths fork ahead of us. The path of green fields and well-trodden ground may also hide a hole to snare the foot of an unwary horse. Its rider then lies face-down in the dust. The path beset by brambles and thorns will breed caution before ever we lay a foot upon it. Thus may a man bravely set out to conquer the way, and more safely reach the end of his journey.*

Hyw understood then why the Welsh lords had followed Llywelyn, even when they intended to fight him. He dismounted to gain better balance, checking his mount's saddle to cover his actions. Mindful of Gawain's cautions, he closed his eyes, placed himself in front of the prince, and threw his mind to the hawk in the sky. He made contact with greater ease than he expected, then felt the shock of wary fear in the bird. At first, he thought the bird was afraid of him, but he sensed it was something outside of their connection. Looking down from the bird's mind, Hyw could see the valley of Clwd below. The battlefield.

Llywelyn, as if looking over Hyw's shoulder, pointed out one Welsh lord or another who had stood with him in battles over the past five years. They watched as the Welsh lords lined up in squares, arms moving to make the sign of the cross on their chests. Row upon row of men crowded together. Where Romans would have linked shields and swords, the Welsh warriors had leather jerkins and lances, and bright war paint on their faces.

No, you fools, Llywelyn cried. *The men don't know this form of fighting. Let them rush and retreat, as they always do.*

The hawk would not go nearer to see the faces of the men who urged the warriors into battle. Then with a roar, the Welsh ran down the hillside. Their lords rode at their sides, streaming proud Welsh colours down into the valley below. The English in their armour rode at them, clanking, from the other side.

As the English swords dove into their lines, the Welsh drove their lances upward. The larger warriors tried to pull the armoured knights from their horses with their bare hands. Then those same warriors were cut down, sharp steel hacking them in two from behind. The battle began to shift. Armour and steel won out over sinew and bone.

The Welsh turned to flee to safety in the hills. Row upon row of their own countrymen stood in their path. The English rode in from the sides and forced them together. Like a wave turning upon itself, they fell to the sword and to their own fear. Llywelyn screamed useless commands. No one heard him but Hyw.

The proud hawk that shared his mind with Hyw was sickened at the smell of sweat and blood. It was held there by Hyw's will, but wanted only to be gone. Hyw tasted copper in his mouth. The hawk would not hunt for prey in this field for many months to come. He felt the bird's disgust at the carrion-eaters, black rooks that dove and plucked at eyes and faces. Hyw felt the pull to flight in himself, but Llywelyn urged him closer.

The hawk shrieked once as Hyw prompted it to circle, slowly drawing nearer. Scores of men lay dead and dying. A hundred—nay, two hundred Welsh warriors lay among them. A mere handful of armoured English knights had fallen. Riderless horses screamed and thrashed, or milled about with fear, banding together in clumps or running wildly across the hills.

Welsh colours trailed upon the ground. English knights on horseback drove Welsh lances into the bodies of the dying. Soldiers hacked at the bodies and flipped something up onto a wheeled cart. Hyw realized it was a cart full of heads and the glint of gold torques that marked a warrior's prowess and skill.

The world blazed red and Hyw felt himself fall into the sun, his wings melting like the stories of Icarus his tutors once told him.

He plummeted downward, his mind full of the sights of war and the screams of his countrymen. Llywelyn's voice was silent.

20

During the following day, Gwilym made no secret of his admiration for Margred. Princess Elizabeth met his hints with that same frozen smile, and Margred grumbled. "She means me to wed a man of more influence," she told Cat at night in their room.

"Would you rather have Gwilym?" Cat asked. "He is a notable poet and often argues disputes of law before Prince Llywelyn's court—I mean, he once did."

"But he's so old, Cat," Margred said, turning away.

"He's not! He can't be more than—"

"Anyway, one old man is much the same as any other. Will you come with us to Market Day in the town tomorrow?"

Cat raised her eyebrows. Margred was skilled at conversation, and this change of subject was more abrupt and clumsy than she had managed previously. Then Cat wondered if it really was a change of subject.

"Will the butcher's son be there?" she asked, teasing. "What was his name again?"

Margred laughed but caught Cat's arm. "You must not mention him! Truly, you must not. Promise me." When Cat nodded, Margred laughed again, a little more light-heartedly, and handed her the bone comb. "Will you braid my hair again?"

On Market Day, it was raining before they left the castle. Mam had asked Cat to buy some fabric and thread, pressing a few pennies into her hand. "That should leave a little something for you, and enough for breakfast for you and Margred," she said with a smile. Cat felt guilty for a moment, wondering what Mam would think of Margred's butcher boy, but she took the money and kept her friend's secret.

Cat covered the beautiful cloak her brother had given her with her old rainproof one, and pulled the hood up over her careful braids, as did Margred. They kept well within sight of Sir Ifan, who accompanied them, but far enough ahead so they could speak privately. Not that they spoke much on the journey to town. Even with the extra clothing, both girls were red-cheeked from the cold by the time they reached the market.

At first it seemed dreary and grey. Puddles dragged at their skirts and plastered their hoods onto their hair. Then the rain stopped for a moment, and the girls were able to throw back their hoods and loosen their fastenings. The market stirred around them. The quiet streets unnerved Cat. She had been looking forward to the voices calling out from stalls around the square, harmonizing to attract their attention and tempt their pocketbooks. But today the sellers showed few wares from their stalls and wagons, and those who were out in the street stepped with silent purpose through the puddles. Margred had to ask the peddler to show Cat her thread when they heard a deep voice chime from a nearby stall.

"Laverbread."

"Ah," Margred exclaimed softly as she turned toward the voice. "I told you we didn't need breakfast at the castle." Looking past Margred, Cat saw the butcher's son beckoning to them with a smile. She wondered why the butcher's stall would serve laverbread, the tasty seaweed rolled with oats.

Margred held her hand out for a penny. He must have known this was her friend's favourite. Perhaps it had been pre-arranged between them? As Margred took the coin and headed for the stall,

Cat lagged behind a little, hoping to give her friend a moment of privacy. The rain dripped from the makeshift stalls to fall in puddles near her feet. A droplet shimmered and coiled in the act of falling. It seemed to expand around her—

—and she found herself standing at the castle battlements. Below her the stones seemed to smoulder with grey smoke. The wind filled her nostrils with the smell of burning flowers, burning flesh, burning torches and the clash and ring of steel on steel. Somewhere nearby she could hear the screams of children, and the frightened cries of men and women. She saw a dark-haired woman running and a man chasing her down, heard the raucous laughter and the screams of what came after.

She saw a man raise his sword and cut the head from a young boy with flaming red hair and then she was screaming his name. "Owain! Owain!" But the wind carried her voice away, up into the air, and she could see it as if the words were flying.

Then it wasn't her voice, at all. It was another sound. "Caw! Caw!" Flocks of jackdaws and ravens filled the air, circling and cawing. One of the jackdaws flew by her, and its yellow eyes bore deep into her soul, and it cawed one word: "Death!"—

—and she felt swallowed in its blackness.

"Cat!" Someone was calling her name and shaking her. "Cat! What happened?"

It was Margred's voice. She struggled as she felt a woman's hand on her forehead.

"She's burning up, poor thing."

"We must get her back to the castle."

Cat frowned. She tried to tell Margred she would be all right. She didn't want to interrupt her friend's plans. Her mouth felt dry and she could not seem to form the words.

Wait—wait! She remembered her vision. She did need to go to the castle. She must find Mam. Cat struggled to open her eyes. But all she saw was the giant head of a raven, its yellow eye staring into hers, and then blackness again.

Cat felt the softness of a down-filled coverlet and smelled the scent of lilies. Princess Elinor, she thought. Oh Princess, save us!

And then she heard singing, and the coo of a small bird. No, not a bird. A child. Baby Gwen, laughing and gurgling, and her mam's voice singing a soft lullaby.

"Huna'n dawel, annwyl blentyn…"

Sleep quietly, dear child. Cat remembered the words to the song she had heard long ago, when she was little older than Baby Gwen or Baby Gwladys. Somehow, she knew that her mother, who sang the words, also had them sung to her. And she floated back through all the babies and the mothers of her ancestors, back to the first mother of her line, Aylwen verch Arianrhod, woman of Troy, first Briton to learn the ways of the *dderwyddon* or Druids—

—and she felt Aylwen's hand on her brow and heard her singing.

"First mother," Cat said. *"Why is this happening to me?"*

"We gained these gifts to help our people," Aylwen said. *"Now these gifts are yours. When we are most in need, the gift returns stronger than before. As it was given to my sons and my daughters, so it was given to you."*

"Why," Cat struggled to speak. *"Why me?"*

"Because you are my last daughter." Cat looked deep into Aylwen's *violet eyes and saw that she was weeping.* "You and your brother are the last of our kind. And when you die, you will blaze a trail across the sky for us to follow. But it is not your time. This is the time when you must help us. You must tell what you have seen. You must awaken, Cat. Waken, Cat—"

"Wake up, Cat," she heard, but it was not Aylwen's voice. It was Adara, her own Mam. "Please wake up."

Cat's eyes flew open, and she saw her mother's face near hers. She reached out, and Mam hugged her. "Oh, Cat," she said, her voice thick with emotion. "I thought—I didn't know what to think!"

"I'm all right, Mam," Cat said, breaking free. "I had a vision. Much stronger than before."

"Of your Da?"

"Much worse." Cat relayed the vision to her mam, recalling every detail. She swallowed bile as she told about Owain, and the raven, and Aylwen's violet eyes. When she had told it all, Mam sat for a moment, staring at the wall.

"Could this be true?" she whispered. "Are we all going to die?"

"Aylwen said to warn them," Cat said, throwing back the goose-down cover and sitting up. For a moment she felt dizzy, and her mam steadied her as she regained her balance. Then she stood. "We must warn Elizabeth."

"And yet, how can we do so?" Mam asked, placing a hand on Cat's shoulder. "How can we tell her what you have seen in a dream, and make her believe us? What I know of Elizabeth tells me she will not be easily convinced."

"There must be a way to prevent what I saw, Mam, and we must find it."

21

"Hyw! Are you injured?"

He heard a voice as if from far away and was surprised to find himself prone on the hillside. He stared up at the overcast sky.

"Wake up! Hyw, are you all right?"

The voice was closer now. James. Hyw's head felt too heavy to raise. He heard James leap down from his horse, and the swish of footsteps as his friend flopped down beside him.

"Did you—" James' voice grew quiet, so the soldiers wouldn't hear. "What did you see? Did you see the battle—"

"No." Hyw struggled to sit up then. James offered an arm. Hyw grabbed it and hung on even after he was sitting on the cold ground. "Your father is right, James. This is not a battle. It's a slaughter."

"Have you seen it, then? Tell me."

Hyw let go of James and plucked a fistful of frozen grass instead, letting the cold sting his fingers. He stared across the hilltop. James laid one hand on his. They sat together for a moment. Then James cleared his throat.

"Your silence tells me all."

Hyw put his other hand over James' hand, linking them like chainmail. After a long silent moment, James added, "I'm sorry for your countrymen."

Hyw was stung into responding. "We are your countrymen

too, or at least we were your mother's. Do you feel no kinship when we are slaughtered?"

James was silent, but he removed his hand and stood, moving to his horse. Too late, Hyw realized what he had said. He jumped up to follow James, but Llywelyn murmured, *Leave it be, Hyw.*

They heard a distant horn. "Come, Hyw," James said, mounting his horse again. "That horn recalls our troops. Ride with me to my father. He must hear more of this."

From the top of a large tent pitched in the encampment, Shrewsbury's standard of three lion heads flapped in the wind. As they made their way toward it, Hyw saw a smattering of soldiers and knights, some in armour, some with bandages over wounds, and some polishing or repairing their equipment. He was relieved to see they'd managed to arrive before Robert and the other knights returned from the field.

Shrewsbury had spread out maps and other parchment upon a makeshift table in the large tent. The lord had removed his armoured leggings and mail for comfort. His dark velvet surcoat hung loosely over his shoulders. Three lion heads with roaring mouths were embroidered on it, in an intricate pattern of gold thread. Shrewsbury stood at his full height, one gloved hand under his chin, staring down at them. He was formidable, and Hyw understood then what it was to be an English lord.

"Father," James said, catching Hyw as he stumbled forward. "Is it over? Do we return to Rhuddlan?"

"A fair question, James." The old lord looked steadily at Hyw as he spoke. "Nay, we march on Dolwyddelan."

They remained camped in the field two days. The old lord had pitched his tents on a sheltered hillside, close enough to the battle to engage quickly and far enough to escape the worst of its sounds and smells. Shrewsbury set James and Hyw to fetch and carry for the squires as they cleaned the blood from blades and armour and made ready for another attack. As he worked, Hyw could hear Llywelyn's questions, pushing him to learn all he could of their plans. Hyw had his own reasons for wanting to know, and he listened for scraps of news. He preferred to stay busy, for whenever he stopped, he was plagued by worries about his mother and sister. He wondered also if his da was alive, and if he would be among the Welsh warriors fighting them at Dolwyddelan.

Knights and squires alike seemed weary and more than a little subdued by the carnage of the battle. Even Robert did not crow over his first kills, although it became known that he would be knighted by the king himself, along with several others who had seen battle on the hillside near Builth.

Learn from those who have survived the longest, the prince commanded. Since soldiers and mercenaries had no squires, Hyw helped one old soldier polish his armour. The man, Alan Acton, came from a border town, so he was familiar with the ways of Welsh and English.

"See the crests and coats of arms?" Alan said. "That be the only means of knowing friend from foe on the battlefield. Once these fellows have their armour on and helmets down, you cannot tell one man from his enemy."

"Whose are the gold lions on a red background?" Hyw asked.

"That's the king himself, Hyw. Three gold lions 'passant guardant.' That means they face you, there, waving their right forepaw, as you see. Anyone who carries those colours carries the king into battle, so to speak."

Hyw noticed the king's lions were shorter than the lions of Gwynedd and had more ruff than the sleek red lions on Llywelyn's personal coat of arms. "Is that on everything the king owns?"

"Aye, that or the rose with gold petals and a green stalk. Those be the king's own, mind you. Our Shrewsbury, he also sports lions, but with three heads instead. He has savvy, our lord. You can see by the grey in his hair and beard. Follow him into battle, young master, and like as not ye'll follow him out again."

Hyw also heard disturbing news as he listened and worked

among the soldiers. Another group had already marched north to take Garth Celyn. At the same time, they would lay siege to several strategic Welsh castles leading through the Eryri mountains, including Dolwyddelan, to cut off any hope of retreat inland. Edward's superiority at sea would prevent the Welsh from sailing over the strait to find refuge in Ireland.

"Some bloody Welsh weasel and his son from Powys are fighting with us, I'm told," Alan told him.

Gruffydd ap Gwenwynwyn and his son. Long have they been the bane of my life, Llywelyn growled inside Hyw. Hyw knew their names from the stories his father had told him. Before Hyw was born, they had tried to assassinate Llywelyn, and then gained sanctuary with the English.

The old soldier leaned closer. "Aye, and they draw point in this march." He grinned, and Hyw realized Gruffydd and his son would face their countrymen first, before the English. The old soldier swore. "Mortimer and his men will no doubt follow, keeping their eyes on those Welshman. Devil take them all."

Llywelyn uttered a soft laugh, but Hyw tried to concentrate on what Alan was saying. After Moritimer's company, Alan expected the troops of Henry de Lacy, followed by the king. Gilbert le Clare would keep close watch as the king's rear guard. Le Clare was the subject of many discussions around the fire at Garth Celyn. He was the scourge of the south, keeping the king's peace with an iron fist.

Shrewsbury's knights would be glad enough to follow the king, Alan told him, grinning. It meant they were cushioned between le Clare's troops in front, and Richard Chester's troops behind to take the brunt of any action the Welsh might muster from the rear. It also gave the more enterprising knights among them one more day to strip the gold torques and other valuables from the bodies of their enemies. Hyw turned his head away and closed his eyes to calm Llywelyn as Alan finished speaking.

Finally, everything was in readiness. After a day's rest and some new booty, Shrewsbury's soldiers were at their peak again. Alan had brought Hyw a young bay gelding as a gift from Shrewsbury. Hyw had kept watch for his father's horses Aeron and Cadarn, but they were not among the captives. This gelding's skittishness showed it had seen battle and probably lost its previous master. He did his best to calm the horse, but he had no will to engage with the beast's mind.

"I'll try to find you a sweet treat later," he murmured in Welsh. The horse turned to look at him almost eagerly. Hyw smiled and patted his neck. Perhaps his former master had been Welsh. "I like a fellow who knows his own tongue."

From that point on, he called the horse *Siwgr*, the Welsh word for sugar. Keeping his voice soft, Hyw mounted without incident. The horse perked up its ears in anticipation.

Shrewsbury raised his gloved hand, and as one, the company rode out.

The January winds blew down from the mountain like the Watchers' wrath. The men broke out cloaks and wrapped themselves, and the horses lowered their heads and plodded along the path that led northward.

Hyw was surprised how slowly the company of soldiers and knights made their way. *These English move like cattle*, Llywelyn muttered inside Hyw's mind. *They need a few Welsh dogs to harry them.*

Hyw and James, at a nod from Shrewsbury, rode ahead to catch sight of the troops passing by. From Alan's prediction, Hyw expected hundreds of troops, but he was sure he could see thousands. Soldiers lined the road in front and behind, as far as Hyw could see. A dozen sturdy horses trundled along beside de Lacy's men, pulling a huge pile of wood of various sizes on a platform. James pointed excitedly at it, and the boys decided it must be meant for the construction of a siege engine. Perhaps a catapult lay below, or was it secured in one of the covered wagons that made their way after it? Soldiers were stationed in front and behind, and made their way slowly along the trail, paced by the tower and horses.

They are foolish to try, Llywelyn told Hyw. *They will soon see why Wales will always be free.*

As they came to a steep hill, Hyw saw the muscles of the horses ripple as they made their way upward, lashed by the whips of the drivers. Some of the older soldiers jumped down and, handing their horses off to the men in front of them, ran back to try to help.

The Shrewsbury standard flew so far behind that James and Hyw had no fear now of losing their place. They jumped off their horses to watch the slow progress of de Lacy's men with the wagon. Twice the platform slithered backwards, the heavy load of wood listing slightly under the thick ropes that held it. Llywelyn laughed softly.

Then de Lacy and his sons rode back to give encouragement to the men. It seemed some of the men were ready to give up, sitting or slumping on the ground. De Lacy spoke to them. Hyw could hear his voice ring across the miles, rising and falling in pitch, although he couldn't hear the words. Then the men cheered, and Hyw could almost see the battle lust rise in them.

Two more horses were added to the team, and two more again. The horses' minds reached out to Hyw, but he resisted. The hawk had been enough for him. He had no wish to learn what other animals thought of war. More men joined the scene as well, and some pushed the platform from behind. Finally, the wagon made the pinnacle. The men broke out in cheers and rejoicing. Hyw could not help but smile at the antics of grown men and grim soldiers dancing around a load of wood like fools at a festival.

Llywelyn, though, was silent.

Screams in the darkness woke Hyw. He startled upright. James stirred and Hyw whispered, "Stay here. I will go and bring back word."

Hyw ran along the path until he slipped in something wet. A soldier behind him brought a lamp.

"Shield that light, man," cried a third. "The devils are upon us."

"What does he mean?"

"The Welsh," cried another. "They attack from the trees, and then disappear."

"Like ghosts."

"Like devils. Like the devils they are."

Hyw searched the darkness with his eyes, something like excitement pounding in his chest. Could his da have been one of the attackers? Before the other man covered the light, Hyw looked down into the gaping wounds of two soldiers on the ground. He recognized the face of one: it was Alan Acton, the soldier who had befriended him. Hyw crossed himself. The poor man.

Fortunes of war, Hyw, Llywelyn said inside him. *That 'poor man' was also your enemy, and the enemy of your people. Yet he treated you with kindness. May he have honour in the OtherWorld, and in the heaven to come.*

"May he have honour," repeated Hyw aloud, crossing himself again and raising one fist to his heart.

"That sounded like Welsh." Someone spoke nearby.

"Nay, 'twas but a Cornish blessing." Hyw flushed with guilt at denying his own language and turned away before the man could raise the light any higher. His guilt turned to anger at the Welsh warriors who had stolen in like thieves in the night to kill the grizzled old soldier. He felt surrounded by enemies on all sides, and his only thought was to make his way back to James. He wiped Alan's blood from his boots and clothes as best he could. And he vowed he would not cry.

22

Cat stood next to the bed. Somehow, there must be a way to prevent what she had seen in her vision. She hadn't told any of them about her gift, other than her mam and Aeneus. Elizabeth may be princess of Wales, but she was English. And the English would surely expect anyone with a hint of such a gift to renounce it. She debated telling Margred, but she wasn't sure what her friend would think of her gift either. What if she found it necessary to tell her priest—what then? Some priests were known to deal harshly with these old ways. She had never considered telling Father Maelgwyn about it.

"No," Cat said out loud. Mam raised her eyebrows. "We need to find a way to tell Elizabeth about the danger without letting anyone know how I learned of it."

"What do we know about the garrison here?" Mam wondered aloud. "We might try to ask the guards how their preparations are going. We are fortunate that Elizabeth keeps the English custom of high table. The captain of the garrison is your da's kinsman, and sits near me. If I show my concern, he might consent to reassure me."

Cat considered what part she might play. Although the girls continued to slip away on their own to practice while the guards were busy training, Ifan often accompanied Cat and Margred on special outings away from the castle. "I'll start with him," Cat said, and Mam nodded.

Word was out in the town that the bard Gwilym was staying at the castle, and on Cat's fifteenth birthday he had agreed to perform in the evening after supper. He was adept at the three bardic instruments—the *telyn*, the long-necked *crwth*, and the *pibgorn*—although his specialty was the *telyn* or harp.

As always, Gwilym began with one of the classical tunes that reminded Cat of Aber Falls with its mists trickling down from the mountains. Cat caught her mam's eye, and Mam nodded slightly as she turned back to the dour garrison captain. He seemed to be explaining something in some detail. Cat looked around her for Ifan. Many of the warriors were moving toward the bard, to show their talent with an instrument or their ability to sing warrior poetry with the master. As Cat tried to catch a glimpse of Ifan among them, Margred stirred beside her.

"I am in the mood for a merry tune tonight," she whispered in Cat's ear.

As supper ended, townsfolk had also begun to trickle into the castle hall, some on the pretext of late deliveries to the castle. The butcher, popular for his voice and his drum, brought a young lamb for the following day's meal. Cat noticed his son Drem with him, and felt sure that was the cause of Margred's restlessness.

Criccieth's house bard took up the *pibgorn*—he seemed to fare much better with music than with insults—and a tall warrior took up the *crwth*. The butcher brought his drum from behind his back, where he had slung it, and sat behind them. As the music picked up in tempo, Margred grabbed Cat's hands, and began to form a circle with some of the other young women who had arrived from Garth Celyn. Perhaps hoping to show Gwilym up, the bard handed the pipes to another warrior and began a lilting Romany love song in his strong tenor. Gwilym merely smiled and moved his fingers fast and light along the harp strings, harmonizing easily to fill in the chorus of the song.

Margred and Cat clapped and circled their companions, jumping lightly from one foot to the other without ever touching their skirts. As they finished, the musicians turned to another dance song, and the servants quickly moved back the tables to make a dance space. Drem joined the group of dancers along with several other young guards and a few more young women. Cat had little time to be concerned for how close Drem might have been standing next to Margred. She felt the closeness of a young man beside her and stepped aside a little to look up at Sir Ifan.

"A happy birthday to you, Lady Catrin," he said. "I am glad to see you are recovered." She remembered he had accompanied them to town and blushed to realize he must have carried her back to Criccieth.

He smiled at her as he placed his hands behind his back. His eyes were very warm brown in the firelight, she thought, as she turned away in the opening steps of the dance. Ifan's hand warmed her shoulder as the grand circle moved clockwise. She barely brushed his hand as they moved back around the dancing space. She tried to train her mind on Rhys, but she felt Ifan's eyes seek her out more than once as they changed partners, weaving around the room to find each other again.

When they finished, she steeled herself to question him, and found him happy to answer her.

"Welsh warriors train each day," Ifan said. "We have the skill and courage to stand against the English."

"I have seen townsfolk and farmers coming to be trained as well," she said.

He hesitated, as if searching for a way to answer politely. "They have been a boon in helping prepare more arrows and javelins for us," he managed.

Under his bluster, she learned he thought the garrison was small, barely enough to hold a castle of this size. By the time she excused herself to join her mam, Cat understood more about her dream but little about how it might be prevented.

"I thank thee for the honour of partnering the fairest flower in the hall this night," Ifan said to her, bowing formally. She found herself a little breathless. Would he try to kiss her, as she had seen some of the warriors doing to ladies in the hall earlier?

"I thank you for the pretty compliment," she responded,

hoping he remembered she was betrothed. She sidled away before he could respond.

Margred and most of the ladies were still dancing, so Cat didn't need to make excuses to join her mam in the room she shared with Elizabeth's ladies. As they compared notes, Cat's concern grew.

"If the English break through the castle gates…" she began, trailing off.

"We must have a plan in readiness," Mam said decisively. "I will enlist our four guards to help us. We can trust them more than any others."

"I – I am not sure if Sir Ifan misunderstood my intentions," Cat stammered.

Mam considered her a moment. "I recall last winter, when we visited Meirionnydd, you seemed close to Rhys."

"I am," Cat said, without hesitation. "Ifan is a worthy man, Mam, but Rhys is my betrothed."

"Then you must set him right. Mention your betrothal, and make sure he knows you intend to honour it."

Cat nodded, and before long they bid each other good night. She made her way to her room. She found the other girls already in bed, sleeping, but no sign of Margred. Cat meant to remain awake until Margred returned, but she was soon lost to her dreams.

23

Finally, they reached Dolwyddelan Castle. Nightly attacks by the Welsh had done little damage to the vast English forces.

There can be but few men left to defend the land, if so few Englishmen were killed, Llywelyn said. *May God bless those who tried, and keep them safe to fight another day.*

Llywelyn thought Dolwyddelan would withstand the siege for many weeks. It was the castle where the prince had set up his communications, and he was sure his brother Dafydd would have taken refuge there. Hyw could tell Llywelyn hoped the English would give up and leave, as had happened so many times before. Yet everything they heard from the soldiers made them fear for the land and its people. Hyw listened to the snatches of conversation around him.

"Even if bloody Longshanks wanted to give up, le Clare and de Lacy would fight on without him."

"Aye, I wouldn't have the two of them against me for all Christendom!"

"These Welsh will burn before the week is out, mark my words."

"And all Wales with them. They say the would-be prince is inside. De Lacy wants his head, and naught will stop him."

The "would-be prince" must be Dafydd, Llywelyn's brother. He had taken sanctuary with Edward more than once, before he turned on the English troops a year ago, to start this war. Llywelyn fretted.

Dafydd must get word to the pope. He is the Prince Regent now. Edward will have dispatched a rider as soon as he had my head in his grasp. If he gets word of my death to the pope before Dafydd makes a claim, Wales is as good as lost.

The English set up camp around the castle. A messenger rode to the walls to offer what Llywelyn called the usual terms of surrender.

Is Dafydd so foolish to think these English have come so far, only to give up and go away again? He cannot win without help.

Hyw did not mention that Llywelyn himself had been just as foolish a few days before. The determination of de Lacy's soldiers and of their leader seemed to weigh heavily on the prince.

Hyw, I must get inside the castle. I must see my brother and discover for myself what the fool has done.

"How can we, my liege? How can we enter without arousing the English?"

I don't know, lad, but we must think of a way. Our people depend on us now.

On the second day of the siege of Dolwyddelan, a string of packhorses made their way up the steep mountain paths toward the English camp, bringing a load of long white cloaks. Word quickly spread that the queen, Edward's wife, had sent them. Edward had his soldiers and their retainers set out cloaks for all the men. Hyw marvelled at the way the men almost disappeared against the snow. The men sent up a "huzzah" for the queen and her ladies.

Hyw pretended to admire their ruse, while inside his heart sank. Llywelyn grunted, realizing the cloaks would give Edward's troops a clear advantage. *We must get word to Dafydd.* Llywelyn cursed the English again.

On the third day of the siege, Hyw finished polishing his pile of soldiers' armour before James. Saying he wanted to stretch his legs, Hyw walked out of the area and then crept along the outcrop of rock until he came to a spot behind the castle. He crouched low and half-ran up the long meadow toward the next ridge. When he got to the top he concealed himself in a thicket of trees. Looking down, he could see Dolwyddelan in all its splendour: the rectangular tower, its dark stone hulk reaching to the grey sky, guarding the entrance to the Vale of Gwynedd, on the path to Garth Celyn.

Ditches cut into the rock on either side of the castle, and the rough terrain isolated it at the top of the ridge. Llywelyn's grandfather and namesake, Llywelyn the Great, had been born here. Llywelyn himself had fortified the stone keep when he returned from crusades. Llywelyn told Hyw it was a strategic location for the protection of North Wales.

Hyw could see shadows moving behind the battlements at the top of the keep and thought Welsh soldiers must be keeping watch inside. On all sides, a steep drop led from the castle to the valley floor. Edward's vast army of men fanned out along the valley like ants scurrying below him. How could he get the prince inside to see his brother, without being killed by either Welsh guards or English soldiers?

Hyw's eyes strayed upwards. Mountain peaks and ridges rose up on all sides of them. He could see points where the ridges came so close, he could imagine one shepherd hailing another, although they grazed their sheep on different mountains.

Strains of a song crept back into his mind, unbidden. *Watchers now sleep beneath the stone.* Legend said the watchers would rise from beneath the mountain to rescue Wales in the hour of her greatest need. Some said the watchers were King Arthur's men, and they would fight to win back the land for the Britons, as the Welsh called themselves. Foolishness, he thought. *How could I believe such foolish stories?* And then his hands balled into fists and he raised them to the mountain tops. He stepped out from the concealing bush and screamed.

"Where are you? Can you not see that the stars have fallen? Can you not see the sun plummeting toward the earth? Lightning strikes your halls! Why do you not awaken? Why have you forsaken us?"

His eyes blurred, and he heard himself sobbing. He stood staring up, and had the sense that Llywelyn stood with him, lost in some agony of his own. Then he heard the prince gasp. Hyw swiped at his eyes with his palm to clear his vision and looked back toward the mountain.

What had been mere wisps of cloud around the tips of the highest mountains had gathered and thickened. As he watched, the clouds themselves seemed to rush toward him, descending into the valley like the last rays of the sun. A white mist swallowed the ridges where he had imagined shepherds a moment ago. The mist rolled across the valleys, filling the dips and crevices until it swallowed the king's men. It swallowed the mighty siege equipment. It swallowed the stone castle of Dolwyddelan. And finally, it crept up the meadow to where he stood and swallowed him.

Around him, the white mist blocked everything from view. Where he expected it to be wet against his face, it was dry and light as air. He breathed it in, and tasted nothing.

What magic is this? he heard Llywelyn whisper.

Then he heard a whining. Looking down, he saw two glowing amber points of light in the mist. When the points disappeared and reappeared again, he realized they were the eyes of a small creature, blinking at him. The creature crept to the edge of the thicket where Hyw had concealed himself. Then it crept a little closer, and through the fog he could see it was a fox. It sat, panting and staring at him.

What are you waiting for? Llywelyn spoke within him. *Use your gift, Hyw. You must go with him to get us through the fog, and into the castle.*

"I dare not."

How can you refuse? You asked them to help. Can you not see this creature is your answer?

Hyw stared at the animal and felt himself drawn into its

amber eyes. Although he knew Llywelyn to be a shade with no more life than a prayer in his mind, he placed himself once again in front of the prince as if to protect him. He felt a shock as the curious mind of the fox met his. Unlike any other melding, this one seemed to require no effort on Hyw's part, as his feet seemed to melt into paws.

Then he was running with the fox, back through the camp of men. At any moment someone might see him, stop him, hang him as a spy or as a witch who had called the fog down upon them. But it was as if the English slept where they stood. The fox maneuvered between them, and Hyw went with him.

Finally they stopped and the fox sat on its haunches, panting as before. Hyw found himself standing in front of a section of the castle's stone wall. It was a secret door, like the one his mother could find in the stone when they were forced to leave Garth Celyn.

I have lived here often in the last fifty years, yet I did not know this was here. Llywelyn seemed puzzled.

"Are we dreaming?"

There is only one way to find out.

The fox whined again, and Hyw sensed it would remain to lead them back again. He reached forward and his hand found the hidden latch. The stone opened to him, and he entered.

24

Cat walked up the stone stairs to the battlements of Criccieth and stood in the early light, looking out over the landscape. She had awakened from a bad dream, and in spite of her recent illness she felt the need to walk. She snuggled deeper into her warm cloak, wondering where Hyw and Da were now, and whether she would ever see them again. As she made her way around the wall walk, her thoughts turned to Rhys again. Would he be looking out at another section of the Eryri Mountains? Perhaps standing on the wall walk at Bere and staring at the mountain they called the Giant's Chair?

She made her way slowly to the seaward side. She wasn't thinking about visions, but about the wind blowing across the sea with the hint of January snow. She stopped for a moment and stared down at the roiling waters. The waves began to circle, swirling over and over, drawing her inside—

—and she found herself on the deck of a large ship. She felt timber under her feet instead of stones, and the press of the sea in the breeze on her face. She heard the voices around her and recognized their accents. Irish! Were they raiders? Or English sympathizers come to attack the castle? She looked around her and saw two other ships sailing a little apart from each other.

The sailors were swinging the sail around to catch the wind. She saw them point toward shore and the castle on the horizon. It was Criccieth. Just then a flaming arrow hit the water near them, and someone cried out in a language Cat didn't understand. Then the captain yelled something and pointed upward toward the Irish crest and colours flying there. Two sailors jumped up and grabbed a piece of fabric, hoisting it up a rope toward the mast. A Welsh lion like the one on Llywelyn's crest unfurled under the Irish.

Too late! Huge boulders and flaming arrows began falling around the men, onto the wooden deck of the ship. Criccieth's forces were attacking to prevent the Irish from landing. The sailors began to run, one screaming as an arrow embedded into his arm and the flames engulfed him.

No! Cat tried to cry out. They're friends! She turned as if to tell someone—

—and she was standing alone on the stone battlement of the castle. She stared out at the sea, but she could not see any ships. What if they were on the way right now? She had to tell someone. She turned from the battlements and went in search of her mam.

Mam nodded as Cat told her about the vision and what she thought it meant.

"We'll get Ifan and the others to watch for ships," she said. "How many did you say there were?"

"I saw three."

"And they're friendly?"

"I believe they are, yes." Cat described the lion in Llywelyn's colours that she had seen unfurled against the mast. Mam tapped her fingertips together in thought before she answered.

"This might be our answer, Cat," she said. "While I tended the babies yesterday, Princess Elizabeth's scout reported Bere is garrisoned and not yet under attack. If the English do get through Criccieth's gates, a stout ship could take us around the bay and up the Mawddach river. We'd be a short ride to Bere from there."

Of course, they could escape to Meirionnydd! Cat tried not to admit how much she wanted to see Rhys again, especially because of Ifan's attentions. Then she realized what her mother had said. "Ride?"

"Aye, if the ship is as large as you saw. We can board the horses, and they will take us to the castle."

Now all we need to do is convince the captain not to sink the Irish, Cat thought, as her mam rushed from the room to enlist her remaining guards. That is, if the ships arrive in time.

⁂

Elizabeth stood, arms folded one over the other, and looked hard at Cat. "And how do you know the English will attack us?" Mam stood beside Cat, and instinctively reached out and took her hand as they faced their princess.

"I do not know, your highness," Cat admitted. "I only believe—" She tried to think of how to explain without telling Elizabeth about her gift. "I believe we should consider the danger."

"Your garrison is less than half the strength needed to protect and fortify the castle," Mam added. "Every report we have says the English come in the thousands. Castle after castle has fallen before them. How long can we hold them off?"

"They're not at our gates," Elizabeth replied.

"Not yet." Cat shouldn't have spoken, but she couldn't stop herself. "If they have taken Garth Celyn, they will make their way here."

Elizabeth considered for a moment, and then shook her head and unfolded her arms. "What choice do we have? Dafydd is holding the line at Dolwyddelan, and when he has repelled the English, he will rejoin us here."

"Of course, he will," Mam said. "But if they come by way of the sea, as they did five years past, then he—"

Elizabeth waved Mam's words away and paced to the window. Cat almost spoke up. Her mam was right. Dolwyddelan Castle protected the route to the south and west, but it was far inland from the Irish Sea. Cat had heard the stories of English treachery in the bard's songs. The English had captured Princess Elinor on her way to Wales, and kept her prisoner for three years. Prince Llywelyn had tried to fight but they came by sea to Anglesey and burned the crops, crippling the Welsh. In the end, Llywelyn was forced to give up half his kingdom and more to get Elinor back. But Mam shushed her with a gesture, and they waited quietly.

Elizabeth finally turned back to them, her face serious and set. "Very well. I will consider it. We should have a plan of escape. After all, we don't have tunnels like Garth Celyn. I will confer with the captain."

Cat was about to say more, but her mam squeezed her hand. "Thank you, your highness. That is wise and prudent of you."

"I will call him now, if you ladies will excuse me." Elizabeth turned from them. Cat and her mam both curtsied and left her to consider it.

"Come with me to the gardens," Mam said. The snow had melted but the wind played havoc in the garden, swirling their cloaks as they walked. Mam asked in a quiet voice, "There has been no sighting of a ship. How sure are you of what you saw?"

"I don't know, Mam," Cat said. She felt tired and unsure, and wondered if she had completely recovered from her illness. "It was the same as the other times, but—well, we were able to change those times, weren't we?"

"I hope we can change this one as well," Mam said. "No point mentioning it all at once. We will need to find a way to tell Elizabeth without endangering you." Then she turned to look at Cat. "You've grown so much in a few weeks. Sorry I am that this had to happen, Cat, but I am glad to have you with me. You're a real help to me, and to the people here."

Cat felt a flush of pleasure and bowed her head to thank her mam for the compliment. As they came to the entrance of the gardens, they saw two guards holding horses for Father Maelgwyn and the castle priest.

"Heading out on their rounds," Mam said. "The people value their visits."

"Good day to you, Father," Cat called.

He looked their way with a start, and an expression passed across his face that seemed almost guilty to her. She hoped he regretted his decision to stop the girls from exercising, while the news of war came closer with each messenger who rode through their gates. She longed to talk with him about it again, but he often went out these days and left confessions and services to the younger priests in training at the castle. He waved to them without speaking as he mounted. Criccieth's priest mounted as well, and they were off through the gates without looking back.

25

Hyw crouched and crept forward through the hidden door in the wall. Mist shrouded the courtyard of Dolwyddelan castle. The banner streaming out above them was Llywelyn's, with three red lions for the Prince of Wales. It was mid-afternoon, yet all seemed as quiet and still as night. He hesitated as he spotted a guard in the yard. Hyw could see the badge on the guard's cloak, showing a blue lion striding forward on a gold field. He frowned.

The lions of Gwynedd, blue for my brother and heir. This is Dafydd's man. He has not yet changed his colours. The mist seemed to magnify the slight disorientation Hyw felt when the prince spoke inside his mind. If he closed his eyes, he would see the prince clearly. Yet he could not help but stare at the guard, who stayed silent and immobile in the swirling mist. Hyw felt the hairs raise on the back of his neck.

It's just like the stories say, marvelled Llywelyn. *This is truly a gift from the Old Ones, Hyw. Now you must trust them. Push onward. My brother waits inside the castle, and we must get to him while we can.*

Hyw made his way carefully behind the guard, who never moved from his position. Two other soldiers also stood still. One held his hand in front of his face as if he was about to pick his nose. Hyw almost wanted to laugh, but he was afraid a noise might break the spell.

He slipped up the stone stairs to the castle door. The mist followed, swirling around him. His vision narrowed and it seemed as if he saw everything through a small round window in the mist. He could not see the castle's great hall clearly unless he turned directly toward it. Then he was inside. The huge fireplace loomed up, leading to the inset window seats. He made his way by the people in the hall, who did not move but seemed frozen in mid-conversation.

More than passing strange. Llywelyn's whisper sounded as if in Hyw's ear, but Hyw was so taken by the sight of the frozen people that he listened without closing his eyes. *Perhaps they are out-of-time, or we are, as in the old stories. This could be a valuable advantage for us, Hyw, if you could but control it.*

"It is not my doing," Hyw whispered back. "And I know not why the Old Ones have favoured us with this time-out-of-time. But I believe it is as my uncle said. We cannot expect to use this to our personal advantage. It would show disrespect."

Llywelyn remained silent. Across from the door, Hyw spotted a stairwell and moved toward it. Mist drifted with him as he felt his way along the stone wall to the upper reaches of the castle. To his left, he saw another stairwell that must lead to the wall walk, and he knew without Llywelyn's whispered warning that Dafydd's warriors would be patrolling. He prayed the mist held them trapped as well.

To his right was a wooden door. It opened as he neared it, and he stepped inside. A man stood near the fireplace, his back to the door. Hyw watched him rub his hands together for warmth. He didn't understand why this man could move when the others could not.

He is my brother. So again, as in the old stories, the Prince of the Blood is allowed to remain unaffected by their magic. Long ago, before Elinor and Gwenllian, I named Dafydd my heir, and now it seems he has claimed the title. I must speak with him, Hyw, if it can be done.

Hyw nodded at Llywelyn's voice. He closed his eyes and concentrated on the prince's will, until he felt a strange sensation, as if the prince had stepped in front of him. Llywelyn's shadow blocked the firelight, and Hyw craned his neck to see.

Dafydd swung around. He snarled and his eyes glared at them. "You," Dafydd growled. "You are dead, and yet you haunt me. I know you are dead. I heard it from your own man."

Hyw realized two things instantly. First, he realized that

Dafydd could see Llywelyn, standing in the doorway. He wasn't sure how they had managed to give that illusion, or how much was due to the magic of the Old Ones. Still, it felt right to allow the prince to lead this exchange, so he determined not to fight it. Second, when Dafydd referred to "your own man," he had to mean Bran. He almost cried out for more information about his da, but he heard the prince's voice rumble in his ears.

"You speak of Bran ap Maredudd of Gwynedd," Llywelyn said, using formal speech to force his brother to answer, according to custom. "Does he live?"

Dafydd smirked, folding his arms across his chest. "So, you do not keep track of your own men. Lucky are the Cymry that I have taken your place."

"Is it so? And is that why your guards stand unmoving, to let me past?"

"Hah! Of course, if you truly are a shade, my men cannot follow where you go. Whereas your men—well, their loyalties must remain with the living, mustn't they? Like your man, who came to me after you fell."

Now it was Hyw's turn to lay a hand on Llywelyn's arm. He felt Llywelyn's efforts to calm himself. "It is only reasonable that Bran would want to serve the Prince of Wales. What reception did you give him?"

Dafydd's face twisted into a snarl again. "What do you think? I bade him prove himself. He leads the resistance in the mountains."

At this Alan Acton's grisly death sprang into Hyw's mind, but he pushed the thought away to focus on the two princes.

Llywelyn drew a breath and began again. "Brother, I did not make my way here to fight with you or be goaded into it. You see me as I am now: but a shade. I cannot harm you in this incorporeal form. Instead, I come as your ally to help save our people."

Dafydd frowned and inclined his head as if considering what Llywelyn said. Encouraged, Llywelyn continued.

"You are surrounded by the English, but in my presence you have a brief respite. The English have white camouflage and plan to attack with stealth as early as tomorrow. Edward sends a messenger to the pope. You must send a swifter one. You may recall the pope supported my claim as Prince of Wales. Whatever you thought then, use that privilege now, to save our country and our people. Ask for men and arms to help you win against Edward."

Dafydd moved slightly. He kept his head down so Hyw could not see his eyes but unfolded his arms as if open to Llywelyn's words.

"What proof have I to offer?" Dafydd replied. "The pope well knows I sided with Edward over you. Nay, don't deny it. I'm sure that in your messages to and fro, you were careful to paint me a villain and a traitor to you. Why would the pope rally to my side now? I would require a talisman. Have you your royal seal that I might send it to prove my claim?"

"Alas, it was stolen from me," Llywelyn responded. "Edward has it now."

"You know this to be so? As a shade, can you not move among his men as you have mine? And steal it back from them? Or failing that, if I appoint a man to follow you, can you not lead my man to the very spot so we may steal it back?"

"I cannot."

"So, you will not?"

"It is more difficult—"

"You know where it is?"

Llywelyn hesitated. "No."

"What good then in coming here? Why should I do as you ask without a talisman to prove you are who you say you are? Why should I believe you are my brother? You could well be a denizen of the devil come to fool me into betraying my people."

"Me, a denizen of the devil? You sound like the English." Llywelyn's voice grew harsh as he moved forward and rolled up his sleeve. "Here is the scar you gave me yourself when you attacked me on the battlefield, fighting with our brother against me."

"Aye and I would again." Dafydd moved forward as well, and he snarled again. "Even as a shade, you plague me with your status and your pope and your futile stance against the English king. It is your fault I have fallen from Edward's favour. This day I sent a messenger to Edward's camp to offer to join forces with him and win Wales. Instead, he sent me the man's head and with it a note: 'Yours will be next.' Had I your princely seal, I would use it to save this country. If you cannot get it for me, what use are you?"

With this, Dafydd reached toward the dagger on his belt. Llywelyn reacted on instinct, but his hand closed on empty air where his dagger once was. In a sudden rush of wind around them, Hyw felt himself meld with Llywelyn again. *Run!* Llywelyn cried inside his mind.

Hyw turned and ran for the stairwell. As he rounded the door, he heard Dafydd's dagger thwack into the wood near his head. Then he all but fell back down the stairs, leaping to the ground. He whispered thanks to his old captain, Aeneus, for the strictness of his physical training and the strength it gave him to withstand the jump without injury.

Dafydd bellowed behind him. The sound dispelled the mist that had protected them. A guard almost bumped him coming in.

"Help the prince," Hyw cried. The guard stepped around him, looking for Dafydd. Then Hyw was running across the courtyard. Guards sprinted past him the other way, toward the castle and Dafydd's yells.

"He has seen his ghosts again," one guard said to another as they ran. They ignored Hyw. He pushed on toward the wall. His fingers found the release for the secret door and he heard the scrape of stone on stone. He shinnied through as it slammed shut behind him.

26

Cat and her mam asked their guards to watch for Irish ships. Each day the men reported to Adara from the wall walk where they "stretched their legs" with Criccieth's watch. They said nothing yet to Princess Elizabeth. Cat wanted to be present when the ships were sighted so she could claim to see something that proved the ships were friendly to Wales. But she couldn't be sure the banner in her vision had been real, or that the Irish would unfurl it in time.

As the days went by and no ships came in sight, the guards relaxed their vigilance. Cat exchanged glances with her mam and occasionally asked about the ships. She continued to exercise with Margred and the Garth Celyn women in their favourite spot. It was sheltered from the worst of the winds churning up the channel, but Margred's younger sisters claimed it was too chilly for them. Cat and Margred found their exercises warmed them and often removed their cloaks or even loosened their ties during their morning "walks."

"Here, Cat," Margred called, setting up the makeshift target again. "Your turn."

Cat chose three small throwing knives as Margred and the other girls stepped out of range. Their practice weapons were meant for young boys to begin their training, and not weighted with the kind of care the warriors took when they fashioned their own weapons. Cat hefted each one and chose what she thought was the best. She set the other two down and lined up carefully with the target. She drew her arm back, and as she released it, she heard a shout.

"Lady Catrin!"

Cat watched the knife thwack into the target before she turned. Father Maelgwyn and the Criccieth priest had reined their horses on the rise of the hill, and he was staring at her.

"Lady Catrin," he shouted again. "I expressly forbade you from this activity. And you other women—Lady Margred! I am surprised to see you participating in this folly."

The two girls said nothing. Cat was immediately aware that she had caught up her dress in her belt to free her movements, and she quickly moved to smooth it down again. Several other girls did the same, trying to hide their faces from him. One of the other women tried to gather up the target and equipment, but it was too late. Cat felt her mouth gaping open, and quickly shut it, trying to think of something to say.

"We were playing a game, Father," Margred responded, her voice level. She had taken off her skirts in favour of the pair of boy's breeches she always wore and made no move to hide herself now. "There's no harm in it."

"A game?" Father Maelgwyn twitched the horse's reigns and the animal grunted in protest. "I will see you both in the princess' solar within the hour, and at confession tomorrow morning."

He spurred the horse toward Criccieth, with the castle priest following quickly behind him. Margred and Cat stared at each other a moment, and then Margred burst out laughing.

"You should see your face, Cat," she said. Cat laughed as well then, and the other women nervously joined in as they all quickly gathered the target and equipment from the ground.

"We will put it away safe, my lady," said one of the women Cat recognized from Garth Celyn. "You'd best hurry to meet yon priest."

Cat and Margred slipped up to their shared room before going to answer the priest in Elizabeth's chambers. They helped each other adjust their ties and changed into fresh tunics. As Margred brushed her hair, Cat used the jug of water in their room to freshen up. She bent over the basin—

—and she saw Hyw and another boy wading knee-deep in a stream. Each held a bucket, and as she looked into Hyw's eyes she felt herself drawn deeper into the waters. The image dissolved as if a pebble had been dropped into the stream, and it reformed into the snowy grounds of a soldier's camp. She saw Father Maelgwyn handing his horse's reins to a guard and taking a folded piece of parchment from the inside of his gown. He handed the paper to the guard, who looked at the seal and nodded.

Then she saw the other priests behind Father Maelgwyn. They also dismounted and made their way toward a grand tent with a banner flying above it that she somehow knew belonged to the English king, Edward Longshanks. A sudden wave of anger and disappointment rippled through her, and the image changed.

She saw Criccieth as if from the battlements again. The castle was surrounded by English soldiers. Father Maelgwyn stood on the stones with his lantern, waving it. A light answered from the soldiers below. Cat shrank back into the late afternoon shadows. The priest gestured to two guards near him, and they moved toward the pulley that would raise the heavy metal portcullis protecting the castle from the invaders.

No! she tried to cry out. No, you mustn't open it—

—and she found herself staring at the basin of water in her room at Criccieth.

"Traitors!" The words came out of her mouth before she could stop herself.

"Who are?" Margred asked.

Cat was too upset to curb her tongue, and too familiar now with Margred's company to want to hide her gifts any longer. "Father Maelgwyn and the other priest—and more besides them—have met in secret with the English king."

"What? He wouldn't," Margred began. Then Cat was telling her about her gift of Second Sight, and briefly about her connection with her brother Hyw. When she was finished, Margred looked thoughtful.

"How does it happen?" she puzzled. "Your visions, I mean. Is it the water? The songs say that's how Queen Mab contacts her people of the Tylwyth Teg."

"It may be," said Cat. "I gave Hyw a token before he left, an arm band woven with some of my hair as a remembrance. And he gave me a cloak. Perhaps that helps us bridge the distance between us."

"And have you had visions of other things as well?"

Cat nodded and explained about seeing English soldiers and their horses on the trail during their escape from Garth Celyn. She downplayed her vision about the attack on the castle for Margred's sake and spoke of the more recent ships she had seen coming to help them. "The horses had been mere hours away, but the ships haven't appeared."

"Then how do you know if the ships are a true vision, or for that matter this new vision of Father Maelgwyn?" Margred asked. "Would the priest not say your suspicions are convenient?"

"How so?" Cat bit back, and then stopped herself. Could her vision have been influenced by their current troubles with Father Maelgwyn? Cat thought for a moment. "In my vision today, when I first saw Hyw, I saw Father Maelgwyn on his horse arriving to speak to the king. It was the same horse he rode today."

"Do you mean he has betrayed us already?" Margred's face was alarmed.

"It may be," Cat said. "There was something—some quality of light—that seemed different in that part. The second part was more hazy somehow, more like the vision I had of the ships."

"So, the priest's actions may happen on the same day as the ships arrive," said Margred. "The priests were gone for almost a week, and the horses were lathered as if they were hard-rode." She appeared to be thinking it over as well.

Finally, Margred stood up. "We cannot accuse a priest without something more, unless you want everyone to know you are a sage and a soothsayer."

Cat shook her head, standing as well. "Nay, Margred, in these times—"

"Fear me not," Margred laughed, taking Cat's hand. "Yet we must try to find out more somehow. Come. Let us face the music we have made for ourselves and see if we can change the tune."

27

The fox was pacing on silent paws as Hyw sped through the closing gap in the castle's defences. The small animal yelped once and ran. Hyw quickly moulded his mind to the fox, and they sped through the trees back to Shrewsbury's camp.

Almost as soon as the camp came into sight, the fox yelped again and vanished. Hyw felt it torn from his mind, replaced by the terror of falling and blackness. He closed his eyes and stumbled.

Steady, boy, the prince said.

Hyw recovered and stood panting, his arms on his knees. "I am sorry we did not accomplish our goal."

There is more than one way to shear a sheep, Hyw. We know two things from this that we did not know. The first is that your father lives. The second is that he has a following. He would never have gone to Dafydd otherwise. He may be camped nearby.

Hyw raised himself and looked around him at the mountains. Hyw wanted to wave, but stopped himself. He realized if his father was watching, he would see his son among the English. What would happen if the Welsh attacked? Would Hyw in the end be forced to fight his father's men to save his own life? Or to save James?

James! What if James asked for him and no one could find him? How long had he been gone? Hyw ran again, this time back to camp.

He found James seated in the dirt with a pile of armour around him. His friend scowled up at him.

"I thought you were going for a walk in the hills."

Hyw spotted his own pile of finished armour, sitting in the same spot as when he left. He thought about the silent, unmoving people in Dolwyddelan castle. They truly must have been stopped in time. He realized it had only been a few moments since he left to go on a walk, and discover a fox, a castle, and a living prince. He could find no words to explain it to his friend, so he grinned instead.

"I ran. Here, let me give you a hand." For the rest of the afternoon, the two boys worked together to finish readying the men's armour. When Shrewsbury's knights came to collect it, one of the younger soldiers feinted toward Hyw.

"Here's your reward for a job well done, boy." Hyw recognized him as a friend of the grizzled soldier Alan Acton, and he recognized the man's play-fight as a gesture of remembrance where words failed him.

"Gerald, save your fight for tomorrow," another guffawed.

"Why—do you go into battle again?" Hyw took advantage of the younger knight's familiarity to ask, and Gerald nodded.

"May the saints preserve us," said another, shivering. "Not soon enough for me. I like it not in this place. The quicker we put the fear of God into these heathen Welsh and return to our own land, the better, to my mind."

"Fear of God," Gerald snorted. "Fear of Edward, you mean."

"Edward who?" said the first man, settling down on the armour and bringing out his whittling knife and a twig. "Gilbert le Clare, more like. It is his army I will join, after this battle's won. I hear they fare towards South Wales again. The land of milk and honey."

"Aye, and with land—even in godforsaken Wales—you could marry your Sal," said Gerald. The men guffawed and made bawdy jokes about the soldier's upcoming wedding night. The soldier jabbed at one of the jokers with his fist, and Hyw felt his cheeks flame as he guessed what the men meant by the jest.

Ask them which direction Edward goes. Llywelyn's voice was clear enough inside Hyw's head. He turned slightly from the men and closed his eyes to find the prince dressed in full war regalia. *Ask them where the king plans to travel next. We must try, Hyw. If we can get word to Bran, we may yet get the royal seal back for Dafydd.*

Llywelyn must feel desperate if he was willing to try to enlist his brother's help again. Hyw turned back to the men and waited for a break in the conversation.

"You are the lucky ones indeed. Le Clare is brave, but my master will follow the king. Where will he go after the castle falls?"

"Who can say, boy?" Gerald looked at him kindly. "He is the king and can do as he pleases."

"Pah," said another. "Once he has Dafydd in his grasp, he will hang him from the Tower of London, beside his brother's head."

Partly to distract Llywelyn from the comment, Hyw rubbed his head. "That puzzles me. I thought Edward and Dafydd grew up together. That they were allies."

"Nay. This Day-vid was the bait Edward used to hook his war-like brother."

"If that be true, then why does the king remain?"

"He means to crush the Welsh now once and for all."

"Aye, he must end the royal line," Gerald agreed, "so there can be no more reason for these Welsh to fight."

Hyw thought swiftly of the baby, Gwenllian. His mother would die rather than see that baby harmed—or killed. He sensed the eyes of the men on him and tried not to show his feelings on his face.

"You may have been Alan's friend, young lad, but I begin to wonder why you are so interested in the king." The older knight had stopped cutting fruit and was staring at Hyw.

He tensed. Just then James' stomach growled. As James made a show of grabbing at his belly, all the men laughed. Gerald reached out to ruffle James' hair. "Time for supper, is it? Enough of your questions, then. A prize for the one who can run the faster down the hill toward yon campfire."

Hyw breathed a small sigh of relief as he led James in the race—slowing enough to let his friend win in the end.

The next day another group of men rode in. They were dressed in hooded cowls, and for a moment Hyw looked for his uncle among them. Then the sun caught the rings on their fingers as they shifted their horse's reins, and in that glint, he realized the men were priests, not simple monks like Gawain. His disappointment grew to fear as the men threw back their hoods. Llywelyn cursed anew, and Hyw ducked his head before he could be seen. Among the group was the priest of Garth Celyn, Father Maelgwyn.

The others are also Welsh. At least one served my brother in years past. Llywelyn's voice was low although only Hyw could hear it. *Bran will know a way to aid our people. No doubt any Welshmen capable of resistance will be with him. We must make contact and warn them. Perhaps he has men inside the castle and can get word to them.*

He directed Hyw up the escarpment beside the stream, and along the nearby meadow. Hyw grabbed a water bucket as he left the others, in case anyone saw him. *Stop here,* the prince said. Hyw could see nothing, but Llywelyn showed him a spot where he believed there were signs of men coming to gather water. He led Hyw over to the hedge. Under some loose branches they found an old pot. It was dented, but not rusted.

Left here for use, but old enough that anyone who finds it would not think it important enough to return for. Nothing but the last man's leavings. Make markings here, as I will show you.

At Llywelyn's bidding, Hyw cleared a bit of dirt and wrote symbols as Llywelyn directed him.

I learned Arabic as a young man on Crusade, and your father knows it well. It was how we passed information to each other after our return, and we have kept that tradition.

"What did I write?"

The words for 'beware' and 'priests.' Hyw traced the symbols in the air and tried to remember them. Then he placed the pot on top so it would not erase the letters. At Llywelyn's bidding he gathered twigs and set them in the form of a fish beside the pot. He used a stone for an eye. *An old trick of mine that your father may remember, if indeed he is here.*

After Hyw replaced the branches to cover his work, he stared around him for a moment. Could his da really be so close? Llywelyn reminded him to run back to the stream for water to take back to the English camp.

The attack on Dolwyddelan began at dawn the following day. Fearing the worst, Hyw and James watched as the soldiers made their way with stealth up the mountain. Again, Shrewsbury would not allow the boys to take part in the battle, and the cooks and stewards kept them busy with chores around the camp all day. Hyw strained to listen, but no sounds of battle carried over the wind.

Hyw was about to try making contact with a hawk or some other bird again when a few soldiers returned and made their way to the camp cook. After a few hasty words, the cook began to move quickly.

"Here boys, you can help." James and Hyw gathered the cook's things and within minutes the camp was rounded up and on the move. They made their way up the hill to the castle.

It was noisy with English soldiers, but Hyw could neither see nor smell blood or signs of fighting. Setting up kept him too busy to ask anyone what had happened. That night, when the men had time around the fire, he and James finally heard the tale.

"We crept up the hill in silence," Gerald said, his eyes glowing in the flames. "The castle gate was open. 'What is this?' our captain said. 'Some kind of Welsh enchantment?' In we came, fearing a trap. But no, there was nothing. Not even a dog in the yard. It was as if they sank into the mountain and vanished." Gerald shivered a little as he told the tale, and Hyw thought it was from more than cold. Yet he could not help but be glad that Dafydd and his people had somehow managed to escape.

Edward's army took up residence in the castle, and the soldiers celebrated long into the night. Dolwyddelan had fallen after only five days of siege.

28

Ifan arrived to escort Cat and Margred as they came out of their room.

"Lady Elizabeth bids you to her solar, ladies," he said. Cat searched for the twinkle she usually saw in his eye since their night of dancing and poetry but could not find it.

"Do you know what it is about, Sir Ifan?" Margred asked for her.

"It is not my place—" he began, but Cat interrupted.

"Nay, Sir Ifan, tell us, that we might be a little prepared," she said.

He looked uncomfortable. "Father Maelgwyn had much to say to the Lady Adara and the princess about your—recent activity."

"He thinks it unseemly." She said it as a statement, and he nodded. "And what do you think?"

"I serve my captain, Lord Aeneus, and would not question his decisions."

"Of course not," she agreed. "But privately, do you agree we should be prepared?"

"I would die before I let any harm come to you," he said, and then added, "or to the Lady Margred, or any of our ladies. Yet these are difficult times. God forbid our enemies should breach our gates. Yet if they do, and aught prevent me from reaching you, if you have the strength to flee from harm—then I think it time well spent."

She nodded, pleased to hear him say so. "Then I am ready to face my priest."

He bowed slightly to them, his mouth twisting in what might have been a smile as he stepped behind the girls. Margred linked her arm through Cat's as they marched toward the princess's rooms.

In the end, they were able to say little in their own defence. Cat was surprised when her mam stood up to Father Maelgwyn.

"Begging your pardon, Princess Elizabeth, but I may be able to shed a different light on this matter." When Elizabeth nodded, Mam went on. "When I was young, we faced a similar threat, and I myself took part in these activities. It was not considered unseemly, but necessary to protect ourselves from the *Saeson*. This we do not talk about, and again I beg pardon, but I myself was grateful for the knowledge to hide well and the agility to move myself from harm's way."

"And, Lady Adara, did you take up weapons?" the priest demanded. His eyes blazed into them. "Did you arm yourself and threaten others?"

Mam looked uncomfortable, and Cat wondered what had happened in her youth to bring the haunted look into her eyes. She shook her head. "I did not learn these skills to threaten anyone, but to protect myself. I still do those exercises in the privacy of my room."

Father Maelgwyn raised his eyebrows and turned away from her, as if disgusted. Princess Elizabeth rubbed her brow and looked at Margred. Cat had not noticed how tired and wan the princess seemed, like Mam looked sometimes when she didn't know Cat was watching. Elizabeth must be as worried about her husband Dafydd and her oldest son, as Cat and her mam were about Bran and Hyw.

"I have been lax, Lady Margred, in protecting you," Elizabeth began. Margred made to protest but Elizabeth shook her head. "When we brought you to us, it was to keep you safe from harm and fear. Although you are not my daughters, I have grown fond of you and your other sisters. But it seems I have not done my duty by you."

She turned to the window, and stood staring out, as if on her own past life. "In our day, a young girl has little say in her own life. You will soon be betrothed, and you will have little say in that."

"It is meet and right—" began the priest, but Elizabeth stopped him with a gesture.

"I do not question it, and my life is testament to that." Elizabeth was talking about her first marriage to an English nobleman, Cat realized, and possibly Prince Dafydd too? They seemed happy enough, but had Elizabeth wanted something else? Someone else? "I see the point in being prepared, and fresh air does the children good. Lady Margred, is this something you wish to do?" She turned to Margred, who nodded. "Very well. This much I can grant you. You may continue, but you must dress appropriately and not masquerade as a boy. And Lady Catrin, you will return everything you have taken." When the girls went to protest, she put both hands on her hips. "You will do this that I have asked of you, as your princess. And if you do, you may take exercise as needed to strengthen yourselves. And may God have mercy on all of us."

"Your highness, I must protest," said the priest. "What if—may God in his wisdom protect us—but what if the enemy does come, and we must close the castle gate? I am trying to protect the young ladies. If they are outside the gate..."

As his voice trailed off, Cat exchanged a glance with Margred. If her earlier vision was correct, why was he warning them now? Did he want to protect them? Or—her scalp prickled—was he planning something much darker? She felt she should say something, but what? She tried to imagine saying, *I've had a vision that Father Maelgwyn will open the gates to the enemies and betray us.* What would the priest do? Would he drag her out to the courtyard and subject her to a trial for heresy, as she had heard another English priest had done?

"I will heed your good counsel as always," Elizabeth was saying. She turned to the girls. "From now, you will exercise inside the gate, and keep a guard with you at all times." Elizabeth scanned the room, and Sir Ifan straightened a little as her eyes fell on him. "Lady Adara, is this your man?"

"He is Sir Ifan, a member of Prince Llywelyn's *teulu* and loyal to me."

"Sir Ifan, may we—as mothers, and as your Princess and your lady—trust you with the safe keeping of our daughters?"

Ifan nodded and came to attention. "You may, your highness. I will lay down my very life to keep them safe from harm."

"I pray it does not come to that," Elizabeth said. She turned and swept from the room. Ifan bowed and retired to the corner of the room again, already on guard. Father Maelgwyn stared at them a moment, and then followed the princess. Cat couldn't help but think it wasn't the end of the matter. She caught her mam's eye, hoping for a private moment with her.

"Come," Adara said to both of the girls. "Several of the young men have been commissioned to fight with our warriors, should they be needed. You two can help me prepare the crests for their cloaks."

That meant embroidery, and Cat groaned inwardly. But it might also offer her a chance to tell her mam about the vision.

29

Dolwyddelan was much smaller than English castles. Most of the army, including Robert as Hyw was relieved to see, camped outside the gates. Shrewsbury and a select few of his guards bunked in the castle with the other lords, and he kept James with him as squire. Hyw slept with the soldiers in the garrison near the castle gate. He made himself useful there and joined James inside at mealtimes and for short periods in the afternoons, when they could catch up with each other's business.

The English troops began building the next day, and Hyw quickly learned they were putting up a second tower to keep better control of the countryside. A man arrived as if he had been sent for and took control over a number of soldiers and stonemasons. James watched intently until the man—an architect—agreed to explain his plans.

The priests came again. For two days, Edward held council with them and his lords. Hyw tried to get close but the tents were heavily guarded. He worried that Father Maelgwyn had seen him, but the man did not stop or make any sign. Hyw was relieved, but resolved not to try to spy directly again. Instead, he used his old trick of offering help to the soldiers. As before, he heard much while he cleaned and sharpened their weapons or oiled their leather leggings.

"Aye, yon priests come to help us find that heathen Dafydd," said Gerald, who had joined Shrewsbury's personal guard after the siege. "Won't be long now before we know which way the wind blows him."

The priests will know his ways and his castles. Llywelyn made a disgusted sound. Dafydd had controlled several castles in North Wales, such as Dinbych and Caergwrle. Hyw recalled Caergwrle was built near a town called "Hope." Could he have gone there? *His castle there fell months ago,* he heard Llywelyn say. *Dafydd will go to Bere, no doubt. It is the most fortified.*

Hyw was torn between his feelings and his fealty. He wanted to leave for Garth Celyn right away to warn them, and he longed to see his mother again. But Llywelyn would not hear of it. *Not yet, boy. We have much to do.*

With that he led Hyw back to the area where they had left the message. It appeared undisturbed, but as soon as he moved the branch Hyw could see the pot had been moved and the word carefully erased. In its place was a symbol Hyw had not written. Llywelyn laughed.

It is the Arabic for 'friend.' It can be none other than your father, Hyw. Now I am certain of it. We must find him.

Hyw watched from the castle battlements as le Clare and his troops packed up to leave. He could not catch sight of Robert or Gerald in the company, although they must be there. It took most of the day for le Clare's army to head down the mountain to the south. The priests also left the castle under le Clare's protection.

Edward had decided to remain for another week. Some thought it was to get the new tower underway, but Llywelyn had other ideas.

He is sending out spies to discover which way Dafydd has gone. Mark you, my brother has a good chance if he stays hidden and makes his way to Bere. He knows the mountains almost as well as I.

And yet the mountains did not hide you from Mortimer, Hyw thought. If Llywelyn heard, he seemed too preoccupied watching le Clare's departing soldiers to comment.

Hyw ran to the castle keep and found several knights at the table breaking fast. James had served his father and sat at one of the lower tables to grab a bite of food for himself. Hyw slipped over to him.

"When do we leave?"

James shook his head and swallowed a piece of unleavened bread. "Father will remain, and so will I."

"What?"

"'Tis true. He pleaded age and gout, and Edward has given us leave."

Hyw looked into James' bright excited eyes and knew he was thinking about the castle building. At least now James could enjoy watching the architect without hindrance. Hyw tried to smile for his friend. "Do you—have you heard where Edward takes his army?"

James nodded, and a look of concern passed over his features. "Hyw, I am worried for you. He plans to march on all of Dafydd's castles, but the talk is that he moves across the north from Garth Celyn to Criccieth."

It was as Llywelyn thought. Hyw felt a hollow fear in his chest. He tried to hide his eyes from his friend but felt James' hand on his arm.

"You must go, of course," James whispered. "You must get there before them all and find your mother."

Hyw could not believe his friend guessed his heart so well. Hyw felt a pang for deceiving James: it was not mother but father that Hyw would be leaving to find. He steeled his heart: he had to protect James at all costs. He looked into the other boy's eyes. "And you must not help me. Your father would never forgive you."

"Yet I will help you all I can." James set his chin with resolve.

Wait a little, Hyw, Llywelyn said. *Let me think.*

"Give me a moment to consider," Hyw whispered to James. He closed his eyes for a moment and found Llywelyn with his hand cupping his chin in thought.

You need to protect him and his good father. If you run now, it may seem they have harboured a fugitive. It will not go well for them. And you will lose a future ally, once this war has ended. Llywelyn stood and looked squarely at Hyw. *I may know another way.*

It was a way fraught with danger, but Hyw found himself relaying Llywelyn's plan to James. They would offer to go for water together. James would return alone, running, and claim that Hyw had been taken by Welsh marauders. The boys modified it with what they thought might work. They could secure some food from the cook, who was always willing to feed growing boys, and wrap it in cloth as before for Hyw to take along with him. They decided to wait until the following day to try their luck.

Hyw decided to lead James downstream but turn and go upstream once they parted, to make doubly sure the plan would work. *What your friend does not know, he bears no responsibility for,* the prince said.

Later that afternoon, when James went to watch the architect, Hyw used the commotion of armies on the move to leave another message. Llywelyn showed him the Arabic signs that would convince the men to keep clear of the area so the English soldiers would not find them. Hyw looked around him for the last time, wondering if his father watched from the thickets, or perhaps from an unseen cave. He tried spying through the eyes of a nearby jackdaw, but he could not spot any human activity in the area.

Hyw busied himself in the barn for the morning. At dinner, Shrewsbury kept James busy on the dais, but Hyw managed to collect some extra food from his table and from the cook.

He waited for James in the courtyard. James brought two water buckets. "I thought I'd never be done." He wiped his brow with one sleeve. Hyw grabbed a bucket from him as the two boys set out, quickening their pace so no one would find more chores for them.

As they rounded the castle gate, Hyw led them downstream, away from the message bush. They waited until they had gotten well past the castle before they slowed to talk.

"Hold on." James reached into his tunic and brought out a

small flask of watered-down English wine for the journey. Then he slipped off his inner quilted vest.

"No, you will need it yourself." Hyw tried to protest.

"I have another. Besides, I need to know you are warm out here in this snow. Surely it will be warmer near Garth Celyn?"

"I'm sure it will be," Hyw replied. It was still January, but the Menai Strait kept the climate at Garth Celyn milder than in the Snowdon mountains. "I will worry about you, too."

"Me?" James laughed, but his eyes were shadowed. "I have a whole army at my back. I will be fine."

Hyw meant something more than that, recalling the shine in James' eyes as he watched the architect at his work. As Shrewsbury's heir, James couldn't train in a building trade, even if his heart might lean in that direction. Hyw couldn't think of the words to explain his feelings, so he punched James lightly on the arm as they set off again. "I know it."

Since Hyw had explored more often than James, he had chosen the spot for them to part company. He slowed his pace as they neared it, and James brought out his finger weaving. They wound each other a wrist bracelet. The small one Cat had made was barely a thread on Hyw's wrist now, and he could not speak as James plaited his sturdier cord into hers. Hyw touched the bracelet as he looked down into the water of the stream, and thought of his sister and mother, wondering how long it would be before he saw them again.

The boys half filled their bucket and then dropped it on the ground, grinding their feet into the slush and mud around the stream as if a great many men had scuffled there. They were careful to leave a few tracks of their own clearly visible.

"We will meet again Hyw. When all this is over, you will come back to Shrewsbury."

Hyw found his voice then and put one hand on his friend's shoulder. "I will hold you to your father's promise. I should like nothing more than to serve you, when you are lord of Shrewsbury castle."

"It is a pact then."

"Now head you back," Hyw told him, "so I can see you safely around the bend before I go."

James hesitated a moment and threw his arms around Hyw in a quick hug. Then he ran, stopping once to wave. Hyw set out upstream, taking extra time to cover his tracks and hoping James remembered to slow down as he neared Dolwyddelan, so he would not raise the alarm too quickly.

30

Adara released Sir Ifan at the door of her room, and the three women went in together to begin embroidering crests. With no others present, Cat had the chance to tell her mam that Margred knew her secret. Mam made them swear to tell no one else. That gave Cat the chance to turn the conversation to her most recent vision of Father Maelgwyn. Mam digested this news, remaining silent for several moments.

"These are dark days indeed," she said, her low voice resonating with sorrow. Before Cat could respond, they heard a commotion outside the open window. Cat and Margred looked out and saw a group of men dismounting in the courtyard. The men wore chain mail shirts and had swords at their sides, so they must be nobles or *teulu*, although Cat didn't recognize them. She looked for their banner and saw the Welsh red lion walking forward, with some black markings on a red background. The breeze caught it, and she could clearly see three ravens, two above and one below.

"Meirionnydd's banner," she exclaimed out loud. She knew it well, since it would someday be her own. Just then, the tallest man turned and looked up at their window.

"Rhys!"

She ran for the door, leaving Mam and Margred to follow. Cat raced down the stairs to the main hall in time to see Rhys and two of his men enter. Cat had eyes only for Rhys, and the look on his face when he caught sight of her was payment enough for her.

"The lord of Meirionnydd, Rhys ap Cadwgan ap Goronwy ap…" droned Princess Elizabeth's bard, reciting his extensive family history as Rhys and his men swept through the hall. Rhys knelt on one knee before Princess Elizabeth, and kissed her hand in fealty, as his men knelt behind him. Gwilym and some of Criccieth's guards stood behind the princess.

"Welcome to Criccieth, Lord Rhys," said Princess Elizabeth, extending her hands.

"Dolwyddelan Castle has fallen to the English," he said in a clear baritone, and the small crowd that had gathered gave a collective gasp. "We come at your husband's command, Princess Elizabeth, to ensure your safety and join your ranks to defend Criccieth."

She gestured for him to rise. "My husband," she repeated, with a look of relief. "Then he yet lives? Does he send word?"

"He does, your highness, and he bid me deliver this letter into your hands." With that, Rhys handed her a sealed parchment. She inspected the seal and then tore it off with her fingernails, moving to a chair by the window to read it.

Rhys turned to Cat and her mam with a look of eagerness on his face.

"Cat!" he exclaimed. "I mean, gentle ladies." He bowed to Lady Adara first, and then to Cat, and then Margred, greeting them each by name.

Joy and relief swelled in her, and on its heels was fear. He had been her friend when they were children together, when she had visited his castle as Cat from Gwynedd whose father served the Prince of Wales. Their marriage was a good alliance for both their families, since she would own land in the Llyn valley through her mam, to join with his land in the neighbouring realm of Meirionnydd. He was only three years older than her, and they were well matched in interests.

Or were they? Now that she was a seer—and a seer who could not control her sight—would he think the same of her as before? Would he think her strange and unnatural?

As he took a step forward, she took a step back. He hesitated, brushing back a few strands of his dark hair with a look of pure puzzlement on his face.

"Lord Rhys," she said.

"Lady Catrin," he said, bowing to her. Then he stepped back and turned slightly to include her mother in the conversation. "And Lady Adara. We had word that Garth Celyn was attacked in the night. Glad I am to see you here at Criccieth. You are safe?"

"Yes, we were not harmed," Mam told him.

"And the infant, Gwenllian?"

"We fled to bring her to safety," Mam said. "Princess Elizabeth has been most generous."

"The babe is under my protection, and that of my husband, the Prince of Wales," said Princess Elizabeth, barely raising her eyes from the parchment.

"Your hospitality is commendable," Rhys said, bowing to her before turning to Cat again. "I must confess, this is my first visit to the great castle of Criccieth. Would you show me around?"

Cat's tongue was suddenly tied in knots and she turned her eyes to her mam. Mam stepped forward. "We would be pleased to show you," Mam said, as she took Rhys' arm. "Have you heard aught of my husband, Lord Rhys?"

"What is the matter with you?" Margred whispered in Cat's ear. "He's very handsome!"

"What can I say to him?" Cat replied. "What will he think?"

"You mean about your gift?" Margred looked from Cat to Rhys' disappearing back. "Will he not see it as an advantage?"

Cat shrugged. "I cannot tell what he might think."

"Then you should tell him everything and find out. Surely, he will help keep watch on Father Maelgwyn with us. Come, we must at least accompany them." With that Margred followed after Rhys and Adara, leaving Cat to catch up.

At supper, Cat sat on one side of Rhys while Margred sat on the other. Cat could think of little to say, but Margred kept him laughing. Cat glanced sideways at him. He had a clean smell as if he had bathed since the afternoon, and she noticed one of the servants had trimmed his dark hair. Just then, Margred's laughter rang out again, and Rhys joined in. Cat began to resent her friend, and then felt guilty for it. She pushed the cheese-and-leek sausage around on her plate without eating.

"Are you well, Lady Catrin?" she heard a voice ask from her left. "Our hostess has dug deep for these wares, in honour of the Lord Rhys. Does it not please you?" She turned to find the bard Gwilym considering her in some concern. She remembered how he had stared at Margred when they first met. He might understand how she felt better than anyone else at the table.

"It pleases me well, Lord Gwilym," she said, taking a bite of the sausage. "Thank you for asking. How have you been finding your stay at Criccieth?"

Rhys turned to them then, frowning a little as he saw Gwilym leaning toward Cat. "I trust the princess has spared only what she could, with war on our heels," Rhys said. "Lord Gwilym, how long have you been at the castle?" he asked, and soon they were exchanging news, although she noticed both managed to say very little.

After the meal, Gwilym caught her eye, and stood up. "I have a special song this evening," he began, "in honour of Lord Rhys and his people." Gwilym strode to a seat near the fire where he had set his instruments. He picked up the harp, checked its tuning and then began to play.

Rhys smiled as he heard the first notes. "Well known and well loved," he said, loudly enough for Gwilym to hear his approval.

"Another King Arthur tale, no doubt," Margred whispered beside him. "He's very big on those."

"Lord Gwilym is a very well-known poet," Cat began.

"And quite smitten with me," Margred put in.

"I'm sure he is, Lady Margred," Rhys said, agreeably.

"Oh!" Cat tried to frown at her friend but Margred laughed. Soon Cat was laughing too, struggling to hide it behind her hand. Gwilym played another refrain on the harp, letting them quiet down before he began. Then his voice lifted and filled the hall, singing of a woman who fought in a major war to help her people. Cat found herself no longer hearing Margred's chatter but listening intently to the words. Rhys and several other men and women joined in, each voice naturally harmonizing with the other. The woman they sang about had second sight. She carried a message to her people, but they turned away from her. Then the ravens surrounded them, and as the birds descended the woman rose to meet them, changing and dividing until she became three ravens.

"Three ravens," Cat breathed. The song did not say so, but she recalled the banner Rhys' man held when she looked down from her mam's window: the Welsh lion with three dark ravens around it, two above and one below.

"You are thinking of my banner," Rhys said, just as quietly.

"Yes," she said.

"The raven is sacred to us," he said. "Some say King Arthur turned into a raven at his death. It's an old belief in Meirionnydd. Have you heard it?" When Cat shook her head, he continued, "The Lady Modron—you might know her as King Arthur's sister, Morgana—is reviled as Arthur's enemy in many parts of the north. But we see her as the other half of Arthur himself."

"How so?"

"She had knowledge others would not hear, and could not understand, as the poet says. But she led Arthur to his power, and she lent him her power at the end. The power of the raven. So, we carry her symbol: three ravens at the ready, surrounding the heart of Wales."

"This story is important to you."

"It is, my lady." He leaned closer to her, his deep blue eyes holding hers. "Almost as important to me as... well, as you are."

Cat felt her face flush, and she turned from him to listen to the poet. Margred seemed quiet now, and Cat snuck a glance at her to see that she was also watching Gwilym. Rhys was still looking at Cat, and she smiled at him as she turned back to hear the end of the song. She thought through what Rhys had said. He seemed to believe strongly in the legend. Would he believe her if she told him that some legends could come to life?

31

The wind howled across the mountain pass as Hyw made his way toward his home. He was glad of James' extra vest, but the cold bit hard into him as the sun went down. He tried to listen for any sound that men from the castle searched for him or followed him, but he soon gave up trying to hide his tracks. So loud was the wind in his ears that he heard nothing else as he trudged along the path.

Then with a swiftness that caught him completely unawares, something heavy suddenly dropped on him and he fell onto the cold ground. A thick cord net. It covered him wholly, from his head to his feet. He realized he had been captured. The more he struggled, the tighter the net grew. He yelled, but only once. Then he felt a sharp pain on the back of his head, and all went dark.

Llywelyn leapt to consciousness with a start. The darkness around him was absolute. He turned to his other senses—or, rather, the lad's senses. He could feel the warmth and blow of horses where men and beasts huddled together. The smell of men in the closeness of the makeshift hut was not unfamiliar to him. Llywelyn knew the locations of many mountain caches, where gear might be hidden from the elements. Many times in the past he and his men had found shelter from a raging gale in such a place.

For a moment, Llywelyn thought they were returning from a hunt or a diplomatic mission. His kingdom had been hard won and harder to keep. He had waged many campaigns over the years. Some twenty years earlier, he had held more land for Wales than any other Welsh prince. He had traveled often, visiting the far reaches of his homeland to bring the Welsh chieftains into his fold, some willingly and some with persuasion. He had led his men against the English too—many times. His three years with Elinor had been a welcome change.

Then he remembered. A heavy sense of loss poured in on him.

He concentrated on the sounds. Some of the snores around him were familiar enough to bring names to mind, and he smiled at the slight intake of breath that meant Bran slept near. He'd survived. And no wonder. The man slept with one eye open, waking at the slightest sound or movement.

Yet Llywelyn felt a vague sense of unease. Something was wrong, but what? Then he realized he could not sense Hyw. Since they had begun this mad partnership, he had always had a sense of the lad's character. Now he felt—nothing. He wanted to growl and rouse him, but Hyw was not just sleeping. Something else too: Llywelyn could not seem to make a sound.

The lad was his anchor in this new state of existence. If he could wake Hyw, then he had not lost grip on his reason altogether. A line from an old story slipped into his mind: "He found himself in the body of the Other, alone and aware and alive as he had never lived before." The pure voice of the bard in his father's court had sung of a king who traded places for a year with Arawn, king of OtherWorld. In the old stories, OtherWorld or Annwn was always the place of waiting. Certainly, he could do nothing but wait now.

Always these stories had seemed little more than antiques, harmless and beautiful reflections of his ancestors' beliefs. Now they seemed too familiar. Like the king in that story, Llywelyn could feel no physical pain. He was able to take part in training and sports. Yet he was trapped inside the body of a lad forty years younger than he was. And he seemed to spend much of his time waiting, although he wasn't sure for what. He shuddered. Could this be some kind of punishment for not banning the old stories from his court? Or, perhaps, for not believing them?

He was no stranger to the cruelty of fate. For twenty years he had held the balance of power in the Marches—the border lands between Wales and England. The Treaty of Aberconwy robbed him of all but Gwynedd, his ancestral homeland. Even then, he held ambitious men back from trampling the law and language he held dear. Was this to be his reward? He almost laughed.

Then he remembered stories about a magic that could erase the soul from existence. Would that happen to him, if the lad died? What if the force of his soul became lost now? Would all he had done and tried to do be lost with him?

And what of his love for Elinor? Living without her for the last six months of his life had been like descending into the abyss. Dying without her like this was intolerable. More than once, Hyw's laugh or wit or stubbornness had brought him back from darkness of a different sort: a brooding madness that seemed to overpower his spirit. Where was Hyw now? Why could he not feel the lad's presence?

He heard someone stir near them, rustling the straw on the ground.

"Hyw," someone whispered.

Could it be Bran's voice? He looked around him but could only see darkness. Then he realized he was trapped in Hyw's unconscious body. If Hyw did not open his eyes, Llywelyn could not either.

"Hyw," the voice repeated, a bit louder.

Now he was sure it was Bran who spoke.

"Why does he not stir?" Bran continued.

"I did not hit him that hard, sir," said another voice. "The English were close by us, following his tracks. He's got a good set of lungs on him. I could not count on the storm to mask the sound."

Llywelyn tried to move or thrash about but he could not get Hyw's body to respond. He tried to call out again. He could hear water in a basin and felt the cool wet cloth as someone wiped Hyw's face.

"He's burning up." It was Bran's voice again.

Llywelyn would not allow himself to panic. As he did in preparing for battle, he took stock of the situation. Even when the lad was asleep, he had felt a connection to him. He sensed that Hyw was lost somehow, that they needed to connect again. Perhaps the blow to the head had done some damage? He could think of only one person who could help them now. They must find Gawain. The monk would know what to do.

Llywelyn needed to convince Bran to find Gawain and bring him here. Perhaps I can speak through him, as I did to Dafydd?

He concentrated all his will on making a sound. Finally, Hyw groaned a little. Good, Llywelyn thought. Now to make him ask his father to get Gawain.

"Uhhh—"

"He's trying to say something."

How could he make them understand? He removed all other thoughts from his mind and concentrated on the monk's name.

"Gah—"

It was all he could manage. The effort exhausted him, as if he'd run a mile at his fastest speed. His heart sank as he heard the response from Bran and the others with him.

"Shhh, Hyw. Don't try to speak now."

"What's he saying?"

"I cannot tell. It's the fever talking."

"Bran, I know you don't want to hear it, but what if the boy doesn't recover? Should we fetch the village priest? We could blindfold him and bring him here."

"There's no need for that."

"But the lad—"

"No."

No! The lad must not die. Llywelyn felt powerless, but his warrior's training forced him to think of a plan. He tried to remember the days they had spent with Gawain, and some of the monk's suggestions for communicating with each other. He slowed his breathing and changed the focus of his thoughts to Hyw. Where are you?

Llywelyn fought down through layers of darkness, calling Hyw's name.

Hyw stared through the brackish water. Tendrils of seaweed drifted around him, encasing his ankles and wrists. The light cast dim shadows, like fish swimming in and out. It was peaceful. Hyw floated quietly, not thinking.

He didn't know how long he'd been there. He thought he might have been sleeping, but something had wakened him. Then he saw a figure in front of him: a man. The man was familiar but Hyw couldn't remember his name. He could see the man's mouth moving but couldn't hear any sound. Strange, Hyw thought. He started to turn away, back to the seaweed and shadows. The man reached out then and grabbed Hyw's arms.

Hyw blinked and found himself sitting on the fragrant wild grasses in a field overlooking Garth Celyn. The man sat beside him. He realized it was the prince. For a long time they looked down at the long stone building that Hyw thought of as home.

Flags flapped gaily in the breeze as it blew in off the ocean and whipped up the mountain toward them. Hyw could see the slate roof and the stone watchtower of the longhouse, and almost feel how cool those stones kept the air inside. His fingers twitched to retrace every inch of its rough sandstone windowsills and pillars. In front of the building, the wide, open space of the yard invited men to practice the arts of war. The little church stood guard over the upper courtyard, and around the outside edges he counted the various buildings: brew house, bake house, kitchens, kennels, and stables.

Always there had been people milling about the yard and buildings. Yet today, the yard was silent and still. There were no people in Garth Celyn. No people. A roar like the wind rushed past his ears. He felt pain, as if the hand of a giant had reached into his chest to stop his heart.

"Why did you bring me here?"

This is what it's all about, Hyw. Our home, and the home of our people. This is all it's about. We must stop them. We must protect our people.

Hyw looked at the man then, and knew he was the prince, Llywelyn ap Gruffydd. "You are dead," Hyw said finally. "The Prince of Wales is dead."

Llywelyn stared at him for a moment, somber and thoughtful. *And yet, I am here. You keep me here. I do not begin to comprehend it. Yet I remain.*

Hyw looked back at his silent home. He thought about the soldiers who trained in the yard, and the women inside the hall with their chores, spinning and weaving stories for their spirits along with wool for their clothing. He thought about the men and women who tilled the fertile fields and fished in the sea and hunted on the land where they sat. He saw again the stalks of grass lit like gold in the dawn sun. He breathed in the mist of Aber Falls again and let the spray soak into the pores of his skin. He felt the cry of the hawk vibrate through the sinews of his body. And finally, he nodded.

Without warning, he found himself under the ocean again. He could not breathe. Seaweed tightened around his hands and feet. He began to struggle. With a flash, a metal sword cut through the bracken. Llywelyn hacked the weeds from him, and together they swam for the surface.

32

It was nearly noon when Cat, Margred, and Ifan came back from their field. Ifan carried the weapons for them. It was a small price to pay, but she was sorry to lose them just as she was developing some skill with the throwing knife. Father Maelgwyn watched them from the doorway of the chapel as they made their way into the armoury. Margred waved at him and turned away, almost flouncing past. She must feel the same as Cat about the traitor-priest and his commands.

Ifan set the pile of weapons down and whistled. One of the younger boys came running, eager to be helpful, and Ifan knelt down to explain where to take each set of weapons. Cat was watching him, appreciating his gentleness with the boy, when she heard the shout.

"Ships!" The shout came from the battlements and she whirled, shading her eyes with one hand to look up. "Ships in the harbour!"

Guards began to run for the battlements. The heavy portcullis chains rattled as the gates shut behind them. Ifan stood as if to join the guards but Cat grabbed his arm.

"Get Lord Rhys and bring him to me. Quickly. We will be in the hall."

If he was surprised, he hid it well. He nodded and was gone. Cat and Margred rushed to the castle as Adara came down the stairs looking for them. Ifan and Lord Rhys came through the side doors from the yard, followed by two of his men.

"Go," Mam told Cat. "Tell him on the way. Join us later.

157

Margred, come with me. We must secure the children and Baby Gwen."

Cat grabbed Rhys's arm and almost pushed him to the doors. "We must not let them fire upon the ships," she hissed.

"What? But they are Irish—"

"There is no time to explain. They are not enemies, and we will need those ships. You must believe me."

He looked at her and then at Ifan who followed them. Ifan's face was impassive.

"Very well, I will try to stop them."

"We must stop them. All our lives depend upon it."

"How do you know?"

"I know," Cat told him. "As Morgana knew, I know."

"She has the message," Ifan finally said. "Will you not hear it?"

Cat glanced at him, and he smiled at her. She thought of the promise she had made her mother that no one else should know, but it was not something she could worry about now. Rhys took her by the shoulders and stared at her face. Ifan's hand went to his sword hilt, but Cat raised her hand to stop him.

"This is—a prophecy?" Rhys looked startled.

"Call it what you will," she said, searching his face. "But we must save those ships."

Rhys let her go then and began to run for the door. Cat followed him, and Ifan kept pace with her.

"Go with him," she told Ifan.

"My duty is your safety, lady," he replied. As they moved from the castle to the courtyard another shout went up, but she could not hear the words. A catapult ground into place. It would not take them long to ready a shot. Could Rhys stop them in time?

***

They could hear the angry voices from the gatehouse stairs.

"I cannot let you go nearer, lady," Ifan said.

"I must see," she told him. He looked around them and

nodded, leading her up above the battlement to an arrow slit in the stone wall.

"Is that you, Gron?" a voice called from higher up the staircase. The arrow holes were manned, she thought.

"Aye," Ifan answered, putting one finger to his lip. He made way for Cat to look through the bottom end of the long slit. She could see Rhys in the centre of a group of men, arguing with the captain of Criccieth's guard. Some of the men around him looked as ready to fight with Rhys as with the Irish. Rhys's men flanked him, also with drawn swords, facing the Criccieth warriors. Cat realized he was outnumbered by a group of men that did not answer to him.

"You must help him," she whispered to Ifan.

He expelled his breath in what sounded like a sigh, and then motioned for her to stay. "I will return for you." With a glance up the stairs to be sure the men held position above them, he went back down to the courtyard. She heard his voice below, and some of the men made way, but she could not see him.

"We have word that these ships are friends," Ifan told them.

"Word?" the captain scoffed. "From whom?"

"Have you not heard, brother?" Ifan replied, keeping his voice calm. "Lord Rhys has just returned from Prince Dafydd himself."

"So he says," the captain growled.

"I saw the letter he brought with him." It was Ifan's voice again. "It bore the prince's seal."

The commander of the guard was silent a moment, but she could sense a shift among the men. One unclenched his fist, and another put away his sword. Finally, the commander nodded. "My apologies, Lord Rhys, but we have heard much about spies in the fallen castles. We would not count our own among them."

"Your diligence commends you," Rhys replied smoothly. "I would not want to think you would believe without cause. But I can assure you, these ships are a necessity to our princess's safety and to that of the children."

Ifan appeared in the stairs and motioned to Cat. She wanted to stay and make sure the situation was resolved, but his impatience hurried her. They made their way to the yard just as Father Maelgwyn came in sight.

"Lady Cat," he said. "What are you doing in the gatehouse?"

"Why, Father," she began, glancing at Ifan. "Sir Ifan was bringing me to make confession."

"Confession?" He stared at her as if she had not been to chapel already that morning.

"Yes, Father," she continued smoothly. "It is a most urgent matter."

"Now? Can this not wait until mass tomorrow?"

"Oh no, Father, as you yourself will see shortly," she said, "and Sir Ifan also would confess. In fact, his need is more pressing than my own."

"My lady?" She could hear the surprise in Ifan's voice, but he covered it smoothly. "I mean, my lady speaks aright, Father, if you could but spare the time."

"I must freshen up first, Father Maelgwyn, but I will be there with my own confession as soon as Sir Ifan has finished."

The warrior knight looked torn as Cat made to walk across the inner courtyard, but she nodded at him as the priest took his arm. "Come along then, and see you find your words more quickly today." As the two moved into the chapel in the lower tower, Cat ducked out of sight. Rhys finally came out of the stairwell and she stepped up beside him.

"My Lord Rhys, I must explain," she began, startling him. He took her arm and moved her toward the gardens behind the hall.

"We will find a quiet place, and then you must," he told her. "And you can explain how you come to be here, and not in your rooms with the other women."

33

Hyw spluttered and coughed. He tried to open his eyes and the light seared them. A rustle and bump told him someone was nearby.

"He wakes. Steady on, Hyw." The voice was familiar. Hyw's eyelids fluttered again, and his hand came up to shield his face. It was caught in the rough hand of another, familiar one. "Glad I am to see this."

Hyw's eyes flew open. "Da!" he cried, and now both arms seemed to come up of their own volition and around his father's neck. "I thought you were dead!"

"And I you," Bran replied. "If the storm hadn't taken you, I was afraid that knock to the noggin had done you in. You must forgive my oaf for his zeal in bringing you to me."

"Nay, 'twas neither." Hyw would not let go of his da's neck. "You got my messages then?"

"Your messages?" His da looked at him searchingly, and then Hyw saw a strange expression pass over his eyes. "You wrote those messages? How? How did you know the letters to write?"

Hyw opened his mouth to answer when he heard Llywelyn's voice at his ear. *Nay Hyw. Do not tell him about me yet. He is not alone. Let us choose the timing better.* "I—I had help."

"Who? Who was it, Hyw?" Bran stared at him intently, but Hyw could not find a way to answer.

"I cannot say, Da."

"Was it—? Is he—?" Bran left the sentence unfinished.

Hyw had to say something, but he wasn't sure how to form the words to tell his da what had happened. "I saw the words in my mind and wrote them so."

Bran expelled his breath. His voice was so low, Hyw could barely hear him. "I thought perhaps—" Bran tried to smile, but it made him look sad and tired. "I heard the grisly tale of his death, but I could not stop myself from hoping. If we got away, surely he could as well. When I saw the letters under the hiding place—well. I thought it was him."

Bran disengaged Hyw's arms then as gently as possible but kept seated near him. Hyw felt a rush of pity for his da and almost told him everything. He heard Llywelyn's voice again, cautioning him. *A warrior of the new Cymru would not easily understand this thing that happens between us. There will come a time when he will need to know. Let the time be right.*

Bran had already moved to look around them, gesturing to the others. "Welcome my son back to the land of the living."

Hyw noticed the hut fashioned from skins and branches, rising around him. Several other men looked on, one with tears showing at the corners of his eyes.

"Glad I am we did not have to fetch the priest, after all," the man said, pawing at his face with one hand.

Another man moved closer. Hyw noticed the glint of a warrior's gold torque around his neck. "How came you from the English camp in one piece, son of Bran?"

"The English." Hyw tried to rise but fell back against the sheepskin bedding.

"Give it time, Hyw."

"No. We must get to Garth Celyn."

"What says he? Does he speak of the *llys?*" Another familiar voice spoke the Welsh name for the royal court, and Hyw saw a face set like stone, frowning.

"Aeneus!" Hyw again tried to rise. Instead, his former tutor in the arts of war and physical strength came to his bedside and hugged him soundly.

"Glad I am to see you whole again, lad."

"And I you."

162

"Now I can keep my word to your lady mother. She sent me to seek you, but I was taken on the road. Then came your father to dispatch the *Saeson*. He called me to him to aid in this resistance. Now I am doubly glad I came."

Hyw moved aside then and, gripping Aeneus' shoulders, spoke to him and Bran. "We must make haste. The king will march on all of Dafydd's holdings."

"Is le Clare in charge?"

"He returned to the south. But one of the soldiers showed me the banners for William de Valence. He leads them now. And the king has men from abroad. He pays them silver coins and offers them land if they can take it away from us."

"I know this de Valence." Aeneus nodded at Hyw. "A cousin to the old king, Henry, and fiercely against us."

"What path do they take?"

Hyw turned back to his father. "I am not sure. Criccieth, Dolbadarn, Bere. Those were the names I heard."

Bran looked thoughtful, stroking his moustache. "Roger Le Strange has long sought the castle Criccieth for his own."

"The Marcher lord? Aye, it could well be. They'd be a fool to attack Bere." Aeneus looked grim. "That castle will stand against OtherWorld's hounds. Even Edward Longshanks himself would pose no threat."

"We need more information." Bran straightened and turned to the others. "We must gather everyone we can. Aeneus, when the weather breaks, choose a man, and go in tandem to locate your brother's group. Flush out as many men as you can find—loyal to Cymru all, and willing to fight for Prince Dafydd." Hyw was happy to hear Wales called by its rightful name again: Cymru. "Let the first be a man who hails from Bere."

"Aye, I was born there." The man who teared up earlier had recovered.

Bran and the men conferred. Their voices droned in Hyw's ears. Finally, Bran nodded and turned back to Hyw. "Here, try to regain your strength." He took up an earthen bowl and held it up to Hyw's lips. The broth tasted like nothing Hyw had ever tasted before. Ambrosia, he thought, food of the gods. He remembered the word from the poetry told around the fire in the evenings. That led his mind back to Garth Celyn again. He choked as he remembered his dream.

"There, now. That's enough. Rest, if you can. We must be ready to move out as soon as the wind lets up."

Bran settled a warm sheepskin around his neck, and Hyw closed his eyes.

Hyw was still shaky the next day. He thought he might see Cadarn and Vox with his father, but there were no horses in the camp. Aeneus gruffly told him the English took them all at the ambush. The two men who had shared their hut left at sunup. At noon Bran said they could wait no longer.

Some twenty men broke camp with them. Llywelyn laughed inside him. *It's good to feel the ground beneath our feet again.* Hyw shook his head and looked around him. He had just come from the English camp where cloth and winter gear were plentiful, thanks to their queen and her ladies. He was amazed some of the Welsh warriors were bare-legged in spite of the recent blizzard. Yet none complained or seemed to notice the cold. He heard the rumble of Llywelyn's laugh again. *That is what it means to be Cymry.*

Bran ruffled his hair. "Look at you. You are near as tall as me now. I swear you have grown at least a handspan."

Hyw grinned and ducked his head. He grabbed up some of the camp gear and followed after the men on their way to stash it in a small cavern in the nearby rocks. It wasn't large enough for a man but held the skins and camp tackle easily. The branches that had fortified their hut served a double purpose to hide the stash. Bran handed him a flask to carry.

"Pure mountain water. Keep it full."

Aeneus nodded. "Drink as much as you can. It's from a stream blessed by the Old Ones. Let them protect you from the frost."

Another grunted. "Edward's men share the same stream."

"Aye, but I've heard them curse the very ground as they do," a wizened old warrior grinned. "That should make their ears burn."

"Enough of your blather." A hulk of a warrior carrying a javelin shook his head at the others and turned to Hyw. He heard Llywelyn's voice again: *Listen to this one. See what he hides beneath his cloak.*

Hyw caught sight of a gold torque slung for safekeeping around the man's thick bicep. He had been one of Llywelyn's *teulu.* "Drink you as much water as you can, from any stream you find, boy. May the Old Ones bless you, if they will. If they do not, then bless yourself. You can last three weeks without food if you have to, but no man can stay upright without water. The harsher the weather, the more you must drink to keep the body limber."

Bran sent a man ahead to scout the trail across the mountains. Shortly after they started out, the man returned. The party moved quietly along the ridges and looked down at a knight with two foot soldiers. Englishmen. Without making a sound in the snow, Bran's men dropped them and slit the knight's throat. One soldier lay immobile on the ground, his leg at an unnatural angle.

"I'm from Shrewsbury," said the other soldier quietly, laying down his arms and kneeling. "You know me." Hyw recognized him as a man from Gerald's company who had not gone to the south with le Clare. Bran stared at him, arms across his chest.

"If we know you, then you will not mind aiding our cause."

"I will do all I can, sir."

Aeneus grinned. "Aye, to keep your life intact you will tell us anything."

"Nay, I will tell you truly."

Aeneus leaned closer and set his blade to the man's neck. "See that you do."

Bran nodded. "Where goes the king's army?"

"He split us up, sir. He will attack each castle until he has them all."

"Why? What does he want from us?"

The man thought for a moment. "We had word yesterday that Dolwyddelan Castle has fallen, but Prince Dafydd was not there."

"So, he seeks Dafydd?"

"Aye, my lord. For he believes without a prince, Wales will yield."

Bran pursed his lips at that, but he continued to ask questions. "And how many strong?"

"A thousand men, or more, sir. It cannot go well for you."

Bran looked over at Hyw, who nodded. The man spoke truly about Edward's army, at least. Bran looked back at the soldier, and set his head to one side, as if thinking.

"Why are you pursuing us? It's not as if we haven't all fought this battle many times. Wales wins, then Edward wins. The knights may fight to the death, but we men—we don't often leave each other bleeding in the snow." The man looked embarrassed but said nothing. Bran persisted. "The king's men have never in my recollection crossed the slopes in snow before. Why now? And why are the soldiers stealing our heads from our bodies?"

"The king's bounty," the soldier mumbled. One of the Welsh warriors prodded him with the point of a javelin. "Edward offers a shilling for each Welsh head."

Bran didn't flinch. "And how many have you brought him?"

The man hesitated a fraction of a second, before he began to protest.

Bran turned away. "Leave Edward a message he'll understand." His voice was harsh.

Hyw felt bile in his mouth as he realized his father's intention. "Wait, Da," he said, putting a hand on Bran's arm. "The one with a broken leg cannot join the fighting again. Nor can the other, if he escorts that one home. Is that not enough?"

Bran considered his son for a moment before he spoke. "Good counsel always makes a leader a better man." Then he bent down to the uninjured soldier. "If you are rescued, see that you tell your captains the Welsh showed you mercy. And consider whether that is worth more than a shilling."

34

As they walked in the winter garden, Cat told Rhys as quietly as she could about her visions and the results. She left out some of the details about her brother, concentrating instead on the final three: the ships, the attack on the castle, and Father Maelgwyn at the gates.

For a long moment, Rhys said nothing. Then he asked, "How soon will the remaining two come to pass?"

"I do not know," she said. "It may be that we can prevent them from ever coming to pass. Mam can explain more."

"Your mam knows of your gift?"

"Yes, it is common enough in her family."

"Ah. It is your inheritance?"

"I believe so." She felt miserable now, cold outside and in, and she began to shiver. He noticed her shaking and rubbed her shoulders.

"I forget myself. We tarry too long outside. Come, let us go inside and warm you up."

"Nay, we must be sure Princess Elizabeth has heard of the ships."

He nodded and they turned toward the castle hall. Ifan joined them at the door.

"I am so sorry, Sir Ifan," Cat began.

He raised his eyebrows at her. "I trust my forced confessions were to some benefit," he said.

"More than you know," she said. Rhys looked from one to the

other, but she went through the door Ifan held open for her and up the stairs without another word.

In Princess Elizabeth's solar, Rhys explained his actions in preventing the commander from firing on the ships, without mentioning Cat's role in it. Mam listened with them, but no other ladies were present. The guards Elizabeth had sent to the harbour returned with news. There were three ships in all, with a crew dispatched from one of Meirionnydd's allies in Ireland. They were large merchant vessels with no cargo, but enough room for men and horses. Rhys glanced at Cat but gave nothing away.

"It is Providence," Elizabeth declared, turning to Rhys. "You will know where my Lord Prince would have us meet him, while the English storm Criccieth in search of him?"

Rhys nodded briefly, and it was Cat's turn to be surprised. "He could not trust anyone with the news beforehand, your highness." He looked at the princess, but Cat couldn't help but think the explanation was for her benefit as well. "I was to escort you by land, before anyone could guess our plans. But this will make it easier."

"If we act quickly," she said, and he nodded.

If certain priests do not hear of it, Cat thought. And if there are no more English spies in our midst.

Within a day they were loading horses and chests onto one of the ships.

"Expect your lord, Prince Dafydd, within the week," Elizabeth told the commander and his men. "The other two ships will remain for a time in the harbour, in case they are needed."

The princess had a private audience with the ship's captain, and Cat wondered if she would tell him where they were bound. At least one of her visions had been avoided, but the first one, with the castle under attack and Owain and the others killed, worried her most. She sensed that without preventing both of her other visions, that could still come to pass.

"What of the priest?" Cat asked Rhys, but he shook his head.

"We have no evidence to accuse him," Rhys told her. "I may believe you without question, but I fear it will not sit so with the commander of Elizabeth's guard."

"Or with the princess," Cat added. "Then how can we stop him?"

"We must be diligent, and the answer will present itself." He did not look at her when he said it, and she wondered if she felt as sure as he sounded.

It took several hours to load the ships with food, weapons, trunks of supplies and personal belongings, and finally horses. Rhys was overseeing the horses as Elizabeth, Mam, and the children made their way toward the ship. Gwilym walked near Princess Elizabeth while Ifan accompanied Cat and Margred.

Suddenly she heard a shout and a scuffle, and several hooded men rushed from the gardens toward them. Something glinted in their hands, and Cat realized it was knives. Ifan drew his sword, as did Gwilym and Elizabeth's guards.

"Run for the ships," Ifan shouted. Owain started to draw his sword, but Ifan stopped him. "Take your mam to the ship." He moved between them and the hooded men.

Cat grabbed Enid's arm, jostling Baby Gwen who began to cry. "Come now," she cried, trying to stay calm but almost dragging Enid toward the ships. Owain ran past them with Elizabeth, shielding her from the attackers with his body just as Cat tried to shield Enid. Margred easily passed them both with one sister in her arms and one on her back. Cat did not stop to look back until she had reached the ship, but when she did, she saw Gwilym moving between the men lying on the field. She could not see Ifan. Then she spotted a figure in chain mail lying at an awkward angle on the ground.

And suddenly she was running. Back toward the knot of fallen men and warriors. To Ifan.

"Cat." She heard her mam's voice behind her, but she could not stop. Not until she reached him. Blood pooled around him, and he looked at her dully, as if he didn't know who she was. She knelt near him, ignoring the dark stain on the ground, and took his head into her lap. He tried to raise his hand to her face, and she grasped it.

"Don't move, Ifan," she told him. "You will be all right." She cradled his head with her other hand. She examined him frantically but found nothing until she spotted the deep wound in his thigh. His blood seeped into the ground, covering her skirts, but she did not move even when she heard Rhys's voice behind her. A mist began rising to surround them.

"Call for the priest."

"He is missing, my lord," another soldier said.

"This one over here." Their voices sounded farther away, and Cat realized they must be looking at one of the hooded men. "This is the priest's man, is it not?"

"It is." The voice was that of the commander, gritty and low. "Father Maelgwyn's servant." Now we have him, Cat thought.

"The priest was a spy for the English," Rhys said. "These men must have been set to capture the princess before she could get away."

"That means the English will be close upon us."

Ifan's head moved, and Cat squeezed his hand. "You've done well, Ifan," she said. "We are safe. Rest, now." Ifan's eyes slid away from hers, and he stared up at the sky.

Beyond the mist, she could see him clearly, standing in a field of green grass, the tower of Garth Celyn rising behind him. He raised his arm as if to wave at her. The sun on his chain mail glittered.

She heard the fluttering of wings close overhead and Rhys' surprised voice. "A raven."

But she could not seem to see beyond the glittering that filled her eyes.

35

Hyw blamed the prickly pine branches where they camped for making him toss and turn that night. Every time he closed his eyes, he could see the English army, endless bodies pouring across the field. They seemed as unstoppable as the Nant Peris river flowing over the rocks near their former camp. Finally, Hyw pushed himself up and drew the light blanket closer around him. They had eaten dried meat from their packs, not daring to light a fire lest it lead any headhunting soldiers to them.

He had just stretched his back upright to ease the tension when he heard the owl hoot the first time. It hooted again before he was able to turn toward it. He felt Llywelyn come alert inside him. Responding to the prince's unspoken command, Hyw cast out with his mind. The being he encountered was not feathered, and he pulled back.

Wake your father.

Moving silently in the semi-darkness, Hyw made his way around the men toward his father's form. Bran turned before Hyw got near enough to touch his arm. With a grimace, Bran automatically punched at Hyw, then tried to pull back his arm when he realized who it was. Hyw leapt back in time to avoid the full strength of the blow, but his father's fist felt like iron against his shoulder. He would bear a bruise from the force of it. Bran sat up quickly.

"Hyw," he whispered. "Careful, lad."

Hyw just shook his head and motioned toward the wood.

171

Together they turned just as the next hooting sounded. Bran rose and took up his javelin. Hyw followed, and his father did not motion him back. Without words or sound, they made their way toward the trees at the far edge of their camp. There they heard the owl-that-was-no-owl hoot again. This time Bran stopped and cupped his hand around his mouth, hooting back in a near-perfect imitation of the night hunter.

Not one man but twenty or more melted out of the shadows toward them. Bran set his javelin point up and at rest, standing with feet firmly planted. Hyw imitated him. The men fanned out behind their leader, who stopped facing Bran. He greeted them formally, giving the names of his ancestors to identify himself. "Dai ap Rhys ap Gruffydd ap Rhys ap Roderic Tewdwr ap Cadell. For Cymru." Although the man's cadence was unfamiliar, Hyw heard the old word for Wales, spoken in their shared mother tongue.

"For Cymru. I am Bran ap Maredudd ap Rhys ap Eineon ap Hywel ap Cadell. Cousin, I bid you welcome." The men relaxed, and the leader came forward to grasp Bran's arm in friendship.

"We go to Dolwyddelan."

Hyw felt Bran's body tighten slightly. Bran considered Dai for a moment, and then shook his head. "It has fallen."

Dai uttered a sound that might have been an oath. "Another fallen. We have come from Carreg Cennen in the south, fallen betimes." Dai spat. "English hounds on our heels. We have left traps and snares on our path to slow them."

"As have we, but as yet we have felt no breath on our necks. The *Saeson* take our heads for shillings."

Dai grunted. "As do le Clare's men." He spat again. "I have lived near two score years, and number my own wife's cousins among our pursuers. This is more than any soul should have to bear. I have seen what I can scarce tell, in the towns and on the roadways where the people flee in vain."

Bran nodded. "You are welcome to our camp. We will share what we have."

Dai placed his hand over his heart, a remnant of Roman times. "As will we."

Bran's small force roused and welcomed the new men. After a brief whispered council, they took up separate sections of the clearing and fell back to a restless sleep until daybreak. As the men shared up what berries and roots they had to break their fast, Dai related some of the horrors of the road. Bran sent Hyw for water, and Hyw was glad to leave them to speak of the unspeakable for a time. He filled skins of water at the nearby creek, reaching out into the woods with his senses. All was quiet.

When he returned, he saw his father sitting with Dai, his shoulders hunched and head down. Llywelyn urged him to Bran's side. *You must rally them, Hyw. Bere must remain our next destination. With both forces combined, they may yet aid in its defence.*

Hyw closed his eyes for a moment. "How can I make him listen to me?"

I know him well, Hyw. You must remind him of the castle. His instinct will do the rest.

Hyw managed to get his father's attention as he handed him a water skin. He took a breath and tried to think of a way to do as Llywelyn had suggested. "Da, what do you know of Bere?"

"Little, Hyw, save what I have seen on trips there in times past. The men say it is still well fortified."

"I know it," Dai looked up at them. "It is held by Cynfrig ap Madog for my lord Rhys ap Cadwgan. I fought with Cynfrig when de Valence attacked some five years past. A good man, with heart. If your forces and mine combine, Bran ap Maredudd, we may yet prove useful in this fight."

"For Cymru." Bran stood, as did Hyw, and they returned to their bedraggled band of warriors.

Bran kept them in the lowlands to make quicker passage through the rugged Eryri Mountains. Hyw had never traveled this route, and he breathed in the fragrant mountain air. *Land of the eagles,* Llywelyn commented inside Hyw's mind. *You'll soon see why.*

They stuck to shadows and treed areas near the Nant Peris River. Bran set the pace over the broken terrain of the river valley. They ran twenty paces, walked twenty in a quick march, ran again, then walked again. The men traveled in silence, stilling their panting breath as much as possible. They could not be sure how long the king's army would tarry to secure each castle, or where they would strike next.

Llywelyn had little more to say, and Hyw was glad of the quiet. During the journey, he'd been too preoccupied to notice any residual effect of his flight through the blizzard and the blow on his head. Now, as his water skin grew lighter and the climb steeper, his head began to ache.

"It's the altitude." One of the men stopped near him during a short break. He was from Dai's group and knew the area. "You'll calm in time. Try this." The man bent forward with his hands on his knees.

Bran stopped near them, concerned. "It is so with several of the men. Yet we must keep up the pace."

"I will try to use the lowlands as much as I can. Water also helps, Hyw." Their guide took a few leaves of an herb from a pouch at his belt and gave a segment to Hyw. "Suck on this." He handed a portion of leaf to the other men as well. Hyw found it bitter at first, but the taste faded.

By mid-morning they passed the small lake at the base of the Yr Wyddfa, the tallest mountain in the range. Their guide's herb had helped ease the pain of his aching head, but Hyw still felt tired and short of breath. He took a moment to stare upward at the mountain. In Welsh its name meant a burial mound, and Hyw shivered.

Bran gestured aside to him, and he was happy to put away his thoughts and search for a likely tree to climb. He would use his gift to check the way ahead. To hide the fact from the other men, Hyw would climb into the tree to act as lookout, then use his gift when he was out of sight.

He steadied himself on a branch and concentrated. It was second nature now to keep the prince safe from any animal minds he might connect to, using the breathing techniques Gawain had shown him. Hyw concentrated, separating a piece of his mind from Llywelyn. He pictured it as stepping in front of the prince, in order to connect another part of himself with a brown eagle. The bird was difficult to control. Hyw sensed it searching for game. He focused his mind on the bird and coasted with it, enjoying a few moments stretched above the trail, staring down at the forest and lake.

The bird rounded in a wide curve. Hyw caught sight of a trail of smoke in the distance. It was far away, a thin streak of grey in the sky, barely enough to make the bird react. Was it a village, or a noble *llys*? Hyw's mind raced to his mam and Cat: were they safe? He forced the bird in that direction until he felt Llywelyn's calming hand on his arm, as if the prince stood behind him, whispering.

We must warn Bran.

Hyw faltered, dropping from the eagle's mind to his own again. In moments, he was standing in front of Bran. Hyw lowered his eyes to hide his feelings.

"I saw smoke, but it is leagues back. More than a campfire, but I could not see—"

Bran laid one hand on Hyw's shoulder and gestured to the men. They rose as one. Their guide took them by a route that avoided the mountain's steeper areas. Even so, the pace was gruelling. They kept it up during the long afternoon, as the sharp rocks stabbed through his foot leathers. His knees and calves ached from the increasing steepness of the path.

The sun was low in the sky before they caught sight of the Desenni valley. It was greening already with spring, and Hyw thought of words he had heard in hymns calling it "the promised land." Bran stopped the group near a brook to refill their water skins and turned to Hyw.

"We may be too far away, but see what you can, before we lose the sun."

Hyw's head pounded now, and he had no strength left to climb a tree. He stood in the shade, staring out across the valley. Far away, towering over the land between them, was the huge summit of Cadair Idris, the giant's chair. He had heard many tales of bards and warriors who spent the night on the mountain, hoping for inspiration, only to discover madness within themselves instead.

As his mind followed his eyeline, he felt rather than saw a small running creature. He made contact: it was a fox. The dappled shadows under the creature's feet told Hyw the path was in shadow, far away on the giant's mountain. He sniffed the air, and felt relief along with the fox when he sensed game. No human scent marred the path. The fox looked up, and through its eyes he saw Bere. Hyw brought himself back to his vantage point reluctantly.

"There are no troops near the castle," he told Bran. He wanted to share some of the experience with his father but wasn't sure how to talk about it. Instead, he pointed toward the path where he had seen the fox. "That way."

"The lad speaks truth." Their warrior-guide from Dai's group stepped near them when Hyw pointed. The man looked surprised. "But to see it from here, he must have sharp eyes. Have you been this way before, lad?"

"Once, but he has a strong memory." Bran responded before Hyw had a chance to speak. The man looked skeptical. Bran handed Hyw his water skin. "Here, son, fill up for both of us."

As Hyw turned away to go to the stream, he saw his father turn back towards their guide. Bran would find some way to explain it. Hyw was tired, he realized, and using his gift taxed him further. He bent to the brook and splashed water over his face and hair, wishing he could explain to his father about Llywelyn.

Give it time, lad. Hyw closed his eyes to find the prince waiting. *You are a strong help to your father. All is not lost while there is yet a Prince in Wales. That castle is a stronghouse, built by my grandfather. If we have any chance to make a stand against Edward, it will be there.*

Fear can keep us alive when all else fails, Hyw. But never give in to despair. These English come and go, but we remain. Our mountains will surely shelter us, until Edward finds someone else to hate.

36

Cat accepted her mam's assistance from the ship she could not remember boarding. Margred and the girls stood near, and Owain stood at the ready near his mam. Cat wondered where Ifan was, before she remembered he was no longer with them. Her limbs felt heavy, but her head felt feather-light, as if the breeze off the sea could blow her away. She looked around for Rhys and spotted him checking the saddles. He motioned to his men to bring horses toward the group and moved toward the princess. When Cat saw him look at her, she waved. His nod didn't reflect the easy camaraderie of the past few days at Criccieth but had a kind of deference. Her heart seemed to clench inside her chest.

Then the horses were between them. She helped her mam and Enid mount. When she gained the saddle, Rhys and his warriors were already forging ahead down the road with Princess Elizabeth and Owain between them. Why did he not look back?

She found herself inside the great hall of a castle, with no memory of having seen the castle from the path.

"The horse," Cat said. It was the last thing she remembered.

"Cynfrig has seen to it," Mam told her, with a questioning look. Cat did not know who Cynfrig was.

177

A man with a kind face and greying moustache took her hand. "You are welcome in this place, Morrigan," he said, moving closer to her to speak quietly. "My Lord Rhys has told me of your feat at Criccieth. It has been many years since one of your kind graced our halls." She stared at him blankly, and he nodded and patted her hand. "You must rest. I will have our Katie show you to your room."

"You are most kind," Cat said. What had he called her? Morrigan? No, she had to correct him. "My name is Catrin. Cat."

It seemed a moment later when she woke, surrounded by quilted softness. She felt the smoothness of the white fabric with her hand.

"It is silk," said her mam's voice, and Cat looked up into her mother's face.

"Where are we?"

Mam looked concerned for a moment and felt Cat's forehead with the inside of her wrist. "We're at Bere. Don't you remember? You must have been more ill than we realized."

She had a sudden flash of the kind man's face and the word "morrigan." It was familiar to her somehow. What did it mean? She felt afraid, but she didn't know what she feared. She felt an urgency to rise and do—something, but she didn't know what. She pushed the quilt off and her mam rose as well.

"How long have we been here?"

"Two days already." Mam caught Cat as she swayed. "Take it slowly. You've barely eaten the last few days, and you've been asleep since yesterday, but I didn't want to wake you. How do you feel now?"

Cat tested herself and looked around. "Better. I think." She dressed with Mam's help and got caught up on the news. Prince Dafydd had come with his eldest son, and she had apparently missed Princess Elizabeth's tearful reunion with her family. Margred and the girls were well, and Owain was practicing in the yard with the other boys.

"And Rhys?" she asked.

"He was here to check on you earlier this morning," her mam told her, smiling.

"He was?" Everything must be fine then.

"And why would he not?" Mam went on. "Nothing stands between you now." When Cat didn't respond, Mam stopped fussing with her hair and looked at her. "Does it?"

"No, of course not," Cat said. But why did she still feel her stomach clench?

In the next few days, Cat found no opportunity to talk with Rhys, even at dinner. They sat in family groups according to the Welsh custom, rather than at long tables as they had at Criccieth. As lord of Meirionnydd, Rhys was expected to serve the others, and Cynfrig and his family helped. Cat sat with her mam, Enid and the baby, and the two remaining Garth Celyn warriors. It was the second evening meal before Rhys happened to serve them.

Mam smiled at him as he and two of the kitchen girls placed the main course of eel and venison in front of them. "It smells tasty," she told him. "Cat should be helping you, Rhys. Then you will know each other's ways before you become hosts together."

"Nay, Lady Adara, I would rather she conserve her health for—what she may need it for," he said, shaking his head. He did not try to catch Cat's eye but turned a general smile upon them all as he backed away toward another table. Cat's smile froze on her face. Was he avoiding her? She watched him joking easily with Margred and Owain as he served them.

"He has great concern for you, Cat," Mam said.

"Perhaps he has too much concern for me, Mam," Cat said.

"Perhaps you should tell him so, then," Mam replied.

Something inside Cat snapped. Enough of this, she thought. If he had reason to avoid her, then he must tell her so to her face. "Perhaps I should do more than that," she said, throwing down her cloth napkin and following Rhys into the kitchens.

"Since I am to be lady of this castle one day, I should offer you assistance in your tasks," she said, moving to the tables.

Rhys stopped what he was doing and raised his eyebrows in surprise. "Nay, Cat—I mean, Lady Catrin," he said, glancing at the Cook and her staff, who had come over to watch. "Your duties are far more onerous than this small task, and I would not have you tax your—strengths."

"I have vast reserves of strength," she said, arranging sliced meats on a plate. "I will admit, what happened as we left Criccieth cast a pall on my spirits, but I did very little. Others did a great deal, while I was merely a witness."

"I beg your pardon, Lady Cat, but I know well what you did," he said, stopping her with one hand. "And I know very well that you were taxed by it."

"I was weary from the voyage, but I am rested now," she told him.

"Perhaps you would take a breath of fresh air with me so we might talk about this together," he said, glancing around them. "Just we two."

She looked around to see a gaggle of kitchen staff staring at them. Cynfrig's grey moustache twitched, and his wife held her hands over her mouth. Cat could not tell if they were upset or—could they be—laughing?

"Aye, Rhys, lad," Cynfrig said, his voice strained. "Take the lady for a quick look at the garden under the moon. We can easily finish what you have begun here."

"Can we indeed?" his wife said, turning away quickly in a fit of what must have been coughing. Then she turned back again. "Aye, I suppose we can."

Cat let Rhys lead her from the kitchen and into the yard at the side of the castle. "Here we grow the fine roots and herbs you tasted in tonight's meal," he said, loudly enough for the others to hear. As the door shut behind them, he turned on her. "What do you mean, you were weary from the voyage? You sat and stared at the water without speaking for most of the trip."

"I did?" she asked.

"You did. And I should know, for I tried every way I could to coax a response from you."

"Every way?"

He pulled her to him. "Nay, not every way. Not with your mam hovering so close." He kissed her. She felt the softness of his lips against her mouth, and the sudden cold when he pulled himself away.

"I beg your pardon," he said. "I did not mean to—I know what you are, Cat. And I know this cannot be, now. You are meant for a higher calling."

"What do you mean?" she said.

"You are the morrigan," he said. "A woman of power. My da had such a woman in our home before the last great war, and I know well what it means."

"What? What is it that you think—"

"I know. I know you cannot marry as other women, or birth children. You must keep your power pure."

"Fie," she said, stopping him. "I know not how you do things in Meirionnydd, but we have no such prohibitions at Garth Celyn. My own mam is a woman of power, yet she loves my da just as other women love their husbands. And she gave birth to my brother and to me, and two other children who died in infancy, just as other women's children die."

Rhys shook his head. "Nay, I am sure it cannot be so."

"It is so," Cat said. "I am here, standing in front of you, to prove it."

Rhys cupped her face in his hands. "Yet I saw you release the young warrior's soul."

"I—I don't know what I did," she said. "I saw Sir Ifan standing in the field outside our home, and I knew he was free."

"You released him," Rhys said. "How can we live as normal man and wife, when you have the power to—the power of the raven?" They stood looking at each other for a moment, and then Rhys turned and disappeared down the dark garden path.

37

Hyw could see the men grow more hesitant the closer they got to Bere. The lush lowlands were surrounded by stark, rugged mountains. As they climbed the craggy slopes to a rock-cut road that stretched ahead of them, the setting sun threw long shadows over the ground. The low howl of the wind through the craggy mountain face made his hair stand on end.

"Gwyn ap Nudd," one of the men murmured. Hyw recalled the name of the legendary king of the Tylwyth Teg. The wind made him think of Nudd's huge baying hounds, said to have the power to drag a man's soul to the OtherWorld. Another warrior behind them on the path made the hooting call of an owl. When the superstitious one jerked around, fearful and wide-eyed, several laughed. Llywelyn laughed with them.

Take heart Hyw. The English soldiers know that legend, as do their masters. Our stories may shelter us here better than the rocks of the castle itself.

The guide took his sword and held it hilt-up toward the valley. He moved it from side to side, using the sun's rays to send a signal toward the castle walls. He repeated the motion three times.

Hyw was standing near him in a thicket. Before long, they

spotted an answering flash that seemed to come from within the mountainside. He squinted until he found the spot where he saw the fox. That rocky slope must hide the great castle.

Their guide nodded down at him. "They know we come, and we are friends. But in these times, you cannot be too careful. We will still need the password, you will see." He pointed to his own temple. "Lucky we are that this is still in one piece."

Hyw could sense Llywelyn's hope rising within him, and almost feel the prince's laugh rumble inside his own chest. *Wait until you see it, Hyw. The English king can try his tricks, but he cannot win here. Would that my grandfather could know his stronghold would stand for us, e'en today.*

An eerie mist dampened the air around them as Hyw and the others followed their warrior-guide over wooden bridges that crossed several deep, rock-cut ditches and culverts. He stopped and spoke quietly into the mist, as if giving a pre-ordained password. A man holding a javelin rose up in front of them, appearing from between the rocks as if by magic. He waved them on, and stood aside as they gained the high-walled path.

When they rounded the last curve, Hyw felt dwarfed by the cavernous stoneworks that led into the castle yard. He felt as if the rock cliffs and slanted pathway pushed them into the inner courtyard. Then the dusk grew rosy in a blaze of setting sun, and colour flooded the castle courtyard as people bustled into view.

Hyw saw townsfolk, women and children, and warriors of all ages. Several wore the traditional Gwynedd warrior garb of a red tunic over chain mail, and Hyw realized some of Llywelyn's army manned the castle. He spotted the dark hair and eyes of a familiar face, and caught a glimpse of the red sash that marked the warrior's privilege. It was Emrys, Hyw's childhood friend, still as wiry and thin as he had been at Garth Celyn.

Before he could wave, a grizzled warrior came toward them. He was short and muscular, but his air of confidence and authority marked him as a leader. His arms opened wide to them. "Welcome to our fortress, Bere." He hugged each man to him in turn. The man's deep-set eyes were troubled but kind. "I am Cynfrig ap Madog, constable here for many years, and glad to be named your host. We ration against the future, but such as we have, we will share with you. Gather you all inside, and dine with us, and with our own Prince of Wales."

Hyw was confused for a moment, wondering how Cynfrig had guessed his secret. He closed his eyes almost out of habit, and saw Llywelyn laughing at him. *Nay Hyw, he speaks of Dafydd. My brother is here. We've made it.*

Too tired to question further, Hyw allowed himself to be led to the castle by his father. They entered together, handing over weapons and washing their feet in keeping with the old customs. Hyw saw Bran run a hand along his chin, rough from quick shaving with his knife on the road. His father would look forward to proper morning rituals again.

Then they were pushed along in the stream of men. Hyw saw several of their companions greet friends, hugging wives and other relations who had taken refuge in the castle. Women sitting in other groupings rose hesitantly to their feet and peered at their group. Some of these women fell still and looked down at their own hands. Even as he felt sorrow for them, he hoped Dai or the others would bring them news of their loved ones to ease their minds.

He didn't realize until the last minute that the constable had led his father toward Dafydd's own family group. Hyw hesitated, but Dafydd made no outcry against him. If Llywelyn's brother remembered him from Dolwyddelan, the only sign he gave was a slight pause as he brought a leg of mutton to his lips, and the narrowing of his ice-blue eyes. Bran made to pay homage to Dafydd, but he waved them off graciously. "We will speak later. See to your wife and children, Bran."

Then Hyw thought of it no more, for at the next table he heard a cry. Up sprang his mother, Adara. The blush of joy on her face lit the room, just as the setting sun had lit the rocks outside. She flew into Bran's arms. Then she turned to Hyw. He was aware of his mother's smallness and hugged her to him.

"Hyw, you're a man in truth now. How tall you have grown."

He grinned down at her. As she turned back to Bran again, he spotted his sister Cat coming toward them. He hugged her to him. "Glad I am to see you, Cat."

"And I you."

She seemed older too, and a little sadder, he thought. He wondered how bedraggled he must look, and how different he would be after a few months away. She hesitated a moment longer, and then turned to greet her da.

Adara turned back to Hyw then. "You are too thin, the both of you," she scolded. "And here we sit, warm and well fed." She broke down then. Bran crushed her to him for a long moment.

"I feared you were dead," Adara mumbled into his chest.

"And how could that be?" Bran's voice was husky. "No one could ever capture this black bird but you, milady."

Hyw thought he glimpsed a shine in his da's eyes as well. Then he noticed Enid the nursemaid beside them, waiting for her turn, and he hugged her with one arm as he kept the other around his sister.

"Where is Gwenllian?" he asked.

"She is asleep, the dear child," Enid said. She knelt and rocked a bassinet beside her. He could only see blankets from where he stood. He didn't want to disturb the babe, but Llywelyn urged him closer. *You see how she has grown anon. Would I could hold her but a moment, though I would not disturb her.* Hyw reached down and stroked the babe's sleeping head, to let Llywelyn feel the softness of her hair and skin.

Finally, Bran set Adara back on her own feet. Cynfrig and his wife brought out more plates of food for all the men, including Hyw's company. Hyw noticed cheese and mutton, along with jugs of white milk. Still blushing, his mam pushed him to a spot near her and added to their plates from her own, beckoning Bran to her other side.

Hyw paused, noticing the easy familiarity of the family gatherings in the Welsh hall. What a contrast from the formal gathering of the English, where the king and his favourites sat on a raised dais apart from rows of knights. Here there were no tablecloths, elaborate fixtures, or cleverly-dressed dishes, but plain food, well-made and nourishing. He tried to imagine King Edward and his wife serving their guests before they ate themselves, as Welsh custom required. He could not imagine the English, even the kindly Shrewsbury, without servants and squires to serve them.

Then he noticed his father's hand shaking as he picked up some of the food. Bran turned to Adara and pulled her to him again, as they sat at the table.

Cat took the opportunity to scramble around them and sit beside her brother. He turned to her, showing her the braided threads he still wore around his wrist. "See, here is the band you made for me long ago. Do you remember?"

"You've added another in with it, here."

He thought of James, and the day they had parted. It seemed much longer than weeks ago. "Aye, that was done with the help of a good friend. It keeps yours in good repair. Always you were in my heart, Cat. This wristband kept you near."

"It did indeed, Hyw," she said, and the look on her face made him wonder if she would say more. Instead, she passed a few morsels of meat from her plate to his. "After supper I would show you around this gloomy place. The wolves howl always here. Have you heard them?"

"It's not wolves, child," Enid put in, "but the wind, howling through the rock face of the mountain."

"I heard it as we came." Hyw gripped her hand. "That very wind and its mournful howl may yet keep us safe from harm." He made up a story for her then, of a sleeping giant knocking the English soldiers off the mountain with his snoring. Before he was finished, Gwladys and young Owain and some of the other children gathered near as well. Lord Rhys also came near, although he remained standing apart.

"Good it is to have you and Da with us again, Hyw," said Cat, laughing at the end of Hyw's story.

"Aye, he has all the warrior's graces." Adara's shining eyes reminded him of all the bardic tales he had heard played and sung by warriors in Garth Celyn, where a man was expected to be as adept at musical arts as he was at combat.

Sure enough, before they had finished the meal, a warrior bard began to sing and play the harp. Cat whispered to remind him this was Gwilym ap Einion, and he pretended to remember the bard from his time at Garth Celyn. Five years ago, he realized. A beautiful young woman came to sit near Cat, and she introduced her as Margred, daughter of Prince Dafydd. People gradually cleared their places, feeding their leftovers to the hunting dogs that shared their space.

Bran rose to follow Dafydd, gesturing to Dai and a handful of other men. They would confer about the war, and Hyw longed to be with them. Above the heads of other groupings, he spotted Emrys watching the men as well. Their eyes met, and Hyw grinned, as did Emrys. He was seated with Dai's group, so he must be related to the warriors they had met on the trail.

Then Adara called his attention back to her. He found himself giving his mother an account of the battle at Dolwyddelan. He hesitated to recount their capture of soldiers, finishing, "We found Dai and his companions as we made our way here."

Adara took his hand gently. "Glad I am you have come back to us at last." He welcomed her touch and the chance to feel Cat warm against his side. Dafydd had been at Dolwyddelan. Had his mam and Cat been with him there?

"Yet how did you come to be here, Mam?"

"We were attacked at Garth Celyn, and we fled to Criccieth, where Princess Elizabeth gave us her protection. Then Lord Rhys came to us, with messages from the prince to commend us to his protection at Bere."

"Does Garth Celyn still stand?"

"I know not. We thought it best to bring the babe to her uncle. After that, we did not plan."

Hyw could see the sense of bringing Gwenllian to Dafydd. *Aye*, agreed Llywelyn inside him. *My brother would never harm the child. Gwenllian is safest with him.* Then Llywelyn asked the question that Hyw realized he should have asked. *Does your mother carry Gwenllian's seal?* Hyw turned to Adara and asked quietly if she still kept the baby's royal seal. She nodded, glancing at Dafydd's table with a gesture that told Hyw to keep this to himself.

So, things were not as cozy as they seemed, perhaps. He looked over at Llywelyn's brother, who was seated with his wife and seven children. Surely Dafydd would have been safe with Edward too, Hyw thought, since they had been friends.

Edward must hate him worst of all now, Llywelyn said softly in his ear, *because in the end, my brother could not kill me. And now he is Wales. You must help him if you can, Hyw, just as you have helped me.*

38

After supper Cat took Hyw by the hand. "Come and let me show you the castle, before it becomes too dark to see," she said, leading him up the stairwell.

"I will," said Hyw. "And who better to tour it with, since you will be its lady one day."

"I suppose I will," she said. Cat had been so dazed by Ifan's death when she first arrived that she had not really taken it in: this would have been her home for the past two years, had her marriage to Rhys gone forward. If she had married, she would not have been there when the unthinkable happened. Cat had a sudden flash of Princess Elinor, smiling and holding out her hand in welcome. Of Elinor's peals of laughter, bringing smiles to the room full of ladies—especially after she understood enough Welsh to catch the clever puns in the songs Cat sang to her. And how quickly the princess learned the harmonies for those songs. She was quick in all her movements, and in her expressions of love for anything and everything from her new country, including Cat. The princess passed along her beautiful gowns to Cat, and fussed over Cat's red hair, bidding her own maid to brush it.

Elinor was twenty when she married Prince Llywelyn, and three years later she came of child for the first time. Cat could still see her mam's pale face when she examined the princess. Mam had squared her shoulders and forced a smile as she made the happy announcement. But Cat had clearly seen what came before, and she was old enough to know what it might mean. When the princess asked, of course, Cat had to stay. Cat would not let herself regret her decision now.

Besides, this castle might still be hers, one day. She looked back across the battlement, smiling at the guard who waved as he walked his rounds. Bere was built oblong, almost triangular, to fit its rocky plateau. One D-shaped tower overlooked the castle well.

"One of the warriors told me these waters grant the powers of sharp sight and strength," Cat told her brother. "He and many others drink from it before leaving the castle."

"So, I will as well," Hyw said. "Quite a bit grander than home."

He meant their longhouse at Garth Celyn. She felt a small pang, thinking of the guard who had helped them escape. How many had died there before the English took it? For a moment they stood together, saying nothing. Cat had to force herself to remember why she'd taken him away from the others.

"There is something else, Hyw," she began. "I'm not sure how to explain. When you left, I had no gift to speak of."

"That never mattered—"

"I know, but after you left, I found I was able to connect with you."

"Connect?" he repeated. "What do you mean?"

She explained her visions, and how she had known he was alive, and about the treachery of the priest Maelgwyn. "After a time, I realized it happened whenever I looked into some kind of liquid, whether a cup of ale at supper or a raindrop. Now I think I see you because of this bracelet I tied to your wrist." She took his hand and pressed the rough wool.

"You used a lock of your own hair," he said.

"Perhaps that is why. Yet something puzzles me. More than once I saw you with the prince, almost as if you were one."

He went pale and took both of her hands. "You saw?"

"What does it mean, Hyw?"

He told her what had happened on the hillside at Builth, about his bonding with Llywelyn and their travels together.

Cat took an involuntary step back in shock. "Our former

prince? And he is with you now?" She searched his face but saw no trace of the former Prince of Wales.

Hyw nodded.

"What does he tell you?"

"Many things," he said. "He knows more of this castle than we do." Hyw pointed to the large D-shaped tower guarding the path at the southern end of the courtyard. "Those walls are ten feet thick. If the English manage to get in, this is where the people should run."

She huffed, almost like a laugh. "How does it work? Does he speak to you?"

"He speaks inside my head, and I can see him if I close my eyes. Come. He says he will show us the castle."

They made their way to the rectangular keep. They took turns peeking out the archer's portals, careful not to disturb the bows and arrows set ready in case of attack.

"These rooms along here—we can rest or sleep here during an attack," Hyw told her as they continued.

"Or tend the injured," she added, and then wished she hadn't said it aloud.

Inside it was strangely quiet, as if the building stood in its own enchanted world that no threat could penetrate. Everyone was still listening to the bards. Cat touched the decorated tiles on the walls, stained glass windows, and lovely stone carvings of armed soldiers and heraldic battles as Hyw reported what Llywelyn told him.

"This is truly the most magnificent castle I have ever seen," Cat breathed. She could not imagine herself as its lady, any more than she could see herself as Rhys's wife.

"Prince Llywelyn says he brought back many of these items from the Crusades," Hyw said, still appearing to listen to his inner voice. "The same place he learned how to speak foreign languages and the strategies of chess."

Wall hangings of legendary battles flickered in the torch light as if they were alive. On one wall, the great King Henry crowned their own Llywelyn as Prince of Wales, only a few decades earlier. Cat wondered what the prince must feel when he saw it now, but she did not ask Hyw.

"Look there," she said instead, pointing to another wall where

Gruffydd ap Rhys of Deheubarth led his troops into the field to win his glorious victory over the English at Crug Mawr. As Cat looked away, Hyw asked her what was wrong, and she told him of her concerns about Rhys and the legend that had caused a rift between them.

Hyw was silent for several minutes when she had finished. "Your gift is of immense value to us now, Cat," he finally said. "Are you sure there is no truth in what Rhys says? This is Meirionnydd's legend, after all."

"There cannot be." Cat was adamant. "If there was, how could you or I be here to discuss it today? Besides, I only have the second sight. In the legends, the morrigan—whatever she is—also transforms into a raven and commands the spirits of the dead. I'm fairly certain I won't be sprouting black feathers anytime soon."

Hyw shot Cat a look. "Yet I have been able to communicate with many animals, including ravens and hawks."

She considered that. "Have you ever shifted shape with any other creature?"

He did not answer right away. "I have been able to allow Prince Llywelyn to—I'm not sure how to explain it. He sometimes appears through me." He told her of the fox at Dolwyddelan, and how it seemed that he had become a fox himself.

Cat nodded, thinking of her vision. "Then do you think you will someday be able to shift into another form?"

Hyw shrugged. "Our uncle mentioned it."

Cat told him of Aylwen, their ancestor, who had told her they had stronger gifts because they were born in a time of need. Hyw said nothing, but she could tell by his face he was considering it. She thought about the morrigan legend again, and what it might mean for them.

It had grown dark while they explored, and in one torch-lit hall they could hear men's angry voices echoing off the castle walls. Cat recalled Da and the other men who had left with Prince Dafydd. Hyw shook his head and she led the way back to the main hall, where they rejoined Mam and the others to listen to bardic songs. Then Owain came to collect Hyw, since he was to share a room with the other boys inside the castle. In spite of her pleasure at seeing her brother again, Cat found herself tired enough to willingly bid him goodnight as she and Margred went up the stairs to their room.

The next morning, Cat poured wash water into her basin. She saw her reflection in the water—

—and she found herself in the castle courtyard. The crash and whump of swords on armour deafened her as arrows sped by. The people ran, screaming. She saw Prince Dafydd surrounded by English knights.

"You we take, and your wife and children, since the king demands they not be harmed," said a large armoured man she somehow knew to be de Valence. "But these others—" He turned with a savage grin and nodded at his sergeant. The man took his sword and moved to Da and Mam. Enid cowered behind them, holding Baby Gwen. The armoured man raised his sword to her mam as another soldier held her da back.

"No," roared Lord Rhys, running at the man in fury. His hands were tied but raised toward de Valence's throat. Suddenly he stopped, his eyes searching. He found Cat's face, and half-smiled. She didn't see the arrow in his back until he fell.

"No!" She reached toward him—

—and she was staring at her own reflection in the basin, a look of horror on her face. "No," she cried aloud.

"What is it?" Margred grabbed her.

"It cannot be," Cat said, staring at her. Margred glanced at her sisters and drew Cat from the room.

"Calm yourself, Cat," she said. "We will find your mam. She will know what it means."

Adara listened to the girls and turned to Cat. "Your da and the others have been arguing about what to do. The prince wants to wage war, but Rhys and some of the others want to avoid it as long as possible. Your vision may be more important than you know. I will make sure your da hears of it, Cat."

"What can we do?"

"I have a thought," she said. "It would seem the simplest way would be for Dafydd and Rhys to part company. Each will get his wish, and your vision will be averted. Rest easy now. If this can be prevented, we will find a way."

39

The next morning, Hyw woke at dawn.

"Psst." He looked up at a young man's face, and realized it was Emrys. His friend's dark eyes snapped with laughter. He gestured for Hyw to follow. Hyw got up, careful not to disturb those still sleeping. In the bustle of the castle courtyard, he waved at his father just as Bran sat down for his turn at the ritual shaving. Other men had already begun their daily exercise, and Hyw and Emrys ran to join them.

"You can train with us today if you wish it." Emrys strapped on his sash. "I serve here with my uncle and his men."

"Who is your uncle?"

The other boys giggled but Emrys shushed them with a gesture. "*Ust.* He is not to know, is he? My uncle is Cynfrig, constable of this castle. But now my cousin Dai has returned, perhaps I may serve with him."

Hyw agreed to train with them, and the boys began with basic agility much the same as Aeneus would at Garth Celyn. Then Emrys turned to him. "I know you spent some time with the English. My da says you cannot defeat an enemy unless you learn his strengths and weaknesses. We would know all we could of those *Saeson*. What can you show us of their moves?"

Hyw thought for a moment, recalling his early days in training before he went to foster in England. "They are different and not so different. They prize their steel and armour well. It is difficult to show you how they train without the—the pieces in the yard."

"What do you mean?"

Hyw tried as best he could to describe the quintain, and the wooden dummies set up for practice with sword and mace. Emrys nodded. "Aye, we have something like it," he said. Hyw thought back to the days before he had gone to foster at Shrewsbury, to contrast the English use of wooden swords to the moves Aeneus taught during field practice. Emrys stood and grabbed two javelin sticks, handing one to Hyw. "Show me how those English move, if you can."

Hyw hesitated, until he heard Llywelyn's voice. *Nay, lad, show him. May it help save his life.*

They skirmished, using the sticks as swords. Hyw struck lightly so as not to break any bones before the battle to come. Emrys, however, knew no such qualms, and played hard. Hyw took a bruise on his arm, and at the next skirmish he also played harder, turning back to front and striking low with the sword at Emrys's feet.

Emrys went down. Around him the others had taken up similar positions with each other to learn what Hyw could show them. As Emrys tumbled, all stopped and went quiet. Hyw wondered for a moment if he had managed to set this group against him so soon, and if he would have a new enemy as powerful as the bully Robert had been in Shrewsbury's court.

But Emrys was not Robert. At sixteen, he wore the sash proudly. He had already seen battle and what the English could do. He got up and dusted himself off. "That was a clever move. Show me again."

By the next day, most of the boys had taken just such a tumble. Then, working as a team, Emrys and Hyw worked out a way to predict the move and leap up over the stick before it struck.

Cynfrig watched them work the move through. He called them over to show some of the other men. Hyw and Emrys fought hard with sticks, and each of them in turn made and sidestepped the blow Hyw had shown them. The men nodded, and soon groups of them began to use the new skill as they had seen the boys do it.

"You have used your time well, I see." Hyw turned to see Bran beside him. His da's eyes twinkled as he stroked his newly-trimmed moustache, and Hyw felt a rush of pride. "It is well that the young teach the old, in this war. Many things have changed, and we must change with them. While there is life, there is yet hope." He tousled Hyw's hair. "Now, before your head swells out of your hair altogether, show me this move."

Llywelyn laughed inside Hyw as they prepared to skirmish with Bran. *Now you know why he is my captain.*

Hyw descended for supper in the castle hall along with his father. Emrys nodded toward him, as did several of the other boys as they made their way to their family table. Hyw saw someone sitting with them in a white robe.

"Uncle Gawain!" he exclaimed, and caught his uncle up in a huge hug.

Now we will hear the news, Llywelyn remarked, and Hyw did not need to close his eyes to know the look of grim anticipation on the former prince's face.

His uncle's normally calm face was clouded throughout the meal, and even Cat's harmonizing with Gwilym on his favourite hymn as the evening progressed did little to brighten his spirits. As Gwilym moved into a longer ballad, Aeneus moved to their table touching Gawain's shoulder as he sat with them. Adara finally leaned closer to Gawain.

"What news, brother?" she began in a low voice. "I know you spoke with Prince Dafydd this afternoon. I bid you, speak freely. What news of home?"

For a moment Gawain was silent, his eyes focused on his hands as if searching for direction there. Finally, he looked up at her and spoke. "I was sent hither by my lord Abbot," he began. "The abbey at Aberconwy is no more. The English king claims our allegiance, and bids us move to Maenan. My lord can do aught but agree, save send me to warn the prince his ancestral lands are gone."

"Gone," Bran said. "How can it be?"

Gawain was silent, folding his hands in his lap. Bran made a noise of disbelief. Hyw heard Llywelyn make almost the same sound.

His mother made no sound, but when he glanced toward her, he saw tears streaming down her face.

"It cannot," Aeneus cried. Adara quickly shushed him, and he went on in a lower voice. "What of the garrison at Garth Celyn, or the men of Ynys Môn?"

"The *Saeson* were merciless," Gawain said, his voice scraping against Hyw's ears. "They ran down all that moved for their shillings. Some of the women and children managed to reach the abbey. I cannot say they were the lucky ones."

40

The next few days went by in a whirlwind. Cat could find no reason to smile, after Gawain's news. Her uncle kept mainly to the chapel except for the evening meal, where he was often silent. She had asked him about the morrigan legends, and he said he would make the time to tell her as soon as he could.

The girls and women were able to exercise freely at Bere at the north end of the courtyard while the warriors practiced farther south. The Bere warriors trained any men and women willing to fight for Cymru. Cat sought out Bronwen, a childhood friend, and bade her join her and Margred. The girls spoke little but worked hard at the exercises set for them by one of the Bere warriors.

"Yours were much tougher," Cat whispered to Margred. Bronwen was impressed when she heard how the girls had formed their own practice at Criccieth.

Cat found throwing knives helped ease her mind. Once when she was lining up the target, Cat felt as if someone was watching her. She let the knife fly and felt the satisfying thwack as it hit squarely in the centre. She turned in time to see Rhys watching her, but in the next heartbeat he looked away. Margred saw as well and put an arm around her as they returned to the back of the line for their next turn.

"Is aught amiss between you and Lord Rhys?"

Cat straightened her shoulders. "Lord Rhys is reconsidering the wisdom of our union."

Mam, who had joined them, heard and pulled Cat out of the line. "Why would he do so? Was it because of Sir Ifan? Did you have feelings for him?"

"Nay, Mam," Cat began, surprised. "Not like that." Cat poured out the story then, telling her mam about the legend and the morrigan who once served Rhys' family.

"I knew her," Mam said. "You know your gift is no problem for you as a woman, don't you?" When Cat said nothing, Mam gave her another quick hug. "You have concerns."

"The legend connects Arthur and Morgana," Cat said. "It speaks of a combination of brother and sister."

"Ah, I see," her mam said. "You think perhaps you and Hyw make two sides of the morrigan." Mam thought for a moment and shook her head. "I also have gifted sisters and brothers who married happily. Your Uncle Gawain took his vows as a monk, but the rest have families."

"But how can I answer Rhys' concerns?"

"Only he can do that," Mam said.

By then it was time for them to join Princess Elizabeth and help her greet some of the townsfolk and farmers who were arriving daily to seek refuge within the castle walls, as word of the English moved down the valleys. Cat and Margred listened for news of Criccieth and those left to defend the castle. Although Margred never said so, Cat suspected she worried for the butcher's son Drem more than her other friends from the town.

Elizabeth, Mam, and the girls welcomed and cared for the women and children, especially those who were pregnant or in need. Most afternoons, Hyw went with Emrys and the other boys to help the Welsh survivors carry their wares, along with oats and other grains in barrels, back to the castle longhouse to feed the people pouring in from surrounding areas. Twice Cat joined the people working in the fields, pounding meat into strips and smoking it for storage and travel, or making breads and cheeses at the cookhouses. Bronwen sometimes came with her and saved a few choice tidbits for Emrys.

"See how she loves me, poor thing," Emrys joked, but Cat could sense the longing in both of them and thought of Rhys.

Cat was on the way to the north exercise yard when Rhys stopped her. After greeting Margred and Bronwen, he asked her to walk with him a moment. His tunic sleeves were rolled up and the glisten on his skin showed he had already been practicing, so he must have been watching for them. She waved at the other girls and fell into step beside him.

He drew a dull grey cloth from beneath the cloak he had slung across one shoulder. She unrolled it to find a set of three lightweight throwing knives. The hilts were burnished with one small green jewel set cleverly in scrollwork, and they fit her hand.

"Be careful," he cautioned her. "They are deadly sharp."

She held one up to the sun and saw it was tapered to a fine thin edge. He touched the leather sheath that held them.

"This sheath belonged to the morrigan," he said. "She was my teacher for a time, and I saw her use her knife more than once. It fixes to your leg with the point inside your boot and seemed to work very well for her."

She was tempted to give it back to him then, but he placed his hand on hers as if he knew what she was thinking. "Please, Cat. If we are separated, I must know that you are safe. I have worried about your safety since Gawain gave us his news. When I saw you in the practice yard, I decided to have them made especially for you. I believe the sheath is special and will help keep you safe."

His eyes blazed into hers and made her think of the kiss in the night garden. Perhaps he remembered also, because he dropped her hands and moved past her to the castle without a backward glance.

41

It was well past noon when Hyw heard a warrior's shout. "They're coming."

He ran with the others to climb the low retaining wall around Bere and strained to see through the light mist that always seem to hang over the lush valleys. He still thought of it as the giant's breath, and felt a shiver run down the length of his back.

Emrys jumped onto the stone wall and mimed a fight. "With some of those moves you taught us, Hyw, they should be more afraid of us than of the giant who breathes down on them now."

All the boys laughed then, the tension broken. Hyw marvelled at the way Emrys could lift their spirits and make them feel bold, even in their fear. *A leader in training,* Llywelyn said softly in his ear. *If he survives what comes, Emrys would be a good candidate for the prince's teulu.* It was a high compliment.

"Look there!" The boys looked where Emrys pointed and spied a flash of metal. With a flush of excitement and fear, they leaned against the wall. Each tried to be the first to see, and the first to point out English troops to his friends. It began with the metallic flash from moment to moment through the thick trees and undergrowth. Then soldiers began to march into the lowlands and muster in groups. Hyw had no need of his gift to track them. By mid-day, the lowlands were full of English banners.

The clouds that ringed the mountain darkened and belched out rain, covering the plain with a muddy mixture that showed the outline of the army clearly. The king's white camouflage coats were useless against the giant of Cadair Idris. Hyw looked for the siege engines the English had taken with them to Dolwyddelan, but in truth they had no need of them. He heard the men guess at the size of de Valence's troops. Camped beyond arrow range, fanning out in the valley, their numbers filled every inch of the Desenni plain.

"There can be nothing left now, of food or game," one man said.

"That will be the end of them, then." Emrys laughed. "How can they remain, without food?"

The man guffawed. "*Saeson.*" He spat. "What do you think they eat?"

"Rat?"

"Sheep droppings." He made a rude gesture and some of the other men huffed a grim laugh at his antics.

"Best stay out of their sights, Gron." Aeneus folded his arms across his chest and stared down at the field of enemy soldiers, unsmiling. "Names will not help you. Hunger makes fierce foes. Who knows what it will do to them? I hear they have mercenaries among them."

"Them I have seen. They dig under the ground and eat the bugs."

Gron launched into a bawdy song, and Aeneus turned away in disgust.

About mid-afternoon, a roar caught Hyw's attention as a younger knight with a banner no one recognized led a hundred or so cavalry and soldiers out of the ranks. After a short flourish, they swarmed toward the Welsh castle. Hyw remembered Edward's words as they left Rhuddlan: any man, no matter his rank, could keep the land he won in this battle. Hyw had seen the hard greed in their eyes as they prepared for the journey.

At first his stomach tightened with what Llywelyn called battle-fear. Hyw felt his hands form fists without waiting for direction from his thoughts. Then, as they reached the base of the rocky cliff, the horses faltered. Emrys laughed a little too loudly. "You see! The fools. They need mountain goats to get up that cliff."

"Or good Welsh ponies," Hyw added.

"Look closer." Emrys cast him a sideways look. Hyw did and noted the line of Welsh breeding in the sturdy horses, realizing his friend suspected their countrymen of aiding the English. "Devil take them."

As Emrys spoke the words, several horses slid backwards. One shaggy mount lost its footing on the rocks and went over backwards, falling onto its rider. Hyw gasped as the horse reached out to him in panic. Vox and Cadarn flashed into his mind, but they were gone. He quickly built around his mind a battlement like the one surrounding Y-Bere. Yet he felt as much as saw the horse flounder, struggling on top of the still form of the armoured man. Had Emrys summoned the horned god from OtherWorld? Hyw made the sign of the cross and felt Emrys make a similar sign beside him. He turned in time to see his expression of horror reflected on Emrys' face.

A few of the horses and some foot soldiers pulled themselves up the cliffs nearer the castle. A volley of arrows from the battlements rained down. The shafts seemed to hit their mark with extra force. It was as if they were drawn by the pull of the valley floor, Hyw thought, or perhaps blown by the giant's breath. Then he noticed half-formed pieces of the siege engines on the valley floor and wondered if these were the same ones the English had dragged to Dolwyddelan. They were of little use on the giant's mountain.

Horses and men fell and pulled back. Twice more the English knight and his followers charged, until he fell back for the final time. Hyw could see the knight bowed over, with an arrow protruding from his shoulder.

Later that day, under a flag of truce, some men on foot dragged off the fallen soldiers. Hyw wondered if they would recover or be buried by their countrymen, never to see their own lands again. He heard a rumble on Cadair Idris, and his skin prickled as he imagined the giant laughing at the tiny men on the field below.

The next day, a rider came to the castle, holding a white flag. Bran went down the path to speak with him, along with two other men from Cynfrig's garrison. Aeneus and the other warriors kept watch from the battlement, javelins at the ready. After a long conversation, the knight rode off again and the men returned to hold conference with Dafydd.

Rumours were rife through the castle most of the afternoon, as the people waited to hear news of the rider. When Bran and the others finally came out of the meeting room, it was as if the whole castle went quiet. All eyes turned to them.

Dafydd came out last and looked around him. "The English know we cannot be beaten. They sent their Lancelot to tell us so." He laughed.

Several others laughed, and then began to cheer. Dafydd let them enjoy the moment. When they had quieted, he went on. "It is right that you know the truth. They will not back off this time. They will starve us out."

"Let them try." Aeneus stood defiantly at the back of the room. "They will need to return to their fields this season, same as us."

Yet too many are not English soldiers, Llywelyn reminded Hyw, in his inner ear. *These men will not drop their swords to take up a plough unless they are given a piece of Welsh land to tend.*

"Nay, their mercenaries will stay," Dafydd echoed the comment. "They can wait us out and trap us here in this stone castle like sheep." Around the room, people shifted. Like many, Hyw had always preferred his *llys* to these stone castles, built to defend Cymru against the English. A handful had already begun complaining they would prefer mountain caves to the cold stone under their feet. Gwilym the warrior poet looked thoughtful.

Dafydd went on. "Lestrange wants me. He offers you the chance to depart this castle in peace, with eighty English pounds divided among you."

A murmur buzzed around the room like a wasp swarm. Lestrange's offer meant surrender.

Aeneus' voice boomed across the room. "They would have our prince? Never!" The room erupted around him. Hyw was dismayed to hear angry voices, as if some disagreed with Aeneus.

No, Hyw heard Llywelyn inside him. *Dafydd must not surrender. He is Wales now. They must not let him.*

Hyw closed his eyes and found Llywelyn seated in front of a chessboard. This was no time to think of games, Hyw thought, but Llywelyn gestured at it. *How many ways can players jump positions?*

Hyw let out an exasperated breath and looked at the board. The white nearly overwhelmed the few remaining black pieces, leaving Llywelyn's king guarded by only one knight. "The knight can jump other players. And I know of a move called castling where the king moves two squares, and the rook jumps across to take its place."

And we have a squire who could take the prince's place, Llywelyn suggested, removing the black king from the board. *Dafydd could flee with the children, while the English remain behind, thinking to capture their prize.*

Hyw recalled taking the knight's position during their training. It was only weeks ago but seemed longer. "My great-grandfather had the ability to change form, but my skills fall far short of that. And I would not put you in jeopardy."

It is too late to fear for me, Hyw. But did not Gawain say that your gift was stronger than any he had seen? Whatsoever you can do to save Wales, you must now do. I charge you to attempt it, no matter the cost to either of us.

Hyw stared at Llywelyn until Dafydd's voice roared out across the hall, startling him into opening his eyes.

"Think you well on this offer, friends. It may be the only way to save you."

42

As the English settled in around them, Cat helped her mam and Cynfrig's family ration their dwindling stores of food. The castle was full of people from the surrounding towns and farms. The food they had gathered, which had seemed so plentiful as they had carried it into the castle, scarcely seemed enough to last the week.

As she served a platter to their family table the next morning, Hyw touched her hand. "I need your help," he said. "This morning, if you can make time."

When she had finished her chores, they made their way to the battlements. Unlike the previous day, Aeneus kept only a few warriors for the watch, strategically placed along the wall walk.

"Most will spend this day in the practice yard, readying for the signal," Aeneus told them. "After yesterday, the *Saeson* will need to rethink their strategy. But their archers will be watching. Mind you both return to the keep."

"The girls will be with Elizabeth and Mam this morning," Cat whispered. Hyw nodded, and they made their way to the room Cat shared with Margred and her sisters. Hyw looked uncomfortable in the small bedroom, as if he had grown too large for it already. He stood at the window, opening the heavy wooden shutter just enough to see out without being seen. She moved impatiently and finally he began.

"Do you remember when you asked me if I had ever used my

gift to become another creature? Would it surprise you to know I've tried?"

She shrugged. "I know the stories of our great-grandfather as well as you. Why shouldn't you see if your gift is as strong as his?"

"Nay, I care not if it is." He went on without waiting for her to answer, tapping his temple lightly. "My liege has asked me to do this thing. For his sake I have tried, but I cannot."

"It will come," she told him. "You know our gifts grow with time and use. What you cannot do now, you may do in a year, or ten years."

"I need to do it now," he said. "In a year or ten, Prince Dafydd may be a prisoner or worse. I must help him now."

"What, would you change into Dafydd himself and go to prison for him? Or into a horse to spirit him away?"

"Nay, but something of smaller size and more spirit," he quipped, drawing her to the window and pointing at a pair of hawks flying together against the grey clouds, just above the castle battlements.

"I don't understand." Cat stared at the hawks, wondering if Hyw meant to fly Dafydd away like Pegasus, the winged horse from the old songs.

"I cannot tell you all just yet, Cat, but if I can manage this thing, I will make sense of it, I promise you."

"But how can I be of service in this task?"

"These powers you have, as a morrigan," he said, "can you call them to you?"

"I do not know. Water plays a part, as you know." She thought of Ifan's death again, and the infinite sadness that enveloped her then. Her powers had seemed such a part of her that she did not fully realize what she had done until Rhys told her what he had seen. Could she call that power to her? Did she want to feel it, ever again?

"And if I did," she said aloud, "how could it help you accomplish your task?"

He shook his head. The look of discouragement on his face made her want to say something more to reassure him.

"Our uncle Gawain may have wisdom to offer," she suggested. "You said he helped you connect with our prince when you began this strange journey. He has some knowledge of the morrigan, but he has not had the time to tell me. We should ask him for his thoughts on all."

"Lucky we are that he remained with us," Hyw said, brightening a little. "Let us find him."

"He has been at chapel every day since he arrived."

"Then let us give him a reason to come outside and enjoy this fine April weather with us," Hyw said, and they started down the stairs together.

Cat asked a passing servant and discovered her uncle was in the chapel. She persuaded Hyw not to disturb the monk's prayers, especially with the English so near. They sat watching, and Hyw gave an audible sigh when Gawain finally crossed himself and stood.

At their insistence, he walked with them through the courtyard as they began to explain. Gawain stopped at the castle well to talk with a group of worried farmers and people from neighbouring towns, reassuring them as he filled his flask. She made an impatient gesture.

"The warriors say this water helps them," he told her. "Perhaps it will be useful to bolster their spirits in the coming days."

She felt guilty for her impatience but joined her brother in pressing Gawain to walk with them again. They made their way to the chapel garden, where Gawain began plucking weeds. Hyw half-sat on the rock fence nearby as he explained their situation. Unable to be still, Cat stood in front of them, shifting from her heels to her toes.

"So can the morrigan—if that's truly what I am—help him?" she finally broke in.

Gawain straightened up and brushed the dirt from his hands. "In truth I know but little of the morrigan," he said. "The Irish have many stories, and some have crossed the sea to us. Like the crow or the raven, she was thought to follow warriors during wartime. Many believed she could predict which side would win and might be convinced to tell them. Yet if a warrior saw her washing his clothes, he believed he would die in the battle. Did she then cause it, or did his own thinking defeat him?" Gawain shrugged. "But Geoffrey of Monmouth writes of a Morgana le Fay, who had healing powers to protect the land and its sovereign."

Cat did her best to listen, but she didn't want a history lesson. She needed to know how it might connect to her, here and now. She could not help but interrupt. "Your pardon, uncle, but much of this I knew. And yet—if I am a morrigan, it would be right for me to protect Prince Dafydd."

Gawain shrugged. "Or Prince Llywelyn, who resides in Hyw. In the old stories, Morgana placed King Arthur into an enchanted sleep to help him to Avalon."

"But I cannot see Llywelyn, let alone give him a sleep tonic."

Hyw sat upright. "Wait," he said. "Some have seen the prince, even so." He scrambled to his feet in front of her and stood for a moment with his eyes closed. Something shifted in the air around him, and for a moment she saw the tall form of the Prince of Wales shimmer into view. "My lady." She heard a deep voice almost in echo with Hyw's and knew it must be Llywelyn's. Then all disappeared again, and Hyw stood where he had before.

Cat gasped. "How did you do that?"

"It is difficult," Hyw admitted. "I must—step aside of myself, as it were, and allow Llywelyn to speak through me. It first happened the day we met the fox of Dolwyddelan, but I cannot manage it for long."

"I wonder," Gawain said, leading them to a spot further away, where they would be sheltered from sight by trees. "You have the gift of foretelling, Cat. I recall that some with this gift may connect their minds with the minds of others close to them. Can you reach Hyw?" Gawain asked. "Can you see the prince as Hyw does, from inside his mind?"

Cat closed her eyes and tried to reach out to her brother, but she saw nothing but blackness. She shook her head.

"There is much talk in the morrigan myths of the powers of three," he said. "And we are three, together. We can but try."

Gawain put two fingers on her forehead in the space above her eyes, and two on Hyw's in the same spot. He nodded, and all three of them closed their eyes. For several minutes, nothing happened. Gawain removed his fingers. He bid her cup her hands in front of her and poured water into them from his flask. Water from her own well.

"Breathe slowly, Cat, as you do when you sing. From here." Gawain laid a hand on her belly, and when he felt her breathing change, moved his fingers to their foreheads again and closed his eyes. She stared at the water in her cupped hands, and heard him begin to sing softly, a song she had never heard before, of the mountains and the watchers.

After a few moments, she began to see a dark form as if through a mist. "I see him!"

Gawain nodded, and dropped his hands. "You each astound me. I have heard stories from our grandfather of powers like yours, but never thought I would see it in my lifetime."

Cat told him of her ancestor vision then, and he looked thoughtful.

"So, might we coax your powers to help both princes, then," he said.

Cat and Hyw tried again, and Gawain gradually moved away from them, as he had when he first taught Llywelyn and Hyw to connect with each other. Cupping the water again, Cat welcomed the mist rising around her. She pushed into and through it to reach the image of the prince.

"My lord," she said, her voice echoing as if they stood in a cave. She looked around her, and they were in a sort of cave. The mist was steam rising from an underground stream that began to trickle in the background. Hyw lounged against a rock at the edge and grinned at her.

In this world, what we think becomes real, the prince said with a smile, and she heard his voice as clearly as she had the day the messenger came to Garth Celyn.

Gawain tested them, taking her aside and asking her to describe the prince's clothing or some other detail to check with Hyw. After the third such grilling, Cat threw her hands in the air in frustration. Droplets of water sprinkled her face and hair.

"What could my seeing Llywelyn possibly have to do with

helping Hyw change into a hawk?"

Gawain turned and looked out at Cadair Idris. "It is something my grandfather once said. Hyw carries a heavy burden in holding the prince's soul to this world. I believe what is stopping him from testing his true powers to their limits is the very thing that allows him to accomplish it." He turned to Hyw then. "When you make contact with the animal, you are doing no more or less than you have always done. But to make the final shift, that will require you to let go of this world and find the body of the animal inside yourself. Yet Llywelyn anchors you here. You must find a way to trust that the prince will follow and accept the shift to a new form."

Hyw looked miserable. "I have sworn fealty."

Cat finally understood what Gawain wanted from her. "So, you want me to help Hyw separate himself from the prince."

Gawain nodded.

"But how am I to do that?"

"I know not, Cat," Gawain said. "I believe it must be something that comes from you, and honestly."

They got no further that morning, and Cat found herself returning to the problem throughout the day.

"What's wrong?" Margred finally asked her, as they prepared for bed. Cat shook her head and said nothing, unwilling to discuss her brother with her friend any more than she already had.

After a night of tossing and turning, Cat stood at the window, opening the shutters the barest crack to look out at the sky. She thought about how Hyw might look outlined by the low clouds, if their plan worked. Her brother had always been more comfortable on the hills than inside a castle, or even in the *llys* at Garth Celyn. Cat stared out for a moment, and then turned and almost ran from the room.

She caught Hyw and Gawain as they entered the hall. "Now is our best hope," she told them, almost dragging them with her to the battlement. It was early, and only the lookouts manned the wall.

They found a sheltered spot and crouched on the courtyard side of the walk, out of sight of both English and Welsh. Hyw sat cross-legged in front of her.

Cat held out her hands for water from Gawain's flask. As soon as she focused on it, she found the connection to her brother's mind. She rode the mist deeper, until she could see the prince. He stood with his arms folded.

"My liege," she began, "you said anything we think here becomes real. Please, allow me to serve you." When he nodded, she hesitated a moment and then held out her hand. A goblet appeared in it. She swirled the dark liquid inside it. It smelled of honey and strawberries, of the mist of *Rhaeadr Fawr* and the gold of sunlight on the hillside near their home. She mixed the waters of her own well into it. Finally, she offered it to the prince with a shy curtsey.

"Will you take this drink, your highness, and allow it to help you sleep?"

Sorcery, young Cat, he said, his voice rising in a question.

She hesitated again. Was this not what she feared most, when her gift first came to her that day in church? That it might be a thing of sorcery and darkness? So long ago that seemed now, although it was only a few short months. She thought of Owain, whose life she saved, and of all the tall Irish ships of their allies. And she thought again of Ifan, waving to her from the green fields of Garth Celyn. The voice of her ancestor, Aylwen, echoed in her mind. *We have gained these gifts to help our people.* All the while she stared into the eyes of the shade she had known as the last Prince of Wales.

"It is the gift of a true heart and will not harm you," she told him, certain of the truth in her words. He reached out his hand and took the goblet.

When the prince closed his eyes, Cat opened hers. Gawain was crouching beside her as before, and she realized he had been singing the same song, almost under his breath. Her brother sat with his eyes closed a moment longer, and then opened them to look directly into hers. Gawain let his hands drop, but his voice grew louder. For a few moments, nothing happened.

Then Hyw cast his eyes upward. A hawk soared near them, adding its cry to Gawain's song. Hyw made a sound like a moan and began to shimmer as he had when the prince appeared earlier. She heard a grinding noise and a loud crackle. Hyw cried out, and his arms stretched to the side, his bones stretching and thinning. He drew his legs up and they seemed to shrink into his body. His clothing fell around him. Red and brown feathers sprouted from his flesh. He cried out, and the cry became the shriek of the hawk. She and Gawain ducked at the wind from flapping wings all around them. They looked up in time to see a great hawk, wings outstretched, where Hyw had been. For a moment he faltered, as if hanging on a current of wind. And then he flew.

43

Hyw, exhausted after his ordeal, relied on his sister and uncle to help him to their family table. Cat scrounged what she could for him from the platters as the voices droned around them. People were abuzz throughout the supper hour. Listening to the talk, Hyw realized the English had sent another rider with another offer: less money this time. And it would be less every day, this one said, until the Welsh gave in or were starved out of Bere.

The meal was barely finished when Dafydd called for Bran again. Hyw settled beside Cat and their mam, listening to the bards amid the people's continued murmuring. From time to time an angry voice broke out, yelling defiance against the English or arguing with a neighbour. Hyw heard no clear agreement among the people, and it left him uneasy. The bards switched to warrior tales, and soon many of the defiant voices chimed in with harmonies that shook the walls of the castle hall.

In spite of his tortured muscles, Hyw found himself strangely alert. He noticed Cat often looked toward her betrothed, Lord Rhys, but the two said little to each other. Cat had seemed happy with the match, but he wondered how the war affected their relationship. Hyw reached out with his arm, almost surprised to see it rather than a feathered wing, and placed it around her shoulders.

The torches had barely been trimmed when Bran returned and gestured for Hyw to come with him. Hyw stood, finding his feet carefully, and almost stumbled as he made his way to his father.

"Are you ill, Hyw?" Bran asked.

Hyw shook his head. "Tired only, Da," he said, his voice almost a squawk.

His father looked at him a moment longer, and then nodded. "The prince would have a word with you," he said in a low voice. "Answer well, and truthfully. I will be outside, if you need me. You have only to call."

Bran led the way into a room at the end of the hall. *Tywysog* Dafydd was seated at a round oak table. His fingers were spread and touching, and he nodded. With that, Bran turned and left the room, shutting the door behind him.

Hyw stared into a pair of ice-blue eyes. Dafydd remained seated at the table, with his fingers steepled in front of his mouth. His hair and moustache shone auburn in the firelight. The muscles bulged on his biceps, and his shoulders were square under his light tunic.

Dafydd gestured to the seat. Hyw stumbled again and nearly fell into one of the large chairs that ringed the table, making everyone equal in importance. This was where Llywelyn had met with the other Welsh princes. Hyw thought of Arthur, the great king, who was known to have listened well to all of his counsellors. Every Welshman was raised to believe in those traditions of equality for everyone, equal service and equal reward, and it was ingrained in the laws they fought so hard to defend. Hyw had a right to sit in that chair, but at that moment he felt small and insignificant.

Never think it, lad, he heard inside his mind. *You have brought us this far. You will see this through. You are the one Dafydd must listen to now, and you are the only one who can make sure he does.*

Hyw nodded and sat up straighter. Dafydd shifted forward and held Hyw's eyes. Hyw stared back, willing himself not to flinch. Dafydd raised his eyebrows as he reached forward to take a sip from his goblet of spiced ale.

"Your father tells me you lived with the English at his bidding. I thank you for your service. It seems you have used your time there well, if Cynfrig's tales of the practice yard can be believed."

"I've done my best to share what I've learned."

Dafydd smiled a little and filled a goblet for Hyw. Hyw swirled the liquid. It was spiced Welsh ale. He could smell the flavour of it. He had been allowed a mug on saints' days and holidays and knew it would taste sweet and strong. He took a sip.

"Are you comfortable with us?" Dafydd asked.

"Yes. Very much."

"Really? It surprises me, since you've been with the English for so long."

"I returned to my father in October."

"Yet you were not with him in January, when last we met."

Hyw looked at him steadily. *There's little point denying it,* he heard Llywelyn advise in his mind. "Your words are true. I was with Lord Shrewsbury."

"And Edward." The words were soft, but the ice in Prince Dafydd's blue eyes seemed to harden, if that were possible. "How was the king?"

In his mind, Hyw heard Llywelyn expel his breath, almost in a hiss. *Even now, he cares about the English king. Even now.* Hyw remembered hearing Dafydd had been friends with Edward since childhood and had spent time there during the attempted English invasion earlier in Llywelyn's rule. He thought about his own complicated relationship with James and wondered how he would feel in Dafydd's place. He also remembered Dafydd's face on the chess piece Llywelyn had shown him many months ago: the face of a pawn. Looking at that same face now, Hyw could see the shadows under his eyes.

"In truth, I saw the king but little," Hyw said. "He seemed hearty, and his wife appeared to dote on him."

"That is well. And was she beautiful?"

Hyw thought for a moment, not sure how to answer truthfully. "The king seemed to think her so." He told Dafydd as best he could about the English king's expression as he looked upon his wife, and how his voice seemed to soften when he addressed her.

Dafydd threw back his head and laughed. "A passable answer indeed, Hyw. You have certainly seen them together."

Good work, lad. He was testing you, and he found you sound. Hyw felt a small flush of pride at Llywelyn's words.

But in the next breath, Dafydd's hand smacked the table with a loud thud. His face changed, and his laughter became a snarl. "Yet somehow you brought the spirit of my brother to me at Dolwyddelan. And before I could wring the truth from him, you vanished. Now I need to know everything you know."

Hyw started at the sound and fury of Dafydd's words. Through it, he could also hear Llywelyn's calming voice like a whisper in his inner ear. *Steady. It's just bluster. Let him wind down.*

Hyw took a deep breath. "You are my prince, and I will tell you anything you wish to know." Hyw answered Dafydd's questions about the English army, its strengths and weaknesses, its horses and weapons. Finally, Dafydd's shoulders slumped forward.

"You were with him—when he died?" Dafydd meant his brother Llywelyn, Hyw realized, and nodded. "I hope he did not suffer overmuch."

Hyw did not know what to say and was glad to hear Llywelyn's voice in his inner ear again. *Tell him I did not.* By the catch in Llywelyn's voice, he could tell the prince was moved. As Hyw repeated Llywelyn's words, Dafydd looked into his eyes. "It was much less than Edward had planned for him."

"Could—could you not send to the king again and bid him stop this slaughter?"

"On the grounds of our childhood friendship? Or because my wife Elizabeth was his choice for me? Or because I had tried many times to kill my own brother for him?" Dafydd laughed bitterly. "Even if he would listen to me, I would not. I am Wales now, and I will take my duty as it falls. Believe me, it would do no good. Edward has a taste for our blood now. I know him well. He is the predator, and Wales is his prey."

His manner and tone changed, and he seemed more desperate than cynical as he continued. "I must take back Garth Celyn, and I will take as many men as I can into the mountains with me to plan our attack. Has my brother anything more to tell me?"

Hyw closed his eyes and found Llywelyn stroking his moustache. *Tell him he must not let them catch him, or his children. Or mine.* Hyw nodded and opened his eyes again, to find Dafydd staring into them. The living prince's eyes were bright and intense, and he held Hyw like the glint of the knife holds the deer. As he had at Dolwyddelan and on the battlements with Cat and Gawain, Hyw felt the pressure of Llywelyn's hand on his shoulder. He closed his eyes and shifted slightly to let Llywelyn through. When he opened his eyes again, Dafydd drew back, startled.

"He is—within you?"

Hyw came back into himself, and Llywelyn receded once more. Dafydd continued to stare at Hyw strangely. "These are the old ways," he said. "You and your family, I have heard you all bear such gifts?"

Hyw felt a moment of fear, wondering if he had revealed too much. "Be assured, Prince Dafydd, your brother means you no harm. Nor do I."

Dafydd sat back and held Hyw's eyes again. "I should fear you, Hyw ap Bran, and the spirit you carry. Men follow me, but I can see in their eyes that they long for my brother. It would be an easy thing for you to help him regain his hold over them."

Hyw tried to protest and heard Llywelyn's voice echo inside him. Dafydd held up his hand. "This war is very different than any other battle with the English we have fought. Edward's hatred leads him, and I am not sure we will survive it. Though your claim might seem fantastical to some, it would be welcome to many. You could divide the people just at the time they need to rally most."

"My lord—" Hyw began. Then Dafydd laughed again.

"I have watched you carefully in the days you have been with us. You hide my brother from the others and make no attempt to reveal your gift. That leads me to think you can be trusted, and my brother knew it. I could not be there to protect him on the field when he was ambushed. Indeed, I am sure he would not believe that I would protect him. Yet I am glad to know his spirit continues. I would ask you this: continue to hide my brother, for his protection. Swear it."

"I swear."

"Tell my brother this: I will take his baby with my family into the mountains, with the majority of our warriors, to move in force to retake Garth Celyn. To cover our escape, Lord Rhys and his steward Cynfrig will stretch the talks with the English. They will hold off the English as long as they can, and then relinquish this castle and accompany their people to safety at the abbey.

He leaned toward Hyw before he continued. "Hyw ap Bran. Your father and mother are set to accompany me, along with my family. Because you carry my brother's spirit in the world, I would offer you the choice. You may remain with Lord Rhys, and earn your place with Cynfrig and his men. Those who continue with us to Garth Celyn will tread the more difficult path. We will find our way blocked by soldiers. We face hardship and endurance and most likely death before we retake Garth Celyn. Think well the path you choose."

Hyw closed his eyes for a moment, and Llywelyn nodded at him. *My brother speaks true, Hyw, and I will do no less. You have made a place here, and these are men to trust your back to. You must make your own decision.*

Hyw opened his eyes and stared for a moment without seeing either of them. "I may have a plan that will best serve you and help all of us."

44

Cat stood in front of Rhys' door and raised her eyebrows at the warrior who stood guard. His face did not change as he reached back and pushed open the wooden door for her.

Rhys was alone, washing up for supper. He turned as she entered. His chest and arms were bare and glistening with water. She had seen him so during practice in the yard, but in the closeness of his rooms she felt herself flush. His muscles were tightly corded and his shoulders were broad, tapering down to a flat stomach. He smiled slightly as he picked up a cloth to wipe the water away.

"I am sorry to disturb you." She found it difficult to begin.

"Your thoughts are always welcome, my lady," he said, reaching for his shirt.

"If that is true, then you will agree with what I have to say," she said, seizing the opening. "You believe me to be a morrigan, and you seem to have experience with someone of my nature. I would know more about how to use my gift, in order to offer what help I can in this war."

"Surely your mother advises you."

"She has some understanding of it from family lore, but you and Cynfrig have worked with a morrigan. You know more about the nature of my gift." She warmed to her topic now, sure of her decision.

"Cat, Cynfrig and I will stay to negotiate with the English. If aught goes wrong—"

This was what Cat had hoped to hear, because she needed to be in the castle when Hyw put his plan into action. "I must stand with you. Is it not what your own morrigan would have done? My gifts cannot serve you from across the mountains. I must be here, with you."

He looked uncertain, but she could see he was thinking through the wisdom of her words. She went on, pressing her advantage. "If there is a battle in our future, as surely there must be, you will be victorious only if I am with you."

Finally, he nodded. "Very well. I—I would rather have you with me, where I can be sure of your safety. And I will marry you, Cat, to give you the full benefit of my protection." He looked away from her again. "But protection is all it can be."

She folded her arms across her chest. "We have been promised to each other since childhood. I have known you in my heart since my princess first brought us together as playmates. And now, even as our enemies surround us, we have found each other again. Is that truly all you believe we can have between us now?" She held his eyes until she saw the deep blue grow in intensity. We shall see, she thought, and nodded.

Her goodbyes to Margred were tearful, but they vowed to see each other again once the war had ended. She shook Owain's hand to wish him well and was surprised when he planted a kiss on her cheek.

Their goodbyes were interrupted by Cynfrig's bellow. "We cannot surrender the castle, my liege. Honour demands that we stand and fight for you and drive these *Saeson* from our land by the Grace of God."

She was still holding Owain's hand, as she looked down to see Cynfrig kneel at Prince Dafydd's feet. Rhys stood near them, undecided. She recalled her vision of Owain slain at Criccieth, and of Rhys and the others cut down in the courtyard of Bere. Owain had become like a little brother to her, and she had grown to care about all of Elizabeth's children. She had to make them understand.

"If I am the morrigan, then they must believe that I know the outcome of this battle."

"Pardon, Lady Cat?" Owain said, and she realized she had spoken aloud. Instead of answering, she squeezed his hand once and let go as she moved past him.

"My lords," she called out. She could feel the flush creep from her neck onto her face as all turned to her, but she kept moving through the room towards them. "You must listen."

Rhys stepped up and opened the curtains of an adjoining alcove. "My lords, would you draw inside to give this lady audience?" He bowed toward Cynfrig and the prince, and Cat ducked her head toward him gratefully. When they had seated themselves at the window seats, they turned toward her expectantly.

"Speak you as the morrigan, returned?" Cynfrig asked.

"The morrigan?" Prince Dafydd's tone was full of scorn.

"If you say I am, then you must believe I know the outcome of this war," she began.

"If she speaks of what she has seen, my lord," broke in Rhys in careful tones, "you must grant her leave, whatever her words might impart about the coming fray."

Dafydd considered them, and finally nodded. "Speak your leave."

She told them of her visions in as much detail as she could, beginning with Owain's death and moving to the scene in the courtyard that had come to her only days before. "You must believe me, my lord. I would not wish harm to you or any of your children, who are as dear to me as my own family now. But I beg you, do not change your course for some ancient sense of honour. Why must it always be kill or be killed? Why can we not live, to fight again another day?"

Dafydd considered her for a long moment, and then dismissed her with a wave of his hand. "Leave us. We will discuss it further."

She left them, hoping they might heed her words.

When she could avoid it no longer, Cat came back to her mam's room. She entered while Hyw was explaining his decision to join them in recapturing Garth Celyn. Hyw had planned to explain Llywelyn to their mam as well. Perhaps it was the looks on their faces, or the connection she now had with her brother, but it seemed clear he had already done so.

"I'm proud of you, Hyw." Mam hugged him.

"I hope you will feel the same of me, Mam," Cat said. "I have decided to remain with Lord Rhys and his people, to offer what help I may."

"Are you sure?" When Cat nodded, Mam reached out her arms and hugged Cat as well. "You have both grown up so quickly," she said, her eyes shining with unshed tears.

"May God keep you safe. And Lord Rhys, of course," Hyw said to her.

"You think little of my own skill," Cat chided, pulling up her skirt and extracting one of Rhys' knives to show him. He examined it carefully.

"He appears to be paying close attention," he told her. "The emerald matches your eyes."

"So I see," she said, wondering a little. She felt a flush creep along her throat as she looked again at the emerald. Had Rhys meant to send her a message of hope with it? She turned slightly to replace the knife in its sheath.

"It is a fitting gift for your skill and position," her brother said, "but I hope you never need to use them."

"Before we take our leave, there is one more thing we must do," their mam said. "Fetch your da, Hyw, and do not tarry. Cat, we must find Elizabeth and the children. Come."

45

Hyw and Bran found them again in the receiving room, along with the prince and princess. Hyw saw Margred and Owain, as well as several of the warriors, including Aeneus, Rhys, and Cynfrig. Emrys waved and grinned at him, taking Bronwen's hand. They had been married the previous Sunday along with several other young couples. Hyw wondered if some announcement was coming.

Mam reached forward and enfolded Hyw in a warm hug. Cat held out a package wrapped in cloth.

"I made it for you, Hyw."

He unwrapped it to find the red tunic and sash she had sewn. "Can it be? The stitches seem straight!" he marvelled. She punched his shoulder to break the tension.

Their da reached out his hand for the sash, and Hyw gave it to him. "I wish we had time for a proper ceremony," Bran said.

"This means more to me than any pomp or ceremony by priest or lord, Da," Hyw told him. Bran half-smiled and drew him toward the prince.

Prince Dafydd nodded to them and stood, clearing his throat. "Our enemies dog our heels, as well you know," the prince began. "Yet we will take the time to honour the old ways, and one of our number who has earned his place among us. We can present it again, properly, when we arrive at Garth Celyn."

There was a murmur of appreciation among the small band as Bran drew Hyw to him. Hyw's throat tightened and his chest seemed to swell as his da unfolded the red sash, draped it over Hyw's shoulder, and tied it at his waist. Then Bran turned to the others, holding up Hyw's right arm.

"My son," he said, and the pride in his voice hit Hyw like the warm sun through a cloud. "Warrior."

Bran then gathered Hyw to him in a fierce hug. He could hear the sounds of his friends clapping and calling around him. Bran's mouth was close to Hyw's ear as he whispered, "I am proud to call you son—for all of your abilities, not just the skill that makes you fit to wear the sash." Hyw choked back the tears that threatened to spill over, and as he drew back he noticed Da's eyes glistening as well.

"Welcome, warrior," the prince said, and raised a mug Elizabeth handed him. "I drink to your future." Aeneus clasped his forearm in Roman style, as Llywelyn had taught his bodyguard, and then hugged him as well. Emrys slugged Hyw hard on the arm and then circled his shoulder with the same hand. Finally, the prince called out.

"Though I am loathe to call this moment to an end, friends, we must depart. Go you to your preparations, as my wife and I will ours. We will greet you one last time in the dining hall."

As they made their way from the room, Hyw drew Cat aside in the stairwell. "This wristband cannot last for much longer." He pulled two chains from his pouch and handed her one. She fingered the scrolled locket before popping it open. "A lock of my hair," he told her. He held open his empty locket, and she used her knife to cut a lock of hers for it.

"As long as we have this, my gift will connect us," she said.

"I will keep it with me always," he said, placing the locket around his neck and under his tunic. "Next to my heart, as you will always be."

A few hours later, under the cover of darkness, Hyw and his family joined the people in the courtyard. Lord Rhys and the people of

Meirionnydd also waited there, and Cat squeezed Hyw's hand once before moving to join Rhys.

Emrys pushed through the crowd to his new wife Bronwen, who threw her arms around him. He would remain with Rhys, Cat, and a handful of Cynfrig's warriors at the castle to negotiate the settlement. Bronwen would travel with their people toward a holding in Meirionnydd, and if all went well, she and Emrys would be reunited in a few days.

Dafydd and Bran began moving their group towards the gate. The princess and her children, including Margred and the other girls, walked with other families who had determined to accompany their men into the mountains, on their way back to Garth Celyn. Aeneus had burned Bere's wooden bridges a few days before so the *Saeson* could not cross, but the men had placed boards over one ditch so the people could get away safely. Emrys moved back to the small group that included the warrior-poet Gwilym ap Einion. Hyw was grateful he would stay to help them bargain with the English.

As he marched with his people along the mountain path, Hyw felt something prickle along his skin almost like vertigo. It took him a moment to realize it was silence. The people sang while walking, while working, even while marching to battle. Tonight they dared not, lest their voices waken the English troops. The silence and the dark made his stomach clench.

Then he heard a groan of wind, as if the mountain giant wept to see them leave. Some of the townsfolk stopped, huddled together. Hyw hesitated. *Let me speak to them,* Llywelyn said. Hyw ran ahead, drawing near to the frightened ones.

"I remember the story, as I have heard it told," Hyw began, keeping his voice low as he repeated Llywelyn's words to them. "On just such a night as this, as the Greeks poured forth from the great horse of their treachery, Brutus and his people stole away in silence from Troy. It was to this land and to these mountains that Brutus led his people. When the Tylwyth Teg heard his story, they bade the giants make room for the people here.

"This night we cannot sing lest we be discovered. This sound we hear is the giant Idris, singing for us. He sings to the soldiers below, camped on the plain. They cannot hide from him. He sings this song to bolster your hearts, to cover your flight from this land into his own. You must believe he will shelter you, and keep the English from you."

He moved up the line to repeat the tale. As he neared his mother and Gawain, she took his hand. "We shall miss your stories, Hyw. Can you stay a while longer?"

"Until sunrise," he promised her, untying his red sash and handing it to her. "Keep this for me, and be assured I will return for it."

She smiled at him, and he made his way past her to the front of the line, where he found his father and the other warriors. It was easier in the cool darkness to use his gift. His mind seemed to reach naturally into the thickets and bushes as they passed. Here a hare scurried for cover, and there a meadow mouse kept her home. Through their eyes, he sensed the roots and dips that might have tripped someone unfamiliar with the territory and passed the information back to the people behind him.

As the sun rose, Hyw pulled away from the group and watched them trudge along the path in silence. They could see for themselves now. When he had walked past the last of his people, he began casting with his senses until he found a hawk flying near. He found a safe place off the path to leave his clothes, touched the locket around his neck, and closed his eyes. He watched Llywelyn take the goblet Cat had given him, swish the liquid, and drink. Llywelyn smiled at him and sat down to close his eyes in sleep. Hyw recalled their circle of three, seeing Cat and Gawain's faces around him as he had on the battlements. Only then did he reach out to the hawk. A gust of wind blew against his face, and he heard the hawk's shrill cry in his mind.

He raised his arms and his bones seemed to thin and twist. He heard the grating of bone on bone and intense pain gripped his body. He felt a moment of panic, but he knew he must not fight this sensation. The pain would pass. He let himself grow light and strong as he lifted off the ground into the wind.

He glanced to the side and spotted the tip of a wing with mottled brown feathers. It took him a moment to realize it was his own. He was no longer one with the mind of the hawk; he was the hawk. Beyond his own wingtip, he could see the hawk he had spotted from the ground, now flying beside him. They soared for a moment, almost circling each other. Then the other hawk dove, leaving Hyw alone in the grey sky.

When he looked down, he could see the people walking along the mountain path. He cried out, and a woman turned toward the sound. Part of him, the human part, recognized her as his mam and he circled above her. She waved, and he flew on.

As he drifted on air currents, he passed over the English soldiers camped below. He could feel the mind of the hawk inside himself—a mind caught in the instant changes of wind and sound and smell. Before he realized he was hungry, his hawk instincts drew his eyes toward the rabbit in the grass below him. Then he saw Bere. He remembered, and with a wing thrust he turned himself east toward it.

46

Cat scanned the skies, watching every bird that circled the battlements. She had seen what it cost Hyw to change as their plan required him to, and she worried that he could not accomplish it without their circle of three. She tried to recall the song Gawain had sung and opened her mind to connect with him. For too long, she felt nothing but her own fear.

Finally, she saw a large red and brown hawk soaring toward her. Although she couldn't see his face or detailing clearly against the grey sky, she could tell it was him by the feel of his mind, like a familiar presence in her peripheral vision. She saw the bird shimmer a little as it moved awkwardly toward the wall walk. It shrieked, and the sound became a cry of pain. The claws pointing toward the wooden platform became a man's bare feet. She heard a grinding of bone on bone and a low moaning as he settled. Flapping wings became arms as feathers became flesh. And Hyw lay, panting, where the bird had landed.

She knelt beside him, giving him a chunk of bread and her skin of well-water to wash it down. She closed her eyes and probed into his mind, finding Llywelyn still sleeping. Gently she hummed the song she had been singing earlier, and the prince opened his eyes and gave her his teasing half-smile. *Do we yet live?* he asked.

"You do, my liege," she answered. "And welcome."

When she opened her eyes again, Hyw asked her the same question. She answered him by ruffling his hair and making the face that always made him smile.

When her brother had recovered, she helped him dress in the clothes Dafydd had left. She'd stuffed the shoulders and waist of the tunic, and helped him drape Dafydd's tabard loosely over it, with the coat of arms clearly showing. She darkened his hair a little with bramble tea. Rhys had contributed a gold torque similar to Dafydd's and a crown, which he said he found in a castle vault. Then she stood back to survey her brother.

"It will do from afar," she said, critically.

"It had better," he said, looking through the battlements at the path far below, where the English company could be seen making their way toward the castle.

Hyw stood in borrowed clothing and watched the soldiers haggle with the warriors. He was himself again, but he felt more than himself. He stood between the battlements, where he could clearly see Rhys with Gwilym, Cynfrig and Emrys on the path, as well as Cat standing off to one side, trying to stay out of the soldier's sight behind them. As Hyw expected, the English captain pointed toward him.

"They will not accept that Dafydd is here without some kind of proof," Hyw had told Cynfrig and Emrys earlier. "They will expect a trick. When they ask you, tell them the prince will wave to you to prove he is there in truth. Then turn and wave, and I will do the rest."

Emrys turned and waved at Hyw. Hyw stood, straightening his tabard so they would see Dafydd's crest, and waved back. He turned his head, hoping the gold of the crown and torque would flash in the sunlight.

Time slowed for Cat as the English captain stared, rubbing his beard with one hand. It isn't working, she thought wildly. She and Rhys stood behind Cynfrig and Gwilym, letting them handle the negotiating. She felt Rhys grope for the sword under his cloak and wondered if they would have to fight their way out. Lucky, she had brought her water skin. Staring down at the water inside it, she tried to make contact with Hyw. She could feel his presence, but she could not enter his mind to send him a message.

Then she thought of Llywelyn. She saw the former prince, standing as if behind Hyw. Her brother said they communicated in thoughts, like silent speaking. She frowned in concentration, focusing her thoughts on them. *Help us. The English captain does not believe the ruse.*

Llywelyn touched Hyw on the shoulder. Cat broke contact and looked up at the battlements. The difference was subtle. Hyw suddenly stood taller and more regally than before, and his hair shone more like Dafydd's than it had. The crown caught the sunlight. Was that the same one she had found for her brother? she wondered. Or was it Llywelyn's conjuring? More importantly, would it help the *Saeson* believe that Hyw was Prince Dafydd?

Finally, the captain nodded. He gave Emrys and Cynfrig a pouch. Cynfrig checked it. That would be the payment for surrendering the castle, and a letter of safe passage, she thought.

As part of the bargain, the English soldiers were to give the Welsh a day to clear the castle before they entered. Cynfrig and Rhys believed they would not wait, so they had agreed to send the people on their way the night before. Now, the little negotiating party began to move toward the road, away from the castle. Cat was drawn along with the others. If all went well, they would join the people who had already escaped before the English knew they were gone.

Hyw would remain where he was, on the battlements, to lull the English into believing Prince Dafydd remained in the castle. She dared not wave but tried to send her thoughts again to reassure him as they made their way into the mountains. The path grew quiet around them and they barely stirred the grass as they passed. Even the giant seemed to be holding his breath.

"Here," someone called. "Up here."

Hyw wiped the sleep from his eyes and stood. The position

of the sun told him it was late afternoon. So, Cynfrig was right. The English had not waited, but were even now storming the castle in search of Prince Dafydd.

In search of him.

Hyw looked down and saw soldiers streaming through the gates. He cast around him and for a moment he panicked. He could not find a hawk, and could not bring the shape into his mind. Could he shift without one? Could he take the form of another bird?

He heard voices at the bottom of the stairs. It was time. He shrugged off his borrowed cloak and clothing. He closed his eyes and raised his arms.

Nothing.

Steady on, lad, he heard Llywelyn say behind him. *Think of the circle of three.*

Hyw could hear pounding footsteps on the stone stairwell but shut his mind to them. Llywelyn began humming the song Gawain and Cat had sung and he focused on it. He imagined them standing with him, singing. Llywelyn drank from the goblet and sank to the floor, asleep.

Hyw reached out for the hawk.

As he let the scent and rush of wind flood through him, he recognized the first man rushing toward him from the stairwell. It was Robert, the bully of Shrewsbury's court, in full knight's armour. His face glistened with sweat and his breath came heavy and panting. And then Robert saw Hyw and raised his drawn sword high to rush at him.

"It is a trick!" Robert's cry of alarm rose like the crash of arms on armour.

But Hyw could not —would not—stop. He felt feathers grow from his skin, and his bones knit and press into the shape the wind loved best.

Robert stumbled a moment as his mind tried to grasp the transformation before him. His face became even more distorted with fear and hatred. "Sorcerer!"

As he took to the sky, Hyw saw Robert suddenly pull a bow and arrow from his shoulder. The arrow zipped past Hyw, almost knocking him off balance. Robert swore, and took a second arrow from his quiver. Hyw struggled against the wind, aware of the young knight setting his feet and drawing back his bow for another shot. Then a second figure trod the wall walk behind him, knocking the bow from Robert's hand.

"Why are you wasting arrows on this bird?" the second man said as Robert's second arrow flew wide. "Where is the prince?"

Hyw circled to identify his benefactor. In the human part of his brain, he knew it was Stephen de Francton. The man had saved him twice. Robert was arguing with him but other human shouts caught Hyw's attention. He circled once more as soldiers picked up the cloak and fought over the gold ornaments. Deep inside him, he heard the rumble of laughter, but he could not tell if it was Llywelyn's or his own.

And he became one with the wind, letting it turn him toward the mountain.

By dawn the people had traveled far into the mountain range. With the hawk's keen eyesight he had easily found his clothes, but he had to run all night in his human form to catch up. Behind them, Bere sat solidly in the rock of Idris, the mountain giant. The English army looked like a dark patch of blight on the once-lush Desenni valley. Like locusts, they would soon have their way and depart. How long would the castle remain? For a moment, he thought he saw Idris himself heave a sigh. Hyw rubbed his eyes and saw the mountain again.

Hyw started toward his mam and da. He could not see his sister anywhere. Cat and Rhys must have found them in the night, and split off from Dafydd's group to take Rhys's people to the safety of Cymer Abbey. Hyw passed Prince Dafydd, who carried one of his sleeping children on his back. The way seemed easier along the mountain plateau, as they followed a path worn by sheep and cattle.

Hyw heard a wavering sound and realized someone had begun to sing. He recognized the clear tones of his mother's soprano, and heard the rich harmonies slide into place as one voice joined another.

The song was a hymn of thanksgiving. He and Llywelyn joined in as he found Adara, and their voices warmed him as the light snow began to fall around them.

Author's note: Castell-y-Bere fell to the English in April 1283, after the longest siege of the war. The English paid £53 to the castle's constable, Cynfrig ap Madog, for the castle's surrender. But Dafydd ap Gruffydd, the last true Prince of Wales, once again escaped their grasp. Cynfrig and the Welsh who held Castell-y-Bere melted into their mountain, never to appear again in the written annals of history.

ḥISCORICAL NOCE

The year 1282 must have begun with great hope. Llywelyn ap Gruffydd (1223–11 December 1282), acknowledged Prince of Wales, and his wife Elinor (I have used Welsh spelling for Eleanor to avoid confusion with the numerous other Eleanors of this time period) expected their first child. A boy would become the heir to the kingdom Llywelyn had spent his life building—and then trying to keep intact.

Elinor was the daughter of Simon de Montfort, a nobleman who became a friend and ally of Llywelyn. In 1263, she was betrothed to Llywelyn, although she was about five years old. In 1267, Llywelyn became the first and only Welsh prince to unite the country and gain the title of Prince of Wales.

In 1275-1276, they were married by proxy. As Elinor sailed from France to marry the Welsh prince, she was captured by Edward I, King of England, who held her in captivity for three years. Trying to get her back, Llywelyn lost a major battle to the English king in 1277. The country split again into North and South Wales, with parts of the south held by lords who served King Edward. The English king forced Llywelyn to pay a stiff tribute in money, and to sign away most of his land to avoid going to war again. Under the Treaty of Aberconwy, Llywelyn kept his title but retained only Gwynedd in North Wales.

Finally, in 1278, Edward allowed the wedding and led Elinor down the aisle to meet Llywelyn, her future husband. Between 1278 and 1282, Llywelyn and Elinor appear to have been happy together. Then in the spring of 1282, Llywelyn's younger brother Dafydd attacked the English, who were, in his opinion, terrorizing his people and castles. Llywelyn tried to avoid committing the country to war by not joining with his brother.

On June 19, Elinor died giving birth to a baby girl, Gwenllian. Llywelyn went into mourning. The Marcher lords on the border between England and Wales increased their attacks against the Welsh. Llywelyn tried to prevent war by appealing to the pope on behalf of his people, and Edward sent the English Archbishop of Canterbury to visit the Welsh court in the autumn. The Archbishop stayed there in the first week of November, during a truce on all sides. During his visit, the Archbishop offered Llywelyn lands and personal gain if he would relinquish his title and surrender to King Edward. Llywelyn and his nobles refused. On November 6, the English forces broke the truce and attacked by water, across the Menai Straight. Llywelyn's forces defeated the English, and many died. The Archbishop later proclaimed the Welsh heathen and in need of subjugation by English forces.

Llywelyn was killed suddenly and unexpectedly on December 11, 1282. There are many stories about how and why he died. Edward hung Llywelyn's head on a pike at the Tower of London, where it remained for close to a decade. The prince's seal, and some letters that may have contained evidence of treachery against Llywelyn, were stolen from his body and taken to the Archbishop. Later Edward melted Llywelyn's seal, along with Elinor's and Dafydd's seals, and made them into a silver chalice, which was sent to an abbey in Lincolnshire for safekeeping.

Llywelyn ap Gruffydd or Llywelyn Ein Llyw Olaf (our last leader) as he came to be known, was the last prince of an independent Wales before its conquest by Edward I of England. That action, and how it came about, is where this story begins.

For me, it began during a family trip to Wales in 2006. My two children and I stayed on a sheep farm near Dolwyddelan Castle, and made several trips through Gwynedd to visit castles and towns in North Wales. We also stayed in a restored 13th Century wattle-and-daub cottage. As we toured castles and historical sites, we read and heard about the country's history. We were especially impressed by the restoration of the Welsh language. The highway and street signs were in Welsh first, English second; and children are taught in Welsh in the schools again. How could a language outlawed 800 years ago come back to thrive in the 21st Century?

My personal ties to this story began years ago, when my mother researched our family name and discovered the Powell family was apparently "keeper of the Holy Grail." After our first trip, I read in J. Beverley Smith's *Llywelyn Ap Gruffudd: Prince of Wales* that the Welsh royal seals were melted into a silver chalice. A "grail" and a "chalice" are both essentially cups, and both have a connection to church and to the Eucharist or communion. My imagination was sparked, and the story began to unfold.

I found inspiration in the historical traditions of *The Brothers of Gwynedd* series by Edith Pargeter and the *Welsh Princes* by Sharon Kay Penman, as well as modern fantasies such as *The Dark is Rising* by Susan Cooper, *Tomorrow's Magic* by Pamela F. Service, and *The Farseer* by Robin Hobb. My daughter Leanne and I also took an introductory Welsh class at Nant Gwrtheyrn. Over the years, I've read and discovered many essential research sources, the best of which are listed under Further Reading.

Like all fiction writers, though, I chose to deviate from the historical research as the story required. For example, through the Shropshire archives, I confirmed there was no lord of Shrewsbury castle in this time period, so I invented one based on the previous Shrewsbury lords. Although little is known about Llywelyn's early life, most Welsh children in this time would have fostered with other families, including the English, so I've used that in the story. A Welsh boy came of age at 14; since Llywelyn's bodyguard or *teulu* were known to wear red tunics, I invented the red sash as a visual way to show this transition. I have also used artistic license in other areas, such as having Bran and other Welsh warriors wearing torques, which may have been rare by the 13th Century, as symbolic of their Welsh heritage. Although Rhys ap Cadwgan and Gwilym ap Einion are fictional, Cynfrig ap Madog is a historical figure credited with managing the negotiations at Castell-y-Bere, which I have called "Bere" in the story, and a well-known bard was also thought to be present (Smith, 575).

I chose to include a few Welsh words, used Welsh spelling whenever possible, and altered names when it seemed useful. For example, Llywelyn married Eleanor de Montfort, whose mother was also Eleanor de Montfort; King Edward's wife was another Eleanor (de Castile) and his mother was Eleanor (de Provence). To lessen confusion, I used the spelling Elinor, which I found in some sources, for the princess.

The poem mentioned on pages 86-87 is "Y Gododdin," which is considered the earliest surviving Welsh poem. I have written words for Llywelyn's poem to avoid conflicts with copyright, but the original can be found in translation by Siân Echard in the Broadview anthology, and by Joseph Clancy, among others (listed below under Further Resources). Similarly, one inspiration for the scene in Chapter Eighteen was the YouTube video *Mari Lwyd* by Trac: Music Traditions Wales; the link and other resources for the greetings, insults, riddles, and other aspects of that chapter can be found in Further Resources.

As well, there are many stories about why and how Llywelyn was killed, and whether or not he was preparing to go to war with Edward. Some stories suggest he was surprised while meeting allies near Builth, and killed by a Shropshire soldier named Stephen de Francton, who did not recognize him as the Prince of Wales. De Francton profited little from it, since others took Llywelyn's head to the king, allowing me to speculate about his character and how events may have unfolded. The English pursued Dafydd to Dolwyddelan and Castell-y-Bere but did not capture him when the castles fell. At various points he had his wife, son, and daughter with him, as well as several illegitimate daughters (although little is known of them, leaving me to invent Margred and the others). My main sources were the Smith biography, as well as the Cilmeri and Castles of Wales websites.

Scholars also disagree about what castle fell on what date during the 1282-83 invasion, and on the location of the royal llys at Garth Celyn (or Garthcelyn as it appears in some sources.) The list of sources under Further Reading provides more information about these topics. In changing or leaving out some details, I hope I have left room for readers to find their own stories.

GLOSSARY

Annwn – Welsh word for OtherWorld (see OtherWorld); Arawn was its king (Cŵn Annwn, or hounds of Annwn, are also known as the Hounds of Hell)

anon – soon, in a little while

bard – singer and/or storyteller: Welsh bards or beirdd also had other duties, such as oral historian, legal advisor, and skilled political negotiator. There were three orders: Pencerdd or master poet, bardd teulu or family poet, and cerddor or minstrel

Builth (bilth or BEE-ehst) – castle in mid-Wales

Cadair Idris (CAH-dayr EE-drrees) - mountain in North Wales, known as the "giant's chair" for the legendary giant Idris; also thought to be the legendary hunting ground of the Tylwyth Teg (or Welsh fae)

Caergwrle (CIYR-goo-lee) – castle in northeast Wales built by Dafydd, near a town called Hope, built on a mountain known as Hope Mountain

Carreg Cennen – castle in south-west Wales

Castell-y-Bere (CAS-tethl-uh-BEH-rreh) or Bere – castle in north Wales built by Llywelyn the Great; it was besieged by English forces and fell in April 1283, but the English failed to capture Dafydd there

Cistercians – religious order in Western Europe started in the late eleventh century, known as White Monks; they lived in solitude and isolation, had no personal property, kept a rigorous way of life, worked the land by hand

coat of arms – distinctive heraldic design representing a particular individual or his retainers, often on a cloak, shield or banner

Cornish – people from Cornwall, a district in northern England crest – a heraldic emblem usually on a helmet

Criccieth (KRIK-ehth) – castle situated on the northwest coast that fell early in 1283

crwth (krooth) – Welsh term for the lyre

Cymraeg (CUM-riyg) – Welsh language, related to Gaelic

Cymru (CUM-ree) – The Welsh word for the country of Wales

Cymry (CUM-ree) – Welsh term for the Welsh people (the Welsh called themselves Cymry, "compatriots," and thought of themselves as people of Britain by virtue of their ancestors, the Brythoniaid or Brythons.)

Desenni valley – valley in Northwest Wales

Dolbadarn Castle (doll-BAH-darn) – castle in North Wales

Dolwyddelan Castle (doll-with-ELen) – castle in North Wales that fell after five days' siege, on January 18, 1283, and was a strategic loss for the Welsh

Dderwyddon (ther-oo-ITH-oyn) – Druids (people of the derw or oak), an ancient people said to possess magic

Eryri Mountains – the Snowdonia mountains were known as the Eryri or land of the Eagles in medieval Welsh

fealty – special kind of service (especially military), loyalty, and allegiance, usually pledged by a knight to a noble

Feast of the Holy Innocents: an early Christmas feast day, dating from the 5th century, celebrated on December 28 to commemorate the children King Herod killed in his search for the infant Jesus

Feast of Saint Stephen: On December 26, people gave leftovers to the poor to honour a deacon known for his good works who was stoned to death in 36 AD; root of the carol, "Good King Wenceslas"

foster – in medieval times, at the age of 7, boys were sent to live with another noble family to train to be knights; they began as pages, then advanced to squires, then to knights garderobe – The toilet in a castle, often a wooden bench with a hole in it

Garth Celyn – The dwelling of the royal family of Wales at Aber and Llywelyn's headquarters; may have been a castle or fortress made of a combination of wood and stone, with a traditional longhouse and other buildings, but the area was levelled by Edward I in 1283 and replaced with English castles; the English manor house at Pen-y-Bryn, built in the 1600s, is thought to contain one tower of it

Gwyn ap Nudd (gwin ahp nee_th_) – King of the Tylwyth Teg (faeries)

Gwynedd (GWIN-e_th_) – district in North Wales, held longest by the Welsh royal families

keep – fortified tower within a walled castle, often with a large hall inside

King Arthur – legendary king in Welsh lore who united the warring chieftains of Wales

lauds – early morning prayers in a monastery, focused on praising God (in contrast to evening prayers which were focused on thanksgiving)

laverbread – tasty mix of seaweed in rolled oats, usually eaten at breakfast

Llyn valley – district in North Wales, in the Snowdon mountains

llys (thlees) – Welsh term for the royal court

Llywelyn the Great or Llywelyn ap Iorwerth (c. 1172-1240) – Llywelyn ap Gryffydd's grandfather, ruler of Gwynedd and most of Wales

Marcher lords – fierce knights who were given land in return for policing the English-Welsh border

Marches – the lands along the English-Welsh border

Mari Lwyd – New Year's tradition, still celebrated today, in which a skeletal horse's head (grey mare) is invited into homes to help bring good luck for the year

marriage by proxy – a marriage where the bride or groom is not present but is represented by another person

Meirionnydd (may-rree-ON–ith) region in North Wales, once a sub-kingdom of Gwynedd

Menai Straight – treacherous body of water between North Wales and the island of Anglesey (Ynys Môn)

Nant Peris River – river in North Wales

nones – ninth hour (3:00 p.m.) in a monastery, a fixed time for mid-afternoon prayers

Nos Galan Gaeaf (nohs KAL-an GAY-ehv) – Welsh term for Halloween: the eve of winter, or the night before Calan Gaeaf (the first day of winter); also known as Ysbrydnos or Spirit Night

OtherWorld – the place, known as Annwn in Welsh, thought by some to be where people went when they died, and by others to be more of a parallel world identical in most ways to our own; in Welsh legends, people sometimes exchanged bodies with people who lived in the OtherWorld

pibgorn – Welsh pipe-horn (phibau) with one reed (sounds a bit like a bagpipe)

quintain – shield rigged to swivel on a wooden pole; when training, boys would ride horses toward the quintain as hard as they could and try to hit the shield squarely with a lance; after the hit, the wooden apparatus swung around behind the rider to unhorse the unwary with heavy swinging sandbags

Rhaeadr – waterfall in Welsh (Rhaedr Fawr is Aber Falls)

Rhuddlan – castle in Northwest Wales near the Welsh-English border

sext - sixth hour (noon) in a monastery, a fixed time for midday prayers in praise of God's works

Shrewsbury – town in northern England, near the English-Welsh border

Simon de Montfort – English lord who fought for an early form of democracy and was brutally hunted down and killed for it by King Henry and his son Edward, who later became Edward I; Llywelyn may have fought beside de Montfort, and in 1263 Llywelyn was betrothed to his daughter Elinor

Sir Gawain – knight in the legends of King Arthur, and Arthur's nephew

solar – private sitting room for a lord or lady in a castle

telyn (TEL-in) – Welsh term for the harp

terce – fixed time for mid-morning (9:00 a.m.) prayers in a monastery

teulu – term for "family," a Welsh prince's personal bodyguard (Llywelyn reportedly had 160 in his teulu, more than any other Welsh prince had before)

torque (tork) - ring of gold thought to have been worn by Celtic warriors around the neck, often crafted with intricate designs

trencher – English tradition: flat loaves of bread, cut in half and used as plates for food

Twelfth Night – English tradition: last day of the 12 days of Christmas, on January 5, celebrated today as Epiphany; often the day when gifts were given, ending the Christmas season

Tŷ Hir – Welsh term for longhouse, possibly the royal dwelling at Garth Celyn

Tylwyth Teg (tuhl-with taig) – The Welsh term for Faeries

Tywysog (tuh-WUH-sog) - Leader

vespers – evening prayers of thanksgiving

vigils – prayer service at night; in some traditions, specifically at midnight

Watchers – legendary characters that sleep within the Welsh mountains, in some Welsh legends thought to be the Old Ones (faeries) and in others King Arthur and his knights; it was said that the Old Ones would return to the people of Cymru in the time of their greatest need

weft – filling yarn in weaving

Y Calan – traditional Welsh song for the New Year

Ynys Môn – Welsh name for Anglesey, island off the northwest coast

Acknowledgements

Like many novels, this story came into being through the help and encouragement of many people, although I take full responsibility for any errors or omissions that may have occurred in the writing of this book.

First and foremost, I want to thank my publisher and editor Jeanne Martinson. Special thanks to my developmental series editor Amanda Bidnall, historical editor Danièle Cybulskie, and Beta readers Sharon Plumb, Maureen Ulrich, Leslie Wibberley, and Michelle B. Heartfelt thanks for feedback and encouragement to Eileen Cook, Donna Barker, Crystal Hunt, Wendy Turner, and many others with the Creative Academy for Writers. Special thanks to Creative Saskatchewan for funding the series.

An earlier version of this book was published as *Hawk* by Five Rivers Press. My special thanks to editor Robert Runte, Naomi Davis, and Beta readers Pegi Talfryn (especially for information about Welsh cultural traditions), Sharon Plumb, Shelley Freese, Barbara Tomporowski, and the Phantasts and Young Adult Critique (YAC) groups.

Others who were instrumental in earlier versions of the book include Kathy Stinson, CANSCAIP, the Highlights Foundation, Patricia Lee Gauch, Steffany Campbell, Dr. Mary Blackstone, Katherine Gibson, Greg Stevenson, David Evans, Sarah Downs (Shropshire Archives), librarians at the University of Regina and Regina Public Library, Alison Lohans; Barbara Galler-Smith; Steven Galloway, the Sage Hill Writing Experience, the Erratics writing group, as well as many others. I also owe special thanks to Glen Huser, my first editor and MFA thesis advisor at the University of British Columbia, and our MFA class. My apologies if I have missed anyone's name.

Thanks to the Access Foundation Professional Development Fund and the Highlights Foundation Scholarship Fund for mentorship funding, and to Visit Wales, Ffynnon in Dolgellau, Coastal Holidays, and Apt 7 Llys Rhostrefor, Benllech for research travel funding.

FURTHER READING

Nonfiction Books

A Collection of Welsh Riddles by Vernam Hall and Archer Taylor
A History of Wales by John Davies
Broadview Anthology of British Literature: The Medieval Period, edited by Joseph Black
Cadw Guidebooks on various castles
Castles of the Welsh Princes by Paul R. Davis
Castles of Wales by Alan Reid
Celtic Gods and Heroes by Marie-Louise Sjoestedt
From Medieval to Modern Wales by R.R. Davies and Geraint H. Jenkins
Llywelyn ap Gruffudd: Prince of Wales by J. Beverley Smith
Medieval Welsh Poems translated by Joseph P. Clancy
Stories and Ballads of the Far Past by Nora Kershaw Chadwick
The Age of Conquest: Wales 1063-1415 by R.R. Davies
The Journey Through Wales: The Description of Wales by Gerald of Wales
Wales and the Welsh in the Middle Ages edited by R.A. Griffiths and P.R. Schofield
Trioedd Ynys Prydain (Welsh Triads) by Rachel Bromwich
Welsh Wars of Independence by David Moore

Online Resources on Y Calan and the Mari Lwyd:

Welsh Culture and Traditions: Nos Galan (New Year's Eve): http://www.britannia.com/wales/culture2.html
The Magic of the Mari: http://www.folkwales.org.uk/mari.html
Mari Lwyd: http://www.omniglot.com/songs/bcc/marilwyd.php
Visit Wales: https://www.wales.com/about/culture/mari-lwyd
Tradition of the Mari Lwyd - BBC Cymru: https://www.youtube.com/watch?v=G_xFo6Hifzk
TRAC Music Traditions Wales, Mari Lwyd: https://www.youtube.com/watch?v=6ptel9C3Zhg

Online Resources on Welsh History

Archeology of Northwest Wales: http://www.archaeoleg.org.uk/areanorthwest.html
Castles of Wales: http://www.castlewales.com (articles and essays)
Cadw: http://cadw.wales.gov.uk/daysout/dolwyddelan-castle/?lang=en
Cilmeri.org: "Death of Llywelyn" (Internet Archive): https://web.archive.org/web/20170702053329/http://www.cilmeri.org/eng/?page_id=5
Llys Rhosyr: http://www.heneb.co.uk/palaceoftheprinces/rhosyr.html
Gathering the Jewels: Castles of the Welsh princes: http://education.gtj.org.uk/en/item10/28986
International Heralds and Heraldry: http://www.internationalheraldry.com
Ye Olde Medieval Insult: http://kol.coldfront.net/thekolwiki/index.php/Ye_Olde_Medieval_Insult
Medievel Insults: http://www.funnyjunk.com/funny_pictures/4254438/Medieval+insults
Medieval riddles: http://www.increasebrainpower.com/easy-riddles.html http://www.justriddlesandmore.com/riddlearchive.html
Sarah Woodbury: "Making Sense of Medieval Wales" video series, https://www.youtube.com/watch?v=IQfG6WlyxEU

Online Maps of Wales:

http://commons.wikimedia.org/wiki/File:Wales_after_the_Treaty_of_Montgomery_1267.svg (Alex D.)
Source: Wrex County exhibition:
http://www.wrexham.gov.uk/english/heritage/medieval_exhibition/struggles.htm
http://commons.wikimedia.org/wiki/File:Gwynedd_after_the_Treaty_of_Aberconwy_1277.svg
Gwynedd General Map (James Frankcom):
http://en.wikipedia.org/wiki/File:Gwynedd_General_Map.jpg

Fiction

After Cilmeri (series) by Sarah Woodbury
Assassins Apprentice: The Farseer by Robin Hobb
Lord of the Rings (series) by J.R. Tolkien
Ranger's Apprentice (series) by John Flanagan
The Brothers of Gwynedd (series) by Edith Pargeter
The Dark is Rising (series) by Susan Cooper
The Once and Future King (series) by T.H. White
Tomorrow's Magic by Pamela F. Service
Welsh Princes (trilogy) by Sharon Kay Penman

Wheel of Time (series) by Robert Jordan
"Y Gododdin" in *The Broadview Anthology of British Literature: The Medieval Period*

BIOGRAPHY

Marie Powell's adventures in castle-hopping across North Wales to explore her family roots resulted in the YA Fantasy series Last of the Gifted. The series includes the books Spirit Sight and Water Sight, and was produced with funding from Creative Saskatchewan.

Marie is the author of more than forty traditionally published children's books, and her award-winning short stories and poetry appear in such literary magazines as subTerrain and Room. Among other degrees, she holds a Master of Fine Arts (MFA) in Creative Writing from the University of British Columbia. Marie lives on Treaty 4 land in Regina, Saskatchewan.

Find her at mariepowell.ca

LAST OF THE GIFTED

WATER SIGHT

MARIE POWELL

BOOK TWO

1

April 1283, Meirionnydd, North Wales

Mist circled the mountain like a massive fist. Squinting upward, Cat could barely make out the legendary giant's seat near the top of Cadair Idris. The fog surrounded her, obscuring Rhys who climbed behind her, but she drew it around her like a cloak. They needed stealth. Below them, the valley was full of English mercenaries, hunting for Welsh heads. It didn't matter that only a handful of warriors remained. Women, children, any of them would satisfy the wretched king.

"Not much further," Rhys murmured.

She hadn't had a vision since they'd fled Bere castle. Not when she stared into the rain that morning, not through her reflection in the stream they crossed earlier, not even in the waterfall when she cupped her hands in it to drink. With English soldiers camped near the lake, Rhys had agreed to show her a stream farther up the mountain so she could try again.

Her foot dislodged a chunk of slate. It clinked down the side of the mountain, disturbing the mist blanket as it went. Her breath caught. She hesitated, glancing back toward the gulley where they had left the others.

Rhys loomed behind her out of the mist. His features held the usual stoic calmness, but the heat radiating from him made her wonder if the anger still boiled inside him at the loss of his castle. He had given it up to save them. His people. Her.

"You are the morrigan," he said. "If you see not, it may be there is naught to see."

She tried to smile at his wordplay. "I'm no legend," she muttered, but he only raised his eyebrows. He thought of her as a wise woman, like his Irish nurse, whose gift of foretelling could predict and prevent their doom. But Cat was Welsh. Her gift came as it chose. She forced herself to breathe out, slowly. For his sake, she would find a way to will it to her.

She reached for the rocks and climbed, one step, then another, feeling her way with hands and feet as she went. She had tucked away her pretty leather-soled shoes so she wouldn't slip on the smooth slate. Her feet were used to their freedom, but the jagged edges caught at her toes, and her calves ached from three days of hiding and backtracking on a route that should have taken them one.

"There," he said as their feet finally found the firmer ground of a small plateau. They could hear the roar of the stream. She drew a long breath and tried to smile again. He took her hand and led her to a large tree, pulling her forward to stand beside him. The mist had cleared a little, and she could see a fork in the rocky streambed.

"Look there." He gestured toward the ledge where the rushing water parted. "Those stones will hold you."

She stepped onto a large flat stone and crouched down. The rocks slowed the water enough that her pale, sombre face stared back, waving in the ripples. She must see what was facing them. She chose a calm spot near an eddy and fought to remember the songs to call her gift. She could hear her uncle's voice in her memory as she stared fixedly at the liquid, whispering the words, not daring to sing aloud.

Nothing stirred. Cat rubbed her forehead with one hand and sat back on her heels. His hand rested on her shoulder, warm and supportive even through the fabric of her cloak.

"The first thing we must do is get our people to safety. Focus on that now, Cat."

Of course, he would say that. He was raised to be their leader, and he always put their people's welfare above his own. Cat longed to help him more than anything else. If only her gift would cooperate.

A water beetle skimmed across the clear surface of the spring. She followed its path, staring at the ripples it made, when her surroundings began to dissolve—

—and she could feel thudding all around her. Hooves pounding toward her on the flat dirt. She shrank back into the dark stone of the abbey walls, sheltered in its shadow. Familiar voices screamed and cried out, somewhere nearby. Rhys drew his longsword from its sheath and sprinted toward the riders. He swung around as the first horseman flew at him and lunged up toward the armoured man. Cat saw the man flinch as Rhys thrust. The bite of its steel tore open the knight's throat. The horse screamed as it careened past Rhys. He whirled but the second horseman was already bearing down on him. Rhys threw his sword and the force carried the knight off his horse.

Then the third was upon him. Rhys leapt upward again, his bare arms outstretched as if to drag the man from his saddle. The knight's sword flashed as dust and churning hooves covered the scene. Then the horses passed. The dust cleared. She saw a crumpled form on the grass—

—and Cat crouched by the stream again. "No!" She twisted up and threw her arms around him, unable to speak.

"What?" he asked, holding her tightly. "What did you see?"

She stared at Rhys. The violence of the vision stopped her voice. How could she tell him? She had clearly felt the abbey around her. The abbey would offer the people shelter. Food, shelter, rest. What they all needed. And it was the place they must go to collect the relics. But if they went, it would end his life.

"Tell me," he said.

She drew away from him. Tywysog Dafydd—the man who would be Prince of Wales—had sent Rhys on this errand. The House of Aberffraw would fall, and all of free Wales with it, if Dafydd could not rally the people to him, as his brother had. Many said the relics had helped Prince Llywelyn keep the people on his side: the Cross of Neith that marked him as their leader in the eyes of the Church, the Crown of Arthur that marked his true heritage, and the Coronet of Wales given by the English King to mark Llywelyn as the Prince of Wales in the eyes of the world. Now these relics would gain Dafydd the support he needed for a final stand against the English. Rhys had to succeed.

"Tell me what you saw."

Cat's heart thumped.

"We must not go," she said. "You must not go." And she told him all of it. He listened, his blue eyes intent on hers, drawing the words from her. When she was done, he said nothing for a moment, a muscle flinching once in his jaw belying his calm.

"And the people?" he asked. "Were they safe?"

She thought back to the voices, the screaming, and slowly shook her head. His face fell for a moment, so short she almost thought she imagined it, before he regained the stoicism she had come to expect from him. Always in the past, her visions had held hope, a way to change the fate that would surely bring them defeat. But there were so few Welsh warriors left now, and the enemy had so many. How could she change this vision?

"My visions," she began, and faltered. "What do you think of your morrigan now?"

"Your visions give us a chance."

"And yet, I wish I had not seen it." She folded her arms across her chest, falling back into their old argument. "I wish you had married me at the castle, if it would prevent me from seeing such scenes."

"I would do nothing to disrupt your visions. You are a woman of power, and you must keep your power pure." He started to put an arm around her shoulder, but she shook him off.

"It may have been so for your Irish nurse, but it was not so for my own mam, and for the other women of our family. Mam married and had children, but her gift remains strong."

He shook his head. "How can we risk it? Your visions may be our only advantage now."

Each time they argued, it ended the same way. If her mam was here with them, maybe she could convince him. But Mam was half a world away, caring for Prince Llywelyn's only child. Cat turned away from Rhys but his arm came around her shoulders and drew her toward him. His quick response surprised her, and she let herself be drawn.

"Do not think you will get away so easily. Once the English return to their own land…" He bent his head to her and waited until she raised hers to meet him. Then he kissed her gently, as he had in the garden at Castell-y-Bere, and this time she responded.

When he drew back, the blue of his eyes had darkened, and his voice was husky. "I know your value, Cat, and not only as a morrigan. We will be man and wife, if you still will it, but we two must wait until our people are safe."

She swallowed and pushed away from him. "Yet we cannot go to the Abbey now."

"We cannot take the people there."

Something in the way he said it made her turn back to him, but she could not catch his eye. "You cannot go," she said. "That much is clear enough."

"And yet I cannot tarry." He looked at her then. "If your vision happens with the people there, then there may be a way to forestall it and secure the relics. One warrior on his own would make better time."

A chill spread through her, and she thought back on her vision, seeking a way to stop him. "It was only you I saw," she said. "The English soldiers came for you."

"It is not clear why the English would attack God's holy church, unless they knew of its earthly treasure. If that is true, I have no choice but to go."

"You cannot go. You must not go. There are others you can send—"

"None the abbot will trust."

"What of Cynfrig?"

The old warrior had been steward of Bere, trusted by Rhys and by Prince Llywelyn himself, before the prince was murdered six months ago. Had it even been six months?

Rhys was shaking his head. "Cynfrig is loyal but he has a wife and children. I cannot endanger him."

"What of Emrys?"

"With his new wife already pregnant?" He shook his head.

Who else could they send? The few warriors who still stood with them had gone with Prince Dafydd to retake their ancestral home at Garth Celyn. Who else had she seen as she watched from the shadow of the abbey's walls? Only Rhys and herself —

And then she realized. The abbey had been sheltering her.

Not Rhys, but her.

She must go. And he must not. It made more sense to her even as she had the thought. Her family had been with Prince Llewelyn when he hid the relics there. Her vision was telling her she must go to collect them, alone. She felt a shudder of fear go through her. Rhys responded by holding her again, and she put her arms around his shoulders, looking up into his eyes. And she knew he would not let her go, if he thought she would be in danger. How could she hide it from him? Yet she must.

She shifted away from him and squared her shoulders. If she must do it, she would need to act quickly.

"What has happened?" he asked. "Did you have another vision?"

"Not vision," she said, shaking her head, "but reason. You must see the people to safety before anything else."

"There I must rely on you and Cynfrig. I will leave you in his charge. He knows the land as well as I and can guide you all to the safety of a nearby holding. It is still my hope that the people might be safe there for a time."

"You must see to the people first."

Rhys held her eyes and nodded. Yes, she thought, looking away. You must see to the people. And I must see to our future.

As they returned to the path, Cat spotted Cynfrig's youngest child already scrambling nimbly over the rubble on the mountain path. The boy had been well warned, so instead of his usual jubilance, the loudest sound he made was his panting as he caught his breath on the plateau. He was soon followed by his mother Haf, and finally the elder steward himself. As the mist cleared, Cat was able to spot the homespun cloaks of a handful of farmers and their families following at intervals on the mountain path. Below them, the army of the English king blanketed the valley like locusts. Cat wanted to lean into Rhys, to reassure herself, but now was not the time.

"In times past, we might have waited out the spring," Cynfrig said, "trusting the *Saeson* to get sick of our mountains and return home to take up their ploughs. But these mercenaries have no such concerns."

"They will not cease their search for Prince Dafydd," Rhys agreed. "We must get the relics to him without delay."

Only the three of them knew of Rhys's errand, but every Welshman knew of the enmity between Dafydd and Llywelyn in life. With the three relics in hand—Cross, Crown, and Coronet—surely the people would believe Prince Dafydd had his elder brother's blessing at the end, and follow him to defeat the English.

She shifted restlessly, watching Rhys step forward to help a farmer and his family up the path. She knew Rhys would want to speak with his warriors in person before he left for the abbey. With luck, Emrys, the other warrior travelling with them, would be bringing up the rear with his pregnant wife Bron. That would give her a small head start. As she expected, Rhys and Cynfrig reached into their meager stores and shared them out with the women and children. She noticed that Cynfrig halved his portion with his wife and son, while Rhys gave most of his to a young farmer and his family.

Cat had to get to the abbey first, and this might be her only chance. She went to Cynfrig as the one person who might help her.

"Often you have called me your morrigan," she said, drawing him aside. "If you believe it truly, you must help me now." As quickly as possible, she told him the main points of her vision.

"Did you see me in your vision?"

Cat thought for a moment. She caught sight of his young son, watching them almost forlornly, and shook her head. "I heard all of you there," she said. "The abbey only offered me its protection. It must be me who goes."

"But Rhys will come after you," Cynfrig told her. "I will not be able to prevent him."

"Then you must delay him at least half a day," she said. "It will take me that long to get to the abbey."

"Only that long?" Cynfrig rubbed his moustache ruefully.

"You know how fast I am. I will take the fox path, and I will be back with the relics before nightfall."

"I cannot guarantee Rhys will not discover you gone sooner than you wish it."

"Then send him by the fox trail, if he tries to come after me. I will return that way to the holding and so meet him on the trail." She watched the older man's face, but he still hesitated. With a glance toward Rhys, who was just then lifting a child over the rubble onto the plateau, she took Cynfrig's hands in hers. "We need him now, more than ever. This way we will have Rhys, alive, and we will have the relics with no one the wiser. If you believe as you say, then you know I must do this. It is the only way."

Finally, he reached into his pouch and put a small package of dried meat into her hands. "God's speed," he said, and moved past her to block her from Rhys's view.

Cat thanked him and moved swiftly up the path toward the fox trail. She touched the locket around her neck that held the twist of hair binding her to her brother Hyw, wishing for the thousandth time that she had his gift instead of her own. If only she could transform into an eagle or a hawk, she could fly to the abbey and back before Rhys noticed she was gone.

The road forked and she looked longingly down the pony path to the holding where Rhys and their people would travel later that day. Then she set her mind and turned to the shorter trail that would take her past it to the abbey. She had wasted too much time already. She prayed that Cynfrig would keep Rhys focused on his people, so he would not look for her until he thought it was time to say goodbye. She willed that she would be on her way back by then.

Find *Water Sight*
Book Two of *Last of the Gifted* at
mariepowell.ca/booklinks

www.ingramcontent.com/pod-product-compliance
Lightning Source LLC
Chambersburg PA
CBHW070857250626
47159CB00003B/1094